She Had To Kill Him

By

Aviva Gat

She Had To Kill Him

To my husband Ori
For his unending support and love

Chapter 1
Mara

There are two ways to get away with mass murder. The first, an expensive lawyer. The second, suicide. Robert Derby used the first one. I'm using the second.

I show up at the hotel, dressed for the occasion. My long dress flowing around my stilettos and the gun strapped to my inner thigh. I approach the hostess at the ballroom door and give her a smile.

"Name?" she asks.

"Amy Barnes," I say. It's a fake. I couldn't use my real name or maybe they would wonder what I was doing here. Maybe they would single me out, a poster girl for their cause.

"Barnes..." the hostess repeats as she scrolls down the clipboard in front of her. "Here we go." She checks off the name and hands me a card. "I love your lipstick," she says, as though trying to make a friendly connection. "It's so... seasonal."

"Thanks," I say as I walk by her and smack my lips together. The ballroom is already filling up with men in suits and women in cocktail dresses. Everyone is standing around, drinking, smiling at each other, all so happy with themselves. *Good for you,* I say to them in my head. *You're all just saving the world, one fancy cocktail at a time.*

I suddenly feel small in the room, like I might trip and get swallowed by the grouting between the wooden tiles on the floor. I hear the sound of static in my head. It's louder than the chatter flowing around me. I close my eyes a moment and take a deep breath as I remind myself why I am here and what I need to do.

A waiter comes up to me with a tray covered in little plates with bite-sized food on them. He gives some explanation for whatever it is he is carrying, but his voice sounds like he is under water. I can't understand him and I just shake my head. I can't eat anything right now. My stomach is churning and my throat feels like it has closed up. I move through the room, carefully avoiding eye contact with anyone. I accidently brush a woman's shoulder. "Oh excuse me!" she exclaims, ever so loudly with a laugh. I keep my head down and keep walking, afraid that our little encounter could blow my cover.

I look down at the card in my hand. *CADD* it says in big artistic font. *One phone call can save a life.* If only Robert Derby had thought of that two years ago. Suddenly, I see him. Robert Derby is making his way onto the small stage at the front of the ballroom, shaking hands left and right. The crowd starts to clap as he stops in front of the podium. I also clap. I need to blend in. I'm studying his face, his thick graying hair, perfectly groomed goatee. He is wearing a tuxedo with a turquoise bow tie.

He raises his hands to quiet the clapping, but the smile on his face shows how much he is enjoying this. He doesn't really want the clapping to end. But then it does, and he stands up a little taller.

"Thank you to everyone for coming today," he says. "As you all know, this cause is very near and dear to my heart. Two years ago, I made the worst mistake of my life. At the time, it seemed so trivial. I didn't even think twice before I got in my car after the office happy hour. I just wanted to go home and pass out on the couch with my beautiful wife." He nods to the plastic woman standing in front of the stage. She smiles back at him, her diamond necklace shimmering in the light.

"But then, just blocks away from my home, it happened," he continues. "BAM! And just like that my SUV collided with that car right in the middle of an intersection. I was lucky. My airbags saved me and I walked away with just this little scar right here." He points to his right eyebrow. From where I am, I can't see the scar on his tanned face.

"Unfortunately, the passengers in the other car were not so lucky." His tone changes and he continues solemnly. "There were three people in that car." He looks down. "May they rest in peace. Their airbags didn't open. I know the airbags are not totally to blame. They were speeding, but I am also at fault, which is why I started CADD. Call A Designated Driver. If I had, maybe the accident wouldn't have happened. Maybe their airbags wouldn't have been tested. Maybe their lives would have been saved." I can feel the sadness wave over the crowd as everyone pretends to have sympathy for those people in the car. The static in my head is still vibrating loudly.

"I can never atone for what happened," Robert Derby continues. "I paid my judiciary dues, but that was not enough. And for that reason, I started CADD, so hopefully I could stop someone from making the same mistake as I did. CADD is going to be a national organization that anyone can call at any time and we will organize a designated driver for them. In the last year, our army of volunteers have driven more than 5,000 passengers and made sure that each and every one of them arrived home safely." He pauses to let the crowd start clapping again.

"Your donations at this fundraiser will go towards growing our network," he continues. "We need to expand our call-center, which works tirelessly to answer calls and get volunteers out on the road as fast as possible. We need to raise more awareness about CADD, so that every bar in America makes sure that its patrons call us instead of getting behind the wheel. I thank you all, from the bottom of my heart, for your support of this cause. Together, we are saving lives!" Again, he breaks for the applause.

"So, ladies and gentlemen, I invite you to browse the items available in our silent auction." He motions to one wall of the room where tables are lined up with various items displayed on them. "We have some very high ticket items, like a cruise to the Bahamas and a beautiful painting of the Golden Gate Bridge. We'll announce the winners at the end of the evening. And please everyone, enjoy the hors d'oeuvres and the open bar. And of course, no one drive home tonight!" The crowd laughs. "Thank you!"

Everyone is clapping, whistling. Robert Derby stands at the podium acknowledging the crowd. Clapping for himself, smiling at his wife, at all his onlookers. Then, he gets off the stage and kisses his wife. I'm still staring at him, trying to see the scar he pointed out on his right eyebrow. Maybe when he smiles there's a faint line, but maybe that's just a wrinkle. Even people as wealthy as the Derby's must get wrinkles.

What Robert Derby didn't mention in his speech was that the three people he killed—the three people he murdered—were my family. My parents and older sister, who were driving to meet me at a restaurant to celebrate my twenty-first birthday. I sat alone at the table, waiting for them to show up. I was angry with them for being late. For not answering their phones. I ordered myself my first legal alcoholic drink, hating them for making me do it alone.

I want Robert Derby to know what it's like to lose everything. To lose everyone he loves. That's why I'm here. He murdered my family and I am going to murder his. Here, at this fundraiser for an organization that he built, using my family's blood as his inspiration. But I can't afford a lawyer who will find some stupid loophole and get me off the hook for it. I don't want to continue living anyway. It's too hard. The static in my head. Knowing I am all alone in the world. I'm going to kill his family and then kill myself.

I rub my thighs together, feeling the gun between them. My heart starts to race as I think about the opportune time to act. Probably when his family is all standing close together. He has a wife and two sons. The problem is, I don't know what his sons look like, so I watch Mrs. Derby and wait to see who she speaks with. None of them resemble Robert Derby.

I can hear my heart beating louder than the static in my head. My pulse is hammering through my chest, electrocuting my whole body and suddenly I can't breathe. I'm choking, gasping for air. I look around, afraid that someone might be looking at me. They might be suspicious that I don't belong or wonder why my heart is beating so hard that it's pushing my chest out with every pulse. No one's looking at me, but then I see a group of children playing with each other on the floor. Dressed in designer suits and dragged here by their parents. My heart calls out to them, but they don't hear it.

What am I doing? One of the voices in my head asks.

He deserves this a man's voice responds.

But there are children here, the first voice says.

You were also a child, is the response.

"I always hate dressing up for these things," someone says behind me. The argument in my brain disappears. I turn around and see a man standing there with two champagne flutes. I look up to his face and catch his blue eyes smiling at me. He's blonde, broad shouldered. He holds one of the champagne flutes out to me. "Are you one of the volunteers?"

I shake my head and take the champagne flute from him. "Just someone who identifies with the cause," I respond. I suddenly feel cool, calm and collected, my old college persona coming through. "If only we could identify with the cause in jeans, right?"

He smirks, fingering the tie around his neck, and clinks his champagne flute against mine. We both take a sip. "Have you checked out the silent auction?" he says in a mocking British accent, holding out his pinky as he waves his flute side to side. "I believe you may find the items quite exquisite."

I let out a laugh. "Indubitably," I mock back at him.

"I'm Garrett," he says, back in his real voice.

"Mara," I respond, giving him my real name. I no longer hear the static in my head and I can focus on the conversation we're having. I'm the cool Mara, the one who can flirt and seems normal.

"Well Mara, would you like to get out of here? Go get a drink somewhere a little less stifling?"

7

Garrett asks me. He's still fidgeting with the tie around his neck.

I take a moment to remember the gun in between my thighs. My plan for revenge. My suicide. I hear the man's voice in my head screaming at me: *What are you doing? We had a plan!* I try to ignore him. I'm stronger than him.

"I'd like that a lot," I say.

Chapter 2
Mara

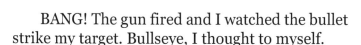

BANG! The gun fired and I watched the bullet strike my target. Bullseye, I thought to myself.

"Nice shot, Mara," my dad said, clapping his hands. I smiled at him and then looked back at the target in front of me, a black outline of a person with concentric circles in the chest. A hole from my latest shot right in the center. "Just remember, in real life, the target is in the leg. The shin," my dad said, bending down to tap his leg. "You just want to neutralize the target, not kill them."

"Hey Sergeant!" Someone called from behind. My dad turned around and nodded at the man as he approached and shook his hand. "Doing some target practice?" The other man was wearing his navy-blue uniform with the star-shaped badge on the left side of his chest. "I'm not used to seeing you in plain clothes!"

"Just teaching my girls some gun safety," my dad said to him. "And what are you doing here in uniform, Officer?" I pulled the earmuffs off my ears so I could hear him.

"Just finished a rough shift with Desmond," the man said. He leaned in closer to my dad and continued in a quiet voice. "Our last call-out was a break-in over on Forty-forth Street. Wife and two babies were in the house, must have surprised the perp. Wife threw a vase at him but that just made him angry." The man looked over at Shannon and me. Again he lowered his voice. "Neighbors called us when they heard the screaming. When we got there, he was beating the wife. Saw us and pulled a gun out. Nicked Desmond in the shoulder, but he'll be all right."

"Babies all right?" my dad asked, placing his hand on the man's shoulder.

"Yes, Sergeant," the Officer said.

My dad nodded at him. "Good job, Officer. Go blow off some steam." The men shook hands again and the officer entered one of the little cubicles and immediately started firing off his pistol.

My dad had been taking us to the shooting range once a month since I was ten years old. A police officer and overprotective dad, he wanted us to know how to handle a weapon. He had seen too many accidents where people had hurt themselves—or worse—because they didn't know how to operate a handgun. He had also wanted Shannon and me to be able to protect ourselves if we ever needed to.

"Can we go home now?" Shannon asked. She was sitting behind me picking at her nails. She shot a couple rounds already and was bored. She could hit the target all right, but not the bullseye like me.

"One more round," I said, as I replaced the magazine and gave it a strong tap to click it into place. I repositioned my earmuffs, lifted the gun and pulled the trigger. BANG! The hole in the middle of the target suddenly tripled in size.

"Good!" my dad said, drawing out the word so that it became four syllables. "Mara, you're a natural. Maybe you could have a career in law enforcement when you grow up."

"Right, I could see Mara arresting bad guys," Shannon said with a chuckle. "You have the right to remain silent. Anything you say can and will be used against you in a court of law..."

"Yes and then Shannon will swoop in," I said and then started my best Shannon impression. "My client will not be answering any questions. He's innocent until proven guilty." We both smiled at each other and giggled.

"I think you two watch too much television," dad said.

"Objection!" Shannon exclaimed, raising her right index finger in the air. "That is speculative, not based on the evidence provided in this case." Our giggles grew louder.

"All right," my dad said with a grin on his face. "I guess it's time to leave. Mom said you both have some studying to do for your finals this week."

"I already studied," I said.

"These are your first finals in high school, Mara," my dad said. "It may be harder now and your grades are more important so you can go to a good university."

"Does Mara need to go to school if she wants to be a police officer?" Shannon said, her tone still exposing her goofy mood.

"If she wants to advance, then definitely," my dad said seriously.

"Dad, I'm not going to be a police officer," I said. "Navy-blue just isn't my color, you know? Maybe if you can get them to change the uniforms to turquoise or purple, then I'll join the squad." I handed the gun to my dad and took the earmuffs back off.

"Ohh turquoise," Shannon responded. "You could be a doctor, they have turquoise uniforms." My dad emptied the cartridge. Then, he carefully opened his silver case and placed the gun in the empty indentation next to two smaller handguns. Then he snapped the case closed and scrambled the dials on the locks on both ends.

"And what about Shannon, doesn't she need to study also?" I said, trying to push the spotlight off me.

"I'm done studying," she said, proudly, as we walked out of the range to the car. "My college apps are in. Senior year doesn't matter. Shotgun!"

"You sat shotgun last time!" I whined, even though I really didn't mind sitting in the backseat. It was easier to get lost during the drive.

"It does," dad said authoritatively, ignoring my whining. "They can rescind their acceptance letters if you don't keep up your grades." I got in the car and strapped the seatbelt over me. After Shannon buckled in, my dad started the engine.

"What if you got shot?" I asked.

"I won't get shot," my dad said.

"Desmond also probably thought that before his last shift," I said, thinking about the officer who had approached my dad earlier.

"We all wear bullet proof vests," my dad said. "So even if I got shot, I'd be fine."

We continued the ride silently. I was staring out the window, looking at the cars passing by. My dad always drove so slowly, it made me wonder how he could ever catch a criminal in his patrol car. It's good he drives slowly, and will never be able to catch a criminal, then he'll never get shot. But what if he does drive faster in the patrol car? With the lights flashing, sirens wailing. My heart started thumping and I felt my hands getting sweaty. The first signs of a panic attack. BANG! A gun went off in my head. I was imagining my dad getting shot, red blood soaking through his police uniform. The vest didn't matter, the bullet lodged itself right in my dad's neck, through the navy-blue collar. "Mara, Mara, Mara," he was saying to me as the blood continued to spill out. "Don't worry, Mara. It's not a big deal, I'll be fine." I shake my head. "No!" I yelled.

"No, what?" my dad said from the driver's seat. "Mara? You OK?"

"No, I don't like that song," I said. "Can you switch the radio station?" My heart is so loud, I am sure they hear it.

"All right, all right," Shannon responded. "No need for the drama!" She changed the station and then looked back at me. In an instant, her expression changed from annoyed to worried. "Mara, are you with us?"

"I'm fine!" I screamed at her. The strength of my voice surprised me. "Turn around!"

"What's going on back there?" my dad said calmly, keeping his eyes on the road.

"Nothing! Leave me alone!" My breath was getting uneven and beads of sweat padded my hairline. In a swift motion, Shannon unbuckled her seatbelt and slid through the middle of the car to the backseat.

"Shannon! What are you doing!?" my dad yelled, but she was already clipping herself in next to me. She grabbed my hands and locked her eyes to mine.

"Mara, did you know that avocados are fruits?" Shannon asked. "Not vegetables. In fact, avocados are actually a type of berry. We learned this in my biology class. Fruits grow from the flower of a tree, so even though they aren't that sweet they are still fruits. There are lots of foods that we think of as vegetables, but are actually fruits. Like tomatoes. Or even cucumbers. Mara, can you think of other foods that we think of as vegetables but are actually fruits? Anything that comes from a flower."

I focused on what she was saying. Foods that come from flowers. That aren't sweet. "Zucchini?" I asked.

"Yes!" she responded. "What else?"

"I don't know!" I racked my brain to think of more foods. "Pumpkins?"

"Yeah!" she said. "Good one!"

"What about eggplants?" dad contributed.

"Yup, those too."

"And bell peppers," dad said.

"Oh, you guys are making me hungry," I said. My heartbeat had started to slow down.

"Also olives," Shannon said. "You never would have guessed that one."

"Nope, definitely wouldn't have guessed that," I said, a smile creeping up on my face. By the time we arrived at home, I was calm.

Inside, my dad took the case with the guns to the safe drilled into the wall in my parent's closet. Also in the case was my dad's police-issued gun and my mother's jewelry. Shannon and I both knew the code—to be used in emergencies only. Before the accident, I'd never used it. Since, I've used it five times. Once, after the accident when the police chief came over to pay his condolences and collect the squad's gun. The second time, to put Shannon's things inside. The third, was when I first thought of my revenge. The fourth, before I went to the CADD fundraiser. The fifth was when I knew I needed my own protection.

Dear diary,

Today it happened again. I think I'm figuring out what to do about it, but every time it's like a brand new phenomenon. I'm the only one who seems to realize this is a recurring thing. Everyone else is just helpless. Especially mom and dad. They don't do anything. They don't even realize this is an issue!

Parents are supposed to know things. To understand things. To have answers when we need them, but the older I'm getting the more I realize they are completely clueless. They don't have the answers. But worse, they aren't trying to find them either. So it's up to me. Like always. I have to be the responsible one. I have to figure out what to do.

Sometimes, I wish I could disappear. But then I think, they need me. What would they do without me? Maybe if I disappeared for a short period of time, just enough for them to realize I'm gone. And then I'd come back and they would be so happy. They would notice me. They would appreciate everything I do. But it doesn't work like that, does it? No one misses you when you disappear for a few hours. They only miss you when they think you're gone for good. And that's something I couldn't do. I couldn't do that to her.

I have to be strong for her. She needs me. Anyway, it's getting late. I can hear her footsteps and I'm sure she'll be in the room soon. I'll write more tomorrow.

Chapter 3
Garrett

It's a relief, stepping out of the ballroom. I roll my shoulders and loosen the tie around my neck so it no longer feels like a noose. I hold out my hand to guide my new acquaintance across the carpeted hallway that leads to a gaudy staircase under an abnormally large chandelier. These hotels always have the same design. They all pretend they are unique, but really the same ugly carpeting tramples the hallways. The same useless chandeliers hang above identical staircases, all designed to make you feel like royalty. Like touching the fake gold railing will lead you to some fairy tale ball, where princes and princesses are doing the waltz and somewhere Cinderella is about to lose her slipper. Well, I've been to plenty of these balls. And never have I found the girl that the shoe fits.

I look to my side where my new acquaintance is walking. Her thin neck is outstretched like she is examining the trim between the walls and the ceiling. My eyes drift toward the walls, but to me, they are the same as every hotel corridor I've seen before. She turns her head suddenly and is facing me.

"Nice hotel," she says. "Must have cost a fortune to have the gala here."

I chuckle. "Depends what you call a fortune."

We reach the top of the stairs and suddenly she grabs onto the railing and leans over. For a moment, I feel like she might fall over, or maybe even throw herself. I freeze, my arms open in front of me like they are supposed to do something. Should I grab her? Wrap my arms around her? But we only just met. If I touch her, well, that opens the doors to so many different harassment charges. My mind is racing with ideas of what I am supposed to do, but then she slides down, sitting on the stop stair.

"Are you OK?" I ask. I step down a few stairs so I'm in front of her. She closes her eyes and shakes her head.

"I can't... I need... I..." She sounds like she is out of breath. Her face is white, so white that if it were a shade lighter, I'm sure I'd be able to see every vein. What if she is about to faint? Should I get water? But I can't leave her sitting like this. I feel paralyzed with inaction, a feeling I'm not used to. I'm a 'do-er.' I'm good at getting things done, fixing things. But I don't know this girl well enough to know what to fix. Her head is down and she is mumbling something under her breath. With a jerky movement, she stretches out her legs and starts fiddling with the straps of the black heels she's wearing. "I have to take these shoes off," she says, looking up at me. Suddenly it's like blood rushes back into her face. Her white skin is tinted pink and she focuses on removing her shoes. I bend down as though to help her, but I just kneel in front of her while she removes the heels. When she finishes, I offer a hand to help her

18

up. "I hate these things," she says pointing to the heels. "I do much better in sandals."

I smile at her and we start walking down the staircase. Thinking about her bare feet on this fancy carpet makes me chuckle. In my circle, women live in their high heels and they never take them off. They wear them to brunch and to the mall, pretending they are the most comfortable things they own. They would rather have their toes break off than be seen with naked feet in public.

Mara is swinging her shoes in her hand as she walks. Her dress is long enough to cover her ankles, but her bare feet show with every step down. An older couple I recognize is walking up the stairs. I can see the woman is staring at Mara's feet, a look of disgust and condescension. I'm glad she's focused though, so she doesn't look up and greet me. I'd rather not deal with a confrontation of fake cheek kisses right now.

When we reach the bottom, I lead Mara to the hotel bar where we sit at one of the high tops. She throws her shoes onto the chair next to her and rests her arms on the table. I wave over the waiter, who brings over a bar menu. Without looking at the menu, Mara turns to the waiter.

"Can we get some shots? Maybe vodka, or whatever. I don't really care what. Something strong." The waiter leans back on his heels. He's good at hiding his surprise. Better than I am, I can't stop myself from staring back and forth between them, wondering how this will play out. I'm intrigued by how many taboos Mara has broken in the short time I've known her. I wish I were as brave.

"Certainly, miss," the waiter says. "Might I suggest the house tequila? It is rather refreshing and has the kick I believe you are looking for."

"Perfect," she responds. The waiter pivots back to the bar and I wish I could see the look on his face. This isn't a bar people order shots at. This is a bar where people drink $100 pours of scotch or cocktails with ingredients they can't pronounce.

A few moments later, the waiter brings two shots with small slivers of lime hanging on the glass rim. Mara lifts one, and holds it up to cheers. I raise the second and clink her glass before downing the shot. She shoves the lime in her mouth after finishing the shot. Another taboo.

"Wow, I needed that," she says. "I need to relax. Do you want to do another one?" I motion to the waiter to bring another round. I can't stop myself from looking around the bar, hoping no one from the gala will wander in here. I don't want to think about what would happen if I were seen here, taking shots like a college fraternity brother.

"Were you alone at the gala?" I ask. I'm sure she's about to tell me that her older boyfriend is there. Maybe they got in a fight and she is trying to get back at him. Or maybe he's much older and doesn't mind her going off to drink with others.

She nods as the waiter brings the second round of shots. "Cheers," she says, raising the glass. A second time she sucks on the lime after finishing the drink. I stare at my lime, a garnish on an empty glass. I'm tempted to put it in my mouth, but my upbringing tells me not to.

"That's pretty brave of you," I say, trying to go back to the conversation I started.

"What?"

"Coming to this thing alone. Were you meeting friends there?"

She shakes her head, the lime still in her mouth. "Those were good!" She lets out a big sigh and she looks so much more relaxed. Her shoulders loosen and her eyes twinkle. "What about you? Were you there with friends?"

I tilt my head, an affirmative responsive without actually telling her. I hate telling people. It changes how they act around me. What they think of me. What they want from me. "I was mostly there for the free booze," I joke, giving her a wink.

She throws her head back and laughs. "Hardly free! Can you believe what those tickets cost? For a charity event!"

Oh, right. Entry costs money. "Want another drink?" I ask. "Maybe a beer this time. We can slow it down."

"I like your thinking," she responds. "I probably shouldn't get too sloppy while I'm operating heavy machinery." She has a coy smile on her face, like she's hiding a secret.

"Heavy machinery?" I respond. I'm trying to flirt, but probably badly. Her face changes, her lips curl downward. For a second, I think she's going to tell me something serious, like she'll be operating a bulldozer when we finish.

"These things," she says with a laugh, lifting up her shoes from the chair next to her. A smile breaks through my face. I love a girl who can keep me on my toes. Who says and does things I wouldn't expect. Who's different from the girls in my world. I order beers from the waiter and suddenly my worries of being seen in the bar disappear. Everything seems to disappear. It's just me and Mara, sharing a beer like we're alone in the world.

Chapter 4
Mara

"Mara," my sister whispered in my ear. Her hand gently rubbed my shoulder and I felt her breath in front of my face. "Mara, wake up."

I blinked my eyes open. Shannon was kneeling next to me, a playful smile on her face. The room was dark, but the outlines of the furniture were highlighted by the moonlight. I was tucked in my covers, the quilt pulled up to my chest. Shannon put her finger to her lips, signaling me to be quiet and then she beckoned me to follow. I slipped out of bed, slowly placing my feet on the long yarn of the carpet that separated our twin beds. She was in the doorway of our bedroom, waiting for me to get up and follow.

"Where are we going?" I asked, forgetting to whisper.

"Shhhhhh..." Again she put her finger in front of her lips and glided out of the room down the hall. I followed her as she led me out the front door and around the house to the back, where our ladder was waiting for us, leaning against the house's one-story frame. She climbed the ladder and took a seat on the tiled roof. I followed her to our spot. The spot we used to go to when we wanted to talk about something secret. When we wanted to be alone. Where our parents wouldn't find us.

When I sat next to her, she pulled out a box of chocolate chip cookies, unwrapped it, and placed it between us.

"What time is it?" I asked her.

"Almost five."

"Why are you up so early?"

"I couldn't sleep." She grabbed a cookie and took a bite, while looking off at the sky around us.

"Are you scared?" I also grabbed a cookie, playing with it in my hands before putting it in my mouth.

"No," she said. "I'm excited. But I'm worried about you. Are you going to be OK when I'm gone?" Shannon's flight was at 10:00 am. She was starting her freshman year at George Washington University. But the way I saw it, she was leaving me.

"I'll be fine!" I said with the cookie still in my mouth. "It's not like you're dying. You're coming for Thanksgiving in like two months."

"But you're going to be OK? You're going to practice what we talked about?"

Since childhood, I had suffered from panic attacks. Before the first day of school, before big tests, or any other stressful situation, I had often found myself hyperventilating, curled up on the floor. My parents saw them as temper tantrums and often would get angry with me for stalling or causing a scene. My sister saw it differently. She would calmly curl up next to me and start talking. About nothing in particular, just anything that crossed her mind. One time she listed off all fifty

24

states and their capitals—that was before her geography exam in sixth grade. Another time, she recited a scene from *Wicked*, when she was preparing for the school play in ninth grade. I could focus on her words, the rhythm of her voice and soon my breathing would become relaxed. Then she would ask me questions. *Do you remember the capital of Wyoming? It's Cheyenne... What's the next line: No one mourns the wicked? No one cries, they won't return.* And eventually she would reach her hand out to me and help me up. And suddenly, the first day of school didn't seem as menacing or the test didn't feel as torturous. I could do it.

Shannon was three years older than me. When she started applying for college, she was afraid to leave me. At first, she only applied to schools in California, wanting to stay close to home, but I knew she wanted to go to DC. So I convinced her to apply, to see what would happen. When she was accepted, she looked like someone who had just been mugged.

"You have to go, Shannon," I told her, even though I was just as scared about what I would do without her as she was for me. But that's the thing about sisters. We both cared more about what was best for each other than we did for ourselves.

The next day, Shannon came home from school with a stack of books she checked out from the library about managing anxiety and panic attacks. She sat with me on my bed and read them aloud, stopping each time there was an exercise that we would do together. We practiced breathing techniques, visualization, muscle relaxation movements. One day, we went to the beach. It was warm, but there was a light breeze that brought goosebumps to my skin even under the sun. "You need a mantra," Shannon said as we stared at the water. "A phrase that will keep you calm when you're stressed." I shrugged, I wasn't sure how someone could come up with a mantra. Then Shannon got up and ran to the water and it hit me: my mantra. *Lead me to the water.*

Shannon hoped that I would get an attack before she left for school, so I could practice the techniques, but unfortunately, or fortunately, one never came. Maybe it was because I was enjoying spending so much time with her. Maybe because all the reading and practicing we were doing was having some effect on me. But when the summer ended and it was time for her to leave, she had to trust that she found a solution for me.

"Of course I've been practicing," I said as I grabbed a second cookie. "You've been forcing me to every hour for the entire summer!" I laughed. "I don't even need you anymore!" But in my head, I was saying something different. I was screaming at her for leaving me. I wanted to tell her she had to cancel her flight and never go to college. That there was no way I could handle this on my own.

The sun started to rise and the light coated us like a thin layer of dust. The rising sun made me angry, knowing the time until Shannon would leave was slowly diminishing with each ray of light that broke through the sky. We sat there, eating the cookies and watching the sunrise until our mom came around the house and called to us from below.

"Girls? Are you up there?" our mom said, shielding her eyes as she looked up.

"Nope," Shannon giggled. "We're not here."

"Shannon, are you all packed? We need to leave soon."

"Mom, you'll have to come up here and get me," Shannon said. "I'm not going anywhere."

"She's packed," I said, smiling at her even though the anger inside me was growing. "She's ready to go." I headed down the ladder and Shannon followed. We ate breakfast together while our dad stuffed her suitcases into the car. And then we drove to the airport and said goodbye.

"Don't forget about me when you get a bunch of cool new friends," I said to her as I threw my arms around her neck. I tried to make it sound funny, but in my mind it sounded sinister and mean.

"Don't you worry," she said, obviously taking it for a joke. "You'll always be my little sister and my best friend. You know how much I love you."

"I know," I said. Her words threw a wrecking ball through my anger. "And I love you too." We stayed tangled in our hug for a few more moments, until our mom put her hands on our shoulders. Then Shannon quickly hugged our parents and wheeled her suitcases into the terminal.

At home, the anger figured out how to rebuild itself. My next panic attack came that evening when I had to go to sleep with Shannon's empty bed next to me. *Lead me to the water... Lead me to the water.* I repeated to myself. I started in a whisper, but the sound slowly grew louder and louder until I was shouting it. *LEAD ME TO THE WATER! LEAD ME TO THE WATER!* I don't know how long I was screaming, but eventually the attack passed.

A few years later, the attacks changed. The first time it happened I was nineteen. I was in my sophomore year at UCLA studying for my biology exam when I heard the static. At first, I was annoyed. The sound kept breaking my concentration, I had to keep rereading the same sentence over and over. I wanted to yell at whoever it was that was making the noise to shut up, but I was alone in the library. The static kept getting louder and louder. My ear drums started to hurt and I began to sweat. *SHUT UP* I yelled to myself, but the static didn't stop. Then the words started to fall out of the book. I tried to catch them and put them back together in their places on the page, but I couldn't remember where each word went. And they wouldn't stick. They kept falling off the pages to the floor where they crumbled into sand. The book was left empty, no words left for me to read, no biology left to study. I failed the exam and changed my major from pre-med to psychology. That summer, I mostly slept. Home in my parents' house felt like being in jail. All anyone wanted to talk about was why I didn't want to be a doctor anymore. What happened with my biology exam. But not my sister. Shannon never asked.

Instead Shannon stayed with me in my bed. Hugging me when it felt right and talking to me. She told me about her friends, who was dating whom, what they were all doing. She talked about the new job she was starting—she had just graduated with a journalism major and was starting out as a reporter at a local paper. She also told me about the news, celebrity gossip, latest political fights. I didn't really listen to what she said, but the rhythm of her voice calmed me. It quieted the static.

"Mara," she told me. "You have to get out of your head. The scary things are in there. The world is a good place if you will just give it a chance." If only she had known.

The summer ended and I went back to school. Psychology was easy for me. I studied memory, social psychology, decision making, statistics and cognitive neuroscience. At the end of the first semester I came home, where my sister was still living with my parents, unable to afford to rent her own place with her new salary.

"I think I have schizophrenia," I confided in Shannon. In my abnormal psychology class we learned about different mental illnesses. When the professor talked about schizophrenia, something seemed eerily familiar.

"Don't be ridiculous," Shannon laughed. "Panic attacks are totally normal. It doesn't mean you are schizo! It's not like you have multiple personalities or something."

I didn't feel like telling her that schizophrenia didn't just mean multiple personalities. But she was probably right. Most likely I had 'medical student syndrome' where someone studying a disease starts to recognize the symptoms within themselves.

Dear diary,

Do you ever feel trapped? Like no matter what you do, you're making the wrong decision. That's what's happening to me right now. There are no right decisions. Every decision is wrong. And I have to live with it. I have to live with making the wrong decision, because there is no right one to be made.

When I left today, I knew it was a mistake. But I had to. What am I supposed to do? Spend my life living for someone else? Yes, my conscience tells me. They need you. But that's why I am trapped. I'm selfish for wanting something for myself. Selfish for not caring about what that does to other people. And no matter what, I'm stuck with that guilt. It's one of the things I hate about myself. My selfishness. My guilt. I guess that's two things I hate.

I thought life would get easier as I got older. That things would make more sense and that I would know what to do. Maybe I'm just still not old enough. Maybe when I'm older, I'll have the answers. But then I look at my parents and they don't. But maybe that's just them. Are all adults as clueless? I won't be. I definitely won't be. Diary, you are holding me accountable. If I'm as clueless as an adult, you need to remind me to get some answers!

Chapter 5
Mara

"Sorry, five more minutes," I say to Garrett when I open the front door for him.

"Take your time," he responds as he gives me a kiss on the cheek and hands me a bouquet of yellow carnations. "I'll just have a look around."

I shoot him a playfully cynical look. "You're going to search my closet for skeletons already?" I put the carnations in a vase, thinking about what I'm going to do with them later. I suddenly notice a bracelet of small bruises around my wrist. I cover them with my hand and try to get their image out of my memory.

"Well I want to see what the arrangement is like, just in case I become one of those skeletons." He winks at me as I walk down the hall to my bedroom to finish getting ready. I'm already wearing a tight tan summer dress and my wavy, light brown hair is hanging loose around my shoulders. I dab a little powder on my face and line my eyes with black pencil, smearing it along the edges to give myself a smokey eye look. I brush a bit of silver eyeshadow on and wave the mascara wand once over the top and bottom lashes. I step back from my mirror and give myself a full once over. I'm ready.

It's our third date. Fourth if you count when we met at the fundraiser a couple weeks ago. The first two dates we met at a bar for drinks. Both times the evening was full of alcohol and witty banter. I still didn't know much about him other than he worked at a family-owned investment company and liked to travel and play golf. I made fun of the golf thing, asking if he wore white sweaters tied around his neck. He did, he said, smiling as though he wasn't sure why it was so funny. This is the first time he is picking me up for a date.

I walk back out to the living room where Garrett is standing in front of the wooden china cabinet filled with wine glasses and other fancy serving plates that are covered in dust. My phone is sitting out on the coffee table with the screen lit up. I quickly grab it and delete the notifications screaming to be answered.

"You have a beautiful home," he says sincerely. "Do you live here by yourself?" He's really asking *do you live with your parents?* It's not the first time someone has phrased it like that to me.

"Yes," I respond. "The house belonged to my parents. They left it to me when they died."

"Oh," Garrett doesn't know how to respond. No one does. "I'm so sorry."

"Why? Did you kill them?" I smile, trying to lighten the mood.

"Uh, no, uh..."

"It's OK, let's just change the subject," I say. I like Garrett so far and I don't want him to run away before we make it to dinner.

"Sure," he responds, trailing off at the end.

"Where are we having dinner?"

It's like a cloud is lifted from above Garrett's head. His beautiful thin pink lips curl up into a smile. "I think you'll really like the place," he says. "I made reservations."

I grab my purse and his hand and lead him out the front door. After locking up, I turn around and see his car parked by the sidewalk. A white convertible BMW. The top is down and the exterior is shining. "Nice wheels," I say. I'm pretty sure I've never sat in a car so expensive.

"Thanks." His smile grows bigger as he opens the door for me. I slide in and he gently closes the door before walking around the front and getting into the driver's side.

"Push the button, Max!" I say in a joking tone.

"What?"

"Sorry, it's a joke, I know your name isn't Max," I say. "It's from a movie. My sister and I used to say it every time we got in the car with our parents."

"Oh," he says, the cloud appearing above his head again.

"Sorry." I make a note to myself not to bring up my dead parents again. "How was your day?"

"Uh, good, actually," he starts. He worked in the morning, then played a round of golf with his father in the afternoon. "We didn't need the white sweaters today," he joked. "How was yours?"

Mine was tedious, I think to myself. I'm a receptionist at a publishing company. That's the kind of job you can get with a bachelor's degree in psychology. I sit behind an oversized desk in a glass lobby and wait for people to call or show up. When someone does, I check if they have an appointment and I notify the person they are meeting or looking to speak with. When someone important shows up, I walk them back to the conference room and politely ask them if they want water or coffee or tea. Usually they just want water. I hate when they ask for coffee because I never know how to make it. How much is 'a little' milk? What is 'two spoons' of sugar?

My grandma helped me get the job after the accident, which happened a few weeks after I graduated. I spent three months in the dark at home before my grandma forced me to get up. One of her friends from her bridge club had a son who was a VP at the company. She knew they needed a new receptionist and she did what all good grandmothers do: guilt you into getting what they want. The next week, I was the new receptionist and I had a reason to get up in the morning. I didn't really need the money, the life insurance settlement for my parents and sister would be enough for me to live on most of my life, but my grandma was right. I needed a reason to get up. It wasn't a good reason, but those phones weren't going to answer themselves.

I've been working there for a year and a half already. Everyone there knows me. Everyone says good morning to me every day and asks me how I am. But they are all stuck up and condescending, probably thinking they are so much better than me, the dumb receptionist.

A month ago, I scheduled myself an appointment with one of the top editors. I had been working on writing a book. A memoir about my history of panic attacks and the loss of my family. It was raw—I'm not a writer like my sister was—but it was emotional and truthful. The morning of my meeting, I had a panic attack and was late for work. I arrived moments before my meeting, clutching my manuscript to my chest.

"I want to publish my memoir," I said to the editor as I placed the manuscript in front of him on his desk. I'd been working on the manuscript for months. I typed all day at the reception computer in between phone calls and making coffees and I usually spent my weekends typing away at home. Putting the manuscript down on his desk was like letting go of a piece of my heart. I wanted to scoop it back up, hold it to my chest and scream that it was mine, but I knew that wouldn't help me. I needed to let go if it would ever flourish. He motioned me to sit down, but he looked at the manuscript in front of him as though it were a carton of rotten eggs.

"I think it's beautiful that you decided to write down your feelings," he said. "But I don't think it's really publishable."

"But you didn't even read it..."

"I don't have to. I've been in this business a long time," he responded. "I know what we're looking for."

"But..."

"You're great at what you do up front," he said. "Keep at it. And when you are ready to write something publishable, talk to me about it." He gave me that smile that said his invitation was not a real invitation. That I should never talk to him again about writing something. I went back to my desk in the lobby and threw my manuscript in the shredder. Since then, work has been torture. Every day I fantasize about how I would quit. Maybe I show up drunk one day and tell everyone what I think about them. Maybe I'll come in with the gun and wave it around like a crazy person. Or maybe I'll just stop showing up. Wait and see if they missed me. They probably wouldn't. They'd keep going on until they realized they missed an important call or that they were unusually thirsty for a Tuesday afternoon. None of the daydreams mattered. I wasn't going to do any of those things anyway.

"My day was fine," I respond to Garrett. "Nothing interesting to report."

"Do you get to meet real authors?" he asks. "What are they like?"

"Mostly they're jerks," I say. "Think they wrote the new bible."

"Well it is about time we replace the New Testament," he jokes. "It's been like what? Two thousand years? It could use an upgrade."

"Oh, yes, definitely," I joke back. "Maybe with an urban fantasy angle. Zombies and vampires. Those are really in right now." Maybe I should have added zombies and vampires to my memoir, I think to myself. There were already enough demons in it.

Eventually we pull into a parking lot and Garrett stops the car in front of the restaurant. Two valets instantaneously open our doors and help us out of the car. Garrett hands over the keys and holds out his arm for me to hold.

"What is this, like the opera?" I'm suddenly self-conscious that I'm underdressed. I link my arm through his and we walk on the red carpet into the restaurant.

"Have you ever been to the opera?" he asks me. "It's actually quite an experience."

I shake my head.

"I'll take you some time," he says. "I think you'll like it. The singing is beautiful."

We approach the hostess, who is wearing a black cocktail dress, high heels, and her hair is pulled up into a tight ponytail on the top of her head.

"Do you have a reservation?" she asks with a polite smile.

"We do," Garrett says. He looks around the room, and then quietly leans in toward the hostess. It's like he wants to tell her a secret, but I hear it. "Under the name Derby."

The name echoes through the restaurant, bouncing off the walls, hitting waiters as they waltz around with trays of plates and cocktails. Derby Derby Derby Derby... the name is getting closer to me, coming for me. I duck my head so that it doesn't hit me smack in my face.

"Mara?" Garrett says. His voice comes out of his mouth armored for jousting and attacks the name, stabbing it right in the heart. It falls to the ground and turns into sand, getting my shoes a little dirty.

"Your last name is Derby?" I say, pausing between each word.

"Yeah," he responds, putting one hand on my lower back and using the other to motion to me to follow the hostess to our table. I pick up my feet and shake the sand off them as I start walking towards our table. I sit down and a menu is placed in front of me.

"As in Robert Derby?" I say after Garrett sits down and thanks the hostess.

"Yeah, that guy from the CADD thing we met at," he responds as though it's no big deal. "He makes the whole family go to all of his fundraisers and everything. He says it's important we support each other as a family and what not. But I guess it turned out, because I got to meet you."

I smile, but the effort needed to move my lips makes me feel exhausted. Inside, the man's voice in my head is screaming *THIS IS THE ENEMY! WHAT ARE YOU DOING? YOU NEED TO KILL HIM!*

Chapter 6
Garrett

"Fore!" my father calls out after swinging the club and launching the white pocked ball across the green. A group of golfers up ahead of us looks up and shields their faces from the sun as they catch the ball with their eyes. I watch the ball fly over them and roll down onto the grass that is so green it is almost fluorescent. The ball lands feet from the flagstick in the hole.

"Nice shot, Dad," I say as we both start walking toward my ball. It landed farther from the hole than my father's, meaning I get the next swing.

"Caleb said you started seeing someone," my father says as we walk. We just started golfing, we didn't even finish the first hole and already I was going to get the third degree. I immediately make a mental note to yell at my older brother the next time we talk. He can't keep any secrets. Especially from our father. "So what's wrong with this one? Did her parents have a nasty divorce? Is she a recovering alcoholic?"

"Nothing's wrong with her," I say, but I'm not even fully convinced of that myself. We approach my ball and I stand next to it, positioning my legs so I can get a good swing. The hole isn't too far away, maybe twenty feet. I lift the club to my neck and take a swing. The ball lifts up into the air and then lands right near the hole.

I've had four dates with Mara so far. The first was right after we met at the CADD fundraiser. We went down to the hotel bar and had a couple rounds of shots and beers. She was witty and sarcastic, not to mention beautiful in her long black dress. I couldn't stop looking at her lips as she spoke. They were thin and covered in a dark lipstick that made her teeth look white as snow. She had curly brown hair tied up in a bun, making her neck look inviting and fragile. Her eyes were the color of the ocean where I went diving at the Great Barrier Reef in Australia. She told me about her job, impersonating the authors who came in—always self-conscious but proud—and the editors—narcissists who were always in a rush. I told her about traveling in the Caribbean and through South America, places she said she'd always wanted to see. There was also something mysterious about her. A few times I tried to ask what was her connection with CADD, usually girls her age didn't go alone to fundraisers. Usually, the attendees were mostly my parents' age. Girls in their twenties who came were usually with parents or rich older boyfriends.

The second date was at a speakeasy that I frequented. They had deliciously strong cocktails that always seemed to impress dates. She wore a purple dress with no straps and black heels that made her tall enough to reach my chin. The third was at a beer garden—when dating I make sure to keep the scenery interesting. It makes for better conversations and more fun for both of us. She wore jeans that suggested she spent hours on a treadmill and a small tank top that showed off an inch of skin around her waist. Last night, I took her for dinner at Spriga, a new restaurant that everyone was talking about. She looked elegant when I picked her up, wearing a tan cocktail dress, red lipstick, and her curls falling loose around her shoulders. On the drive over, she was relaxed, leaning back in the chair and cracking jokes with humor as dry as the Sahara Desert. Then she heard my last name. *Derby.* It always changes things. When people hear it, they can't help but change how they act around me. It's why I didn't tell Mara when we first met. It's why I didn't want her to know, but I made the dumb mistake of making a dinner reservation with my real name.

At dinner, Mara became stiff, making me feel awkward and self-conscious, but not in a bad way. In the type of way that made me feel like I had butter on my cheek or spinach in my teeth—which I didn't, I checked. It was the kind of uncomfortable that made me want to dive in further and see how deep the discomfort could be rooted and when it would uplift. I guess I'm attracted to discomfort. Always have been. Maybe it's a side effect of the life my parents gave me. Mara's reaction to my last name was different than any I experienced before. Usually people act nicer or like they want something from me. They don't usually make me so uncomfortable.

"Well, Son, just let us know in advance when you're going to bring her home to meet everyone," my father says. "So your mother can hide the silverware and lock up all the china cabinets."

I roll my eyes as we start walking toward my father's ball near the flagpole. I'll never hear the end of it. My last girlfriend, Carmen, stole a gold-plated teaspoon. My mother is convinced she also took a Swarovski crystal ballerina that used to be on the mantle, a silver serving spoon that disappeared from the salad bowl one night Carmen was over for dinner, and a five carat taaffeite that left its base naked on the coffee table in one of our sitting rooms. My mother may have been right, but I didn't believe it until I found the spoon in Carmen's purse when she asked me to fish out her lipstick. She pretended it was an accident and I wanted to believe her, but there were already too many cracks in our relationship. I let her keep the teaspoon when we broke up. "She'll probably use it to get the rest of her family over from Mexico," my mother had said once I told her about the teaspoon. It didn't seem worth it to explain that Carmen was born and raised in California and that her parents were both lawyers. Her stealing had nothing to do with lack of funds.

The girlfriend before her was Brittany. She was one year clean and sober when we started dating. Substance abuse ran in her family, she had told me, it wasn't her fault she got addicted so easily. For a year, my parents didn't serve wine whenever we came to dinner. When I noticed a few grains of white powder on the bathroom floor after she had excused herself, I became suspicious. But I could help her, I thought. Get her back into rehab, give her a reason to stay sober. When I approached her about it, she cried and told me how right I was. How much she loved me for staying with her when she needed me the most. Then I found her in bed with another junkie. Half of me still wanted to help her—it was the drugs, not the real her who was cheating. But the other half knew there was no use.

"You know, Ainsley Worthington is single," my father says as he swings his club. "She just returned from vacationing in Europe. Why don't you take her out? I never understood why it didn't work out for you two. Or better, we could invite her and her parents over for dinner this week. I'm sure she'd love to see you." His ball sinks into the hole. "Birdie!" he exclaims, proud of his golf score.

Ainsley and I shared a nanny when we were babies. Our mothers always joked that we were betrothed from birth. As we got older, it started to seem less of a joke and something our parents actually expected. I ended up taking Ainsley to the prom of my prep school. We lost our virginities together that night, but it was the first and last time it happened. Since then, we awkwardly said hello to each other whenever we attended the same functions. I knew she had a serious boyfriend for a while, a Kennedy or Franklin or someone like that. I guess it didn't work out.

"Stop about Ainsley, Dad," I say as I take the final swing at my ball. "It's never going to happen." My ball rolls around the hole and stops just inches away. I walk over and putt it in.

"One-over, not bad," my father says.

We grab our balls and walk to the next hole on the course. Our caddies follow us so silently that I barely notice they are there. I had to admit Ainsley was beautiful. She had blonde wavy hair and deep blue eyes. I imagine for a moment what life would be like with her. Joint family dinners at the Club. Weekend getaways to Paris. Paparazzi at the different fundraisers we'd attend. It would be big smiles all the time. Fun. Comfortable. But like I said, I'm attracted to discomfort.

Mara is different, I think to myself. She isn't like my previous girlfriends who all turned out to be train wrecks. There is something about her, though. Something I can't put my finger on. But whatever it is, I am drawn to it, like a moth to a fire, hoping I don't get burned.

Chapter 7
Garrett

After golf, we meet my mother at the Club House. She's already there, sitting at our usual table in the far corner of the restaurant. The table sits in a right angle of floor to ceiling windows facing the green. My mother is sitting with her back toward us staring out at the golf course, a glass of rosé in her right hand. My father kisses her on the cheek when we approach. She seems startled but composed. He sits down and I repeat his actions, kissing my mother gently on the cheek before taking my seat.

"How was golf?" my mother asks. Her voice sounds like she had kept it in the freezer before extracting it for this conversation.

"It was fantastic," my father responds. "Just a marvelous day." My mother smiles, taking a sip of her wine. Since the accident, my father has been overly enthusiastic about everyday experiences. A cup of coffee could be exquisite, a concert euphoric. An average round of golf, fantastic. It makes me wonder if I'm missing something in all our shared experiences. Or maybe it's his way of coping.

"Wonderful," says my mother. "I'm happy to hear." A waiter comes by to take our drink order. My father and I both order a single malt whiskey on the rocks.

Before the accident, my parents had led parallel lives that rarely intersected. My father spent most of his time growing our real estate investment business, entertaining clients any free time he had. My mother spent her days playing tennis or lunching with wives who were always in constant competition. My mother had done well in the competition, her husband's investments were successful, her two sons had Ivy League degrees (Caleb went to Yale and I to Princeton), and her eldest was engaged to a girl who came from a good family in Boston. They even had a neighboring villa with the Kennedys on Martha's Vineyard, my mother also touted as though that was one of Caroline's starring qualities. When the accident happened, the points she had received from her achievements became worthless. She was the absolute loser in the competition, no matter how she looked at it. So she stopped playing tennis and lunching with the girls.

I remember the day of the accident. I had spent the day at the office, crunching the numbers for a new commercial building we were thinking of buying. My father was giving a tour of the office to a group of European businessmen who were thinking of investing with us. He took them through the lobby where we had white models of some of our recent projects; a 60-floor commercial building designed to look like it was turning on its axis; a residential complex centered around an Olympic-sized pool; and a hotel with a convention center slated to host the next Comic Con. The investors nodded and smiled at each model, making my father's pride grow with every step. Our portfolio was impressive. Derby Ventures was growing by the millions daily and at that rate the business would have been worth billions by year end.

At five, I packed up my bag to go home. My father asked if I wanted to stay and go out for drinks with the businessmen and him. He was taking them to the lounge around the corner—the one famous for their dirty martinis. "Next time," I said. I was eager to get home to Brittany, who had just moved into my apartment after six months of dating. It was too soon, according to my parents, but she was already sleeping over several times a week and was having trouble affording her apartment from the money she made as a dancer. It seemed like a logical solution, we'd be able to spend more time together and she wouldn't have to worry about money. I wanted to see her before her evening shift started.

I went home, where Brittany was sitting on the couch in lingerie watching TV and waiting for me. We had sex and then ordered sushi for dinner. After eating, I watched her get ready for work. She blow dried her blonde hair so that it was big and curled on the ends. She lined her eyes with dark makeup and covered her face and chest with bronzer so that she looked like she just came back from a day at the beach. She painted her lips so they looked fuller and immediately drew attention. "I think you look more beautiful without any makeup," I told her.

"And that's why you're the kind of guy who doesn't go to clubs," she responded. She was right. I didn't go to clubs and I didn't want her to either. I didn't like that she was around alcohol all the time and that she got paid to let other men look at her. I had asked her to stop working there, find a different job but she declined. "I'm good at what I do," she said. "And besides, I don't want to be one of those girls who can't support herself, you know? How would I feel if I just let you take care of me?" I respected her for that, for wanting to work and make her own money. My parents always told me to look out for girls who expected me to pay for everything. Not that I would have minded paying for everything, but it was a testament to her character that she didn't expect it.

After she left, I sat down on the couch to watch TV. I wished I had a beer, but there was no alcohol in the apartment since I started dating Brittany. No need for temptations. I thought about going out to grab a six-pack, but I was too lazy. I'd just watch a couple hours of TV and then go to sleep. Then my mother called.

"Your father has been arrested," she said, sounding more annoyed than worried. "Saul is already on the way to the police station." Saul Backman was our family lawyer. One of them, at least. He dealt with any non-business-related issues we had. Like when the gardener 'slipped' in our driveway and broke his back. Saul negotiated a $500,000 settlement. Less than our annual retainer, but more than the gardener had ever made in 20 years of working.

49

"What happened?" I asked. I was trying to imagine how drinks out with the European businessmen could end in an arrest, but nothing came to mind.

"He ran a red light, allegedly," my mother said. "And apparently there was another car in the intersection that got hit. Your father couldn't pass a breathalyzer." My mother clucked her tongue.

"What should we do?"

"Oh, nothing. Saul will handle it," she paused. "I just wanted you to hear it from me first, in case the media catches on."

The media did catch on. The next day the newspapers all ran the headline: *THREE KILLED IN CAR ACCIDENT ALLEGEDLY CAUSED BY REAL ESTATE TYCOON DERBY.* According to the article, my father's blood alcohol level was 0.08, exactly the legal limit. The article mentioned that my father had been released on bail shortly after arriving at the police station and that he would be expected in court the following week. Family lawyer Saul Backman was quoted, "Mr. Derby sends his condolences to the family of the deceased." The names of the victims were not yet released.

After reading the article, I called my mother. "What a mess," she said after answering the phone. "Investors want to pull their money. Everyone wants to talk to Robert today to make sure this doesn't affect business. We had lunch plans with the Langstons, but they canceled. Probably don't want to be seen with us at the Club.

We would have had to cancel anyway, your father has a black eye and a ugly gash on his forehead. How embarrassing."

In the arraignment in court that week, my father was charged with Driving Under the Influence and Negligent Vehicular Manslaughter. He pled not guilty to the DUI, although admitted to a wet reckless since his BAC was right at the legal limit; and not guilty to the second charge. Saul said a wet reckless was very minor. It meant admitting to driving recklessly, but denying intoxication. Penalties would be minor, especially with my father conceding to it. The court then set a trial date.

During the trial, Saul Backman showed the court what an upstanding member of the community Robert Derby was, his contributions to charity, and how his business transformed communities. He acknowledged that Robert had drank one martini before driving, but that he was still in control and operated his vehicle responsibly. The second charge was the main topic of the trial. Saul's argument has several tiers: the first dealt with the traffic light at the intersection. He argued that it was not clearly visible, blocked by a tree branch that made it difficult to see from the lane my father was driving in. The second tier, dealt with the recklessness of the other driver. According to cameras in the area, the other car had been speeding prior to entering the intersection. Saul was able to convince the jury and the judge that the accident was, in fact, caused by negligent behavior on the other driver's part. In the end, my father was convicted of a wet reckless and acquitted of vehicular manslaughter. He paid a $1,000 fine and received a limited suspension of his driver's license for one year, meaning he could drive to and from work during the suspension. There was also a civil case initiated by the family of the deceased, which was settled with a $100,000 payment.

The fact that my father got off so easy should have been celebrated. But, my parents were silently extricated from their group of friends. My mother was sure the trial's end would bring her back into the tennis matches or lunches she missed, but instead, she heard her friends whispering behind her back when she attended the club. Long time investors pulled their money from my father's business, for various reasons— one needed the money to invest in his son's business, another said he feared a downturn in the real estate industry and wanted to pull the cash. After months of ostracization, my father founded CADD—his ticket back into the elite community of Los Angeles' wealthiest families. All it took was an expensive gala to launch the organization. A-list celebrities were compensated handsomely to attend, and once the tabloids started reporting about LA's most controversial gala, my parents' old friends started to reappear. They all bought tickets to the gala, donated to the cause, and patted themselves on the back for being so magnanimous. He told his story at the gala, detailing how it changed him and why he was becoming a champion for this cause. Just like that, my father's fall from grace led straight to the top of the pyramid. The investors came back—they all suddenly had new cash on hand—and my mother again became one of the gossipers rather than the subject of gossip. Well, she was still the subject of gossip, but gossip that caused jealousy and many introductions to new friends.

"Garrett has a new girlfriend," my father says to my mother as the waiter brings over our whiskeys.

"Oh dear," she responds. "What's wrong with Ainsley? Haven't you heard from her lately?"

I sigh and take a sip from the wide glass cup that has two tennis-ball shaped pieces of ice inside. My parents order salads and lobsters for each of us.

"This one's different," I say to them. "You'll like her. She's not like Brittany or Carmen." Although I'm not sure if everything I said is true. She's definitely different. But whether they'll like her? That seems doubtful.

"I sure hope so, Dear," my mother says. "Why don't you bring her over for brunch this weekend? It's supposed to be beautiful out, we could eat on the terrace."

Chapter 8
Mara

"You can't do that!" Shannon screamed at me. She threw her hands to her face and made a growling sound.

"Why not?" I asked, the scissors still wide open in my hands.

"Because it's mine! You can destroy your own books," she yelled and grabbed the book that was sitting in front of me. When she raised the book in the air, triangles of paper with rows of text like ants fell from the book to the floor. "Look what you did!" She raged as she shook the book in front of my face.

Moments ago, I was cutting the corners off the pages in her book, *Anna Karenina*. She was reading it for school, for her Russian Literature class that she was taking during her first semester. She had left the book on the couch and I found it. I started flipping through it, reading small passages here and there, but then, something told me how to make the book more beautiful. More meaningful, even; so I went to the kitchen and grabbed a pair of scissors. I started snipping away, thinking to myself what a beautiful piece of artwork I'm creating, imagining origami-like designs spilling out of the book cover.

"I'm sorry?" I questioned, like I was fishing for the right thing to say.

"Why can't you ever be normal?" Shannon exclaimed. She rolled her eyes and threw the book on the coffee table. "I'm home for three days! THREE DAYS! That's it! Why can't we just have a normal Thanksgiving like a normal family!" She paused and looked down at the book. "I'll have to get a new one now. UGH!" She stormed out of the living room and into our bedroom where she slammed the door.

"Girls!" I heard my mom shout from the kitchen. "What's going on? Anyone want to come help me?" My mom had been in the kitchen since before either of us was awake. She had a turkey in the oven, yams ready to bake and green beans being blanched. As usual, my grandma would be bringing over the pies.

I got up from the couch and walked to the bedroom, knocking on the door before opening it. Shannon was laying on her bed, facing the wall. She was sniffling, her breath uneven and her back bobbing up and down with every sigh.

"I'm sorry," I said, suddenly feeling very badly about destroying her book. I felt stupid for not realizing that what I was doing would upset her. How could I be so awful? I walked over to her bed, sat on the edge and put my hand on her shoulder. I hated myself for making my sister cry this way.

"No, it's OK," she responded. "I'm sorry I yelled." She rolled over to face me and wiped her nose with her sleeve.

"It's OK," I repeated what she said. "I shouldn't..."

"Are you OK here? Without me?" she cut me off. I hadn't seen her for three months, since she left for college. The first week she called me every day, the second week she only called a few times. By the third, we were just texting. "I haven't been such a good big sister lately." She dabbed her sleeve under her eye, wiping away the small black smudges of mascara.

"The mantra works," I lied. I could have told her how mad I was at her for leaving. I could have told her about how the attacks sometimes got so out of control that my mom would lock me in my room because she feared what I would do. I could have told her that two weeks after she left, I tried to shave a part of my head—that was the reason for my new hairstyle, not that I just wanted a change—with our dad's razor. I could have told her how I was suspended for a week in school because I threw scissors at that bully Jenny May. Or that mom had started taking me to a shrink who wanted me to take crazy pills, but mom was against me taking the pills. She said those pills were for people who were really sick, suicidal even. Not for teenagers who were just acting out. Besides, the side effects could be so much worse than what the pills were supposed to cure, it wasn't worth it, mom reasoned. But I didn't want Shannon to know any of that. "Really, the mantra works." I tried to convince her as much as myself. I curled down next to her in the bed, my face inches from hers.

"Tell me about college," I said. "Is it like the movies? Do you go to crazy parties?"

Shannon giggled. "Sort of. Missy and I usually go out together on the weekends." Missy was her roommate, with whom she shared a small dorm room with matching beds, desks and dressers. "But there is also *class*. You know, where you *learn*. It's not like that's why people go to college or anything."

"Oh, you go to *learn*?" I laughed. "I thought that myth was already debunked and people had given up on the whole 'getting a major' thing."

"A few kids are still doing it." Shannon smiled. "Although it really does get in the way of partying and getting drunk every day."

"Let me guess, you are one of those kids? You didn't want to stop being a nerd in college?"

"Still, and always will be a nerd," Shannon said proudly. "I'm actually going to double major."

"So you have to take twice as many classes?"

"Almost. But the classes are interesting. It's not like high school, where you just take whatever they tell you. In college you can learn about whatever you want."

"What are you majoring in?"

"Journalism and Comparative Literature."

"Aren't those like opposites? Like, news and fiction?"

Shannon laughed. "I guess."

"Well half the news today is fiction anyways, so at least you'll be able to write interesting news, even if it is fake."

Again Shannon laughed. She put her hand on my shoulder, and suddenly became serious. "Mara, college is really hard."

"So major in sociology or something like that," I continued joking.

"No, I'm serious," she said, trying to transmit the direness to me. "It's hard being away from home. I miss you, and mom and dad. It's lonely."

"But you have Missy. And don't you have other friends?"

"Yes, but..." She paused and scrunched her eyes close like she was seeing something in her imagination. "Everyone is trying to find themselves. It's like we're all lost together, bouncing into each other, hoping that someone else will put us on the right path." Her voice sounded very far away.

"But you like it, don't you?"

"Most of the time." She sounded sad.

"GIRLS!" our mom's yell punctured the door. "Can someone come help me?"

Shannon and I lay silently on the bed facing each other. We both knew we were going to get up and help our mom, but we were still savoring our moment. It was like the moment wasn't finished, still dragging on deciding what would happen next. But our mom's call forced the moment to disappear, even though its scent still lingered in the air.

"Come on," Shannon said, lifting her head. "We have to go." I followed her to the kitchen where our mom had stacked plates, silverware, cups, napkins, and a tablecloth on the counter. She motioned to us to take them to the dining room to set the table. There were just five plates. Five forks. Five knives. Five napkins, five cups. One tablecloth. We set the small oval table in the living room, spacing out five of the six chairs. My mom had also laid out the Thanksgiving decorations that Shannon and I had made when we were young—handprints made into turkeys, tiny pumpkins with finger paint and beads glued on top, acorns with feathers stuck inside. And some of Shannon's later art projects: laminated dried flowers. Sometime in high school this became a hobby for Shannon. After every dance, or any time she received a corsage or flower, she would hang the flower upside down with a tack pinned to our wall. Our parents hated that she was making holes in the wall, but Shannon didn't care. Once the flower was dry, she would have it laminated and decorate it with silly sayings or the date of the memory the flower represented. She kept these flowers in her desk. If the flower came from someone she really liked, the flower would stay on top of her desk or sometimes even in her purse. Somehow, my mom got a few of these laminated flowers to add to our Thanksgiving decorations.

It always surprised me that our mom saved these things. I imagined being fifty years old and still eating dinner around the same decorations, with my mom telling my kids what grade I was in when I made each one. Shannon would tell everyone which flower she got from Justin at freshman year homecoming and which was from Brett at the Spring Fling. By then, our table will be bigger. We'll be more than five, I thought to myself. I had always hated that our family was so small. I was envious of my friends who spent the holidays with aunts, uncles, and cousins. One day, that would be us.

Then the doorbell rang. Grandma was the only one coming, so I rushed to the door to open it, swinging my arms around her. "Careful, Dear!" she squawked, holding a pie in each hand. But she didn't need to tell me. I had years of practice hugging her when her hands were full. Any bumps or shifting of weight could cause one of the pies to fall and the glass pan to shatter. But I knew that. I knew exactly what was breakable.

I took one of the pies from my grandma and followed her into the kitchen, where my mom was still finishing up. "Do we have time for some gossip before dinner?" my grandma asked, winking at me and then at Shannon who was standing in the doorway. "Let's all grab something to drink and sit in the living room! You too, Susan! You need to take a break to gossip with the girls." My mother rolled her eyes and grabbed a bottle of sparkling cider. "No! Not that! Come on, the girls are old enough for the real stuff," my grandma scolded my mom. "I'm sure they've had it before." She pulled a bottle of champagne from her bag and I wondered how she had been carrying that in there. The contents of a grandma's bag are always things of awe. I started feeling giddy about having a real drink with my grandma.

"It's illegal," my mom said.

"It's champagne! And it's just a little at home. Supervised!" my grandma reasoned. "Where's Mark? Mark! Are you going to arrest me if I give alcohol to these minors?"

My dad appeared in the doorway. "It's a pretty serious misdemeanor," my dad said in his cop voice. "What have we got here?" He approached my grandma and grabbed the bottle, reading the label. "Wow, Ruth, you really splurged. What did this bottle cost? Five dollars?" My grandma grabbed the bottle back from him.

"If you're going to make fun, you can't have any! Susan, get four glasses! This bottle is for girl time gossip. Sorry Mark, but you're not invited!"

"All right, Ruth, since it's a holiday, I'll let this slide with just a warning, but don't let me catch you again!" My dad winked at my grandma and then left the kitchen. Us four girls each grabbed a glass of champagne and we went to sit in the living room.

"Well this is beautiful," my grandmother said, picking up one of Shannon's laminated flowers that was sitting on the coffee table.

"Shannon got that flower from Dennis!" I blurted. "He took her to prom!"

"Mara!" Shannon snapped.

"How lovely," my grandma responded. "Dennis has fine taste in flowers. Are you still in touch with him, Shannon?"

Shannon shook her head.

61

"Of course not, Dear," my grandma said. "I'm sure there are much more interesting boys in college!"

"I better check the turkey," my mom said, finishing her glass of champagne and returning to the kitchen.

My grandma leaned in close. "Tell me, Dear, are you dating anyone? Do you even call it dating these days? Or is it hooking up? Are you hooking up with anyone?"

"Grandma!" Shannon laughed. "I'm not dating or hooking up with anyone!"

"That's a shame! You are so beautiful! You too, Mara! Both you girls. You're too beautiful. It will be a problem for you with boys in the future."

When dinner was ready, we all sat around the table. My mother poured everyone a glass of sparkling cider, pretending that we hadn't just finished off a bottle of champagne. My dad carved the turkey, while we went around the table to say what each of us was thankful for. I was thankful for Shannon coming home to visit. When the meal was over, my dad cleaned the turkey carcass and saved the wishbone for me and Shannon to break. Every year, we broke the wishbone together, each of us hoping for the bigger side. That year, I wished that Shannon would come back to me. I felt guilty for wishing it, knowing it was selfish of me. But it didn't matter. We both held one end of the wishbone and stared each other in the eyes as we counted off. One... two... three... CRACK! I stepped back to brace myself when the bone broke and looked at the tiny piece in my hand. Shannon had won, a big smile growing on her face. I wondered what she had wished for.

Dear diary,

This week at home has been hard. On one hand, it reminds me about how things used to be. How easy life was back then (isn't that funny, diary? That back then, I thought life was hard and complicated?) But now I know how silly and young I was. These last few months, being on my own, I've learned so much. I've had to take care of myself, which sounds like such an ordinary and obvious thing for a person to do, but it's much harder than anyone ever tells you. No one prepares you for it. No one ever explains to you what that means. It's not about laundry or changing your sheets, no, those are easy things. Taking care of yourself is learning how to comfort yourself. Understanding that your feelings are loneliness and not something else. Because that's what I'm feeling, right? Loneliness? I've never had those feelings before, so recognizing them is hard. And it's even harder to figure out what to do with them. It's funny how people can be so lonely, even when there are other people around. Or maybe I'm the only one who feels that way. Maybe other people aren't lonely around other people. Maybe something is just wrong with me.

I'm feeling even more lonely this week at home. Even though we're together again in the same room, just like before. But it's not like before. There is something different. She's changed. I've changed. I'm not sure what I'm supposed to do around her now.

Anyway, I feel the tryptophan from the turkey kicking in. I better get to sleep.

Chapter 9
Mara

"He wants me to meet his parents," I say to my grandma as she pours me a cup of tea and lays out a plate of cookies fresh from the freezer. I grab a cookie, they are still cold, but soft enough to chew. My grandma used to bake cookies. I remember the smell of melting chocolate chips, cinnamon, and vanilla that used to waft through her kitchen. But these cookies are from the grocery store. She buys the day-old cookies for half price and stuffs them in her giant freezer in the basement.

"Isn't that good?"

"It's weird," I respond. "I've only gone out with him four times. It's not like we're serious." In my head, I add that we barely even kissed yet. The day we met at the fundraiser, he kissed me on the cheek when we exchanged phone numbers and said goodbye. The next two dates ended with a gentle kiss on the lips. When our last date ended, he walked me to my front door. I expected him to come in—most guys who buy you dinner expect to come in after—but he just kissed me goodnight. It was a longer kiss, our lips interlocked and tongues connected, but then it ended and he walked back to his car. I was part disappointed, part relieved. I went inside and collapsed on the couch, tears filling my eyes as I started to hyperventilate. *Lead me to the water,* I whispered to myself repeatedly.

But I didn't feel calm. I felt angry, panicked, torn. I looked over to the carnations sitting in the vase on the counter and immediately went to grab them. I flipped them upside down and found a tack to pin them to the wall. There, I thought. I can dry them out like Shannon would have.

I like Garrett. He is a gentleman, respectful. He is also goofy and smart and had something calming about him. On the other hand, his father killed my family and got away with it. His father is evil, and when I came up with my revenge plan, I had assumed his whole family was too.

"Well isn't it time you dated someone who is serious?" my grandma asks me. I'm twenty-three and I've never had a real boyfriend. I've been on lots of dates, during college and after, but nothing ever lasted. The closest to serious I ever got was with a boy named Tom who I met about a year after the accident. I slept at his place a few times, the last time I woke up in the middle of the night soaked in sweat and screaming. I was convinced he had broken in to rape me, so I punched him in the face, giving him a bloody nose. I ran naked out the front door and later found myself at home, safe in my twin bed. It must have been a nightmare. Or PTSD. I never heard from Tom again. He blocked my calls.

I try to imagine telling my grandma about Garrett. *Oh Grandma, you know Garrett's dad, Robert. He killed your only daughter, her husband and your oldest granddaughter. But don't worry, he's actually a really nice, stand-up guy and his son Garrett is just wonderful. I'm sure you'll get along great with the whole family, once you get over the murderer thing.* Nope. Definitely cannot tell my grandma.

Heartbroken doesn't even begin to describe how she felt after the accident. She was eighty-two at the time, but still drove, cooked, cleaned, did everything by herself. In the last two years, she aged twenty. She became an octogenarian, wore her nightgown all day and sat in front of the TV with her hearing aids, waiting for the end to come. At first, she was the one always pushing me to accept what happened, to continue living my life, but I realize that was her way of not falling apart. She had to be strong for me. She made it her mission to get me out of the house and get me a job. Once that was accomplished, she had to deal with her own grief.

Since the accident, I usually spend my weekends with my grandma. I never really had friends to hang out with. In high school, most people thought I was weird. I was a loner, sat in the back of the classroom, listened carefully. At lunch, I would sit in my spot near the bathrooms and quietly eat the sandwich my mom made me. The bathrooms were quiet during lunch, kids didn't waste their precious free time in there. They waited for the bell to ring, and by then I would be gone. Shannon used to go to the mall with her friends on the weekends. My mom always asked if I wanted to go too, but I'd rather stay home.

In college, I had roommates, but I used to go home on the weekends and spend time with Shannon. Sometimes she would invite me out with her friends, take me to parties. That's how I met Brandon. It was New Year's Eve my freshman year of college. "Little Shannon," he called me as he handed me shot after shot. He kissed me at midnight and by 1:00 am we had snuck out of the party to go to his apartment where I lost my virginity. He drove me back to the party by 2:00 am, where Shannon was waiting outside with a scowl on her face. She screamed at me for not telling her I was leaving and slapped Brandon on the face for taking advantage of her little sister. I hung out with Brandon a couple more times, but when winter break ended, he disappeared. I thought my heart was broken, but now I know that was barely a crack.

"I just don't think it will work out with him, Grandma," I say to her. I know she would love to see me in a relationship, would love to see great-grandchildren, but not with Garrett. "So I really don't see a point in meeting his family."

"Then why are you dating him?" She asks, taking a small sip of her tea. "There are plenty of nice men you could meet. You're a beautiful woman." She touches my cheek. "You don't want to be alone forever."

I know what she is actually saying. *I'm going to die one day and when that happens you won't have anybody left.* She's right. And that's part of the reason I wanted to end it all. What's the point of living if all the people you care about are already dead? If being alive is just a reminder of everything that you're missing?

"It's complicated," I say as I take a sip of my tea. It's still scalding hot and it burns my lips. But I take another sip anyway, letting the liquid burn my tongue. When I was little, we used to have tea parties whenever we visited my grandma. She collected teacups, all elaborately designed with elegant handles, trim, and matching saucers. My grandma would let Shannon and me pick out a cup and she would carefully extract it from its spot in the glass-windowed oak cabinet. She would fill our glasses half with tea, half with orange juice and we would sit at the kitchen table, legs crossed, pinkies out, elegantly sipping our tea as we discussed the week's happenings. My grandma always listened so carefully, hanging on every word when Shannon would tell her about a fight between her two best friends, Chloe and Sophie, or I told her about what TV show I was watching. *Why do you think Chloe said that? What would you have done differently if you were the main character in that show?* Her questions were always thought-provoking and made me feel that she thought of me as a grown-up, instead of the little kid I was drinking a mixture of tea and orange juice while wearing Minnie Mouse pajamas. But I guess that is why fifteen years later, my grandma is still the person I speak with the most.

The last time the cabinet of teacups was opened was right after the funeral for my parents and sister. She convinced me to stay with her for a while, so we could support each other. When we got to her home, she asked if I wanted to pick out a cup for tea. I went to the cabinet and opened the door. Right in front, was Shannon's favorite cup. Ivory white and shaped like a flower with dark red trim lining the top and handle. The saucer had one large rose painted off the center. I grabbed the cup. It had a fingerprint on it, probably my grandma's from putting it away. But at the time, I thought it was Shannon's. Anger bowled through my bones, making my skin bubble and pop to let out the steam. I raised the cup and threw it as hard as I could across the room, smashing it against the back wall. It hit with a melodious crash, the porcelain shattered and fell to the floor. My grandma came into the room, a look of panic on her face, as though she was afraid she had just lost me too. I started screaming *SHANNON WAS HERE! SHANNON WAS HERE!* My grandma hugged me while I fought her. *SHANNON WAS HERE!* And then I collapsed to the ground. I don't remember her cleaning up the pieces and we never drank tea from my grandma's pretty cups again.

Today my cup is a white mug that says *Flyleaf Media Co.* in black block letters. It's the company I work for. They gave me the mug when I started and I gave it to my grandma as a thank you gift.

"Life is complicated, Dear," my grandma says. "But that's why it's worth living. If it were easy, what would be the point?"

I smirk. That only applies when complicated is a problem that can be figured out. A riddle, a Sudoku puzzle. What about when there is no right answer at the end? When you'll never know if you did the right thing. I grab another cookie and think about whether I could possibly meet Garrett's dad. Whether I would be able to smile at him and have a polite conversation.

My phone buzzes and I see the message pop up on the screen: *Where are you? What's going on?* I click the screen off. The man's voice in my head says meeting Robert would be an opportunity.

Chapter 10
Robert

No one knows more about the fragility of life than I do. Everything is breakable. Relationships. Family. Bones. I am reminded of this every day when I look in the mirror and see the faint scar that cuts from my hairline through my right eyebrow. If you didn't know me before, you probably wouldn't notice it. But it's there. Just a hair-thin line one dust under my skin tone. When I smile, it pulls, a reminder that every smile has a price.

I slather my face with shaving cream, rubbing the thick white foam on my cheeks and neck. Then I take my razor and glide it over my skin careful not to nick myself as I clean the stubble from my face, leaving only the goatee. The goatee once was brown, but now it is streaked with gray—a change that still surprises me every morning. When did it happen? I can't exactly say.

When my face is clean I put on my black Ermenegildo Zegna suit, with a blindingly white shirt and dark maroon tie, and head to the garage. I grab the keys for the Porsche, which is parked between the Range Rover and Audi S8. I slip in the car and open the garage door leading out to our half-mile-long driveway. It's a beautiful morning, drops of dew line the grass on either side and birds are chirping up above. A few clouds scatter throughout the sky, but they'll be gone by noon. I stop where the driveway meets the street and get out to the mailbox. Sure enough, another unmarked letter is there. I let out a sigh as I look around to see if anyone is watching. Maybe someone is, but not that I can tell.

For the last few months, we've been getting these once a week or so. The first one said *Watch your back*. The next one said *I'm coming for you*. All of them are just plain text printed on a white paper, stuffed in a white envelope with no address, return address or postage. The first few letters, I took to the police. There were no fingerprints, nothing that could clue who sent them. The police said wealthy people get death threats all the time. But I don't think I'm getting these letters because of my money. I'm sure that's not what it is. Just like I'm sure these letters aren't just empty threats. Someone is angry enough that they're willing to personally stuff threats in my mailbox.

I get back in the car and open the letter. The police said I shouldn't read them. They'll just make me paranoid, but I have to know. Maybe there will be a clue one day, a word or a phrase that will let me know who sent this and why. *You'll get what you deserve*. I crumple up the letter. I'll throw it away at the office. Bonnie doesn't need to know we're still getting them.

I start the drive to the office, trying to stay calm by listening to the news on the radio when my phone rings. I press the button on the steering wheel to answer.

"Robert speaking."

"Oh, morning," Sylvia says. "Listen, James from TeleVoice called again. They said they're shutting us down at the end of the month if we don't pay."

"So pay," I respond, even though I know it isn't that simple.

"We don't have the cash right now."

"What about that anonymous donation that came in last month? The $150,000. Can we use that?"

"We already used that for the commercial and the TV slots for the national ad campaign."

"Can we draw anymore on the bank loan?"

"I can talk to Steve, but I doubt they'll give us any more leeway."

"All right," I say. "I'll talk to James. See if they can be a little more flexible."

"OK," Sylvia responds. She waits silently on the phone.

"Is there anything else?"

"We need to plan another orientation for the new volunteers. We have a waiting list of more than a hundred who want to join."

"All in the Los Angeles area?"

"Mostly, but a few in Northern California. Jamie was thinking we should do an online orientation instead of at the hotel. It could save us money and we'll need to do it anyways once we go national."

"Good idea," I say. "Have Jamie start to set that up." Again there is silence on the phone. "Sylvia, is there something else?"

"Am I going to have a job next month? I love what we do, but I can't work without a salary. Do you know what preschool costs today? Camden just started at Sunnyside. You'd think you'd get a better discount when you have two kids there, but nope."

"Don't worry, Sylvia," I say. "I'll pay your salary myself. CADD needs its executive director no matter what the financial situation. Once the national ad campaign starts, we'll get more donations."

I hang up and make a mental note to call James when I get to the office. What I didn't tell Sylvia was that the anonymous donor from last month was me. I've been giving various 'anonymous donations' to CADD in hopes that it would start the ball rolling. Once the charity started getting big donations, other donors were sure to follow, or so I hoped. Who knew starting a nonprofit would be such a money drain? I had thought after an initial cash infusion, and a few big events, money would start coming in from different directions. After all, everyone I knew was always bragging about how much they gave to the Make-A-Wish foundation last year, or how much they needed to donate at the end of the year to get the optimal write-off for their taxes. Everyone was happy to come to the galas, be photographed in their dresses that cost more than what it took to operate CADD for a month, bid on the two-week Caribbean cruise at the silent auction. But giving selflessly to support the cause was just not as fashionable as people pretended it to be. I make another mental note to talk to my banker about pulling out some equity on the house. Time to make another anonymous donation.

I pull into the garage under the sixty-floor office building that I spend most of my days in. I take the elevator to floor forty-nine and step out into the lobby, where I drop the crumpled piece of paper that's still in my pocket. Across from me it says DERBY VENTURES in big gold block letters plastered on the wall.

"Good morning, Dana," I say to the receptionist as I walk through the glass doors that lead to the hallway down the middle of the office. On both sides of the hallway are glass walls that separate conference rooms and offices where my employees are already crunching numbers in front of their computers. I nod to everyone as I pass by and stop in front of Garrett's door.

"Hey, how's it going?" I ask, standing in the doorway. He doesn't look up from the computer right away. It's like there is an invisible harness holding his eyes to the screen. It takes him a moment to pull his head away, moving it slowly as though looking up is taking all of his strength.

"Fine," he responds. "Scott Wilson wants to meet. He asked if he could come in around noon today."

"About what?"

"He didn't say."

"Can't be good."

Garrett presses his lips together and slides them over to one side. "Probably wants to talk about 523 Heirbloom. There was a story about the fire in the Times this morning."

"All right, tell him noon is fine." 523 Heirbloom was one of our recent investment projects. A dilapidated commercial property in downtown that we were renovating. Earlier in the week an electrical fire sparked in the middle of the night. The fire was in the back, down a dark alley between buildings that were all closed up for the night. By the time the fire was discovered and the fire department came, much of the electrical work had been destroyed, as had been the warehouse space. Until then, we had been right under budget for renovations and right on time to finish and sell the property to Scott Wilson by the end of the year. He had already fronted 10% of the sale costs to show his good faith.

"What's going on with 456 Juniper?" I ask Garrett as I pinch the bridge of my nose.

"Caleb's meeting them today," Garrett says. "He thinks they're going to sign." 456 Juniper is a three-story office building we want to buy. Caleb's been negotiating the sale for months.

"Great," I respond and tap twice on the glass door. "I'll be in my office if there's anything else."

"Sure, Dad," Garrett responds. "Also, I wanted to tell you, I'm bringing Mara for brunch tomorrow."

"Mara?"

"Yeah, the new girl I'm dating," Garrett says. "We talked about her at the club yesterday?"

"Already? Don't you want to wait longer, make sure this is serious before you bring her to meet the family? You don't know her that well yet and you know what happens when your girlfriends see the house." I walk into Garrett's office and take a seat on one of the chairs across from his desk.

"Dad..."

"I'm just saying, you need to make sure she's not with you for the money..."

"Dad..." Garrett repeats himself. "Can you just give her a chance? Don't hate her before you meet her?"

"I don't hate her, I'm just saying, you're always jumping into these things," I say. "Take it a little slower. We'll meet her when it's serious." I sigh. I don't want to see my son starting a relationship with another broken girl. Maybe it's my fault for always sheltering him, but Garrett is naïve when it comes to relationships. In a room full of eligible women, he is always sure to pick out the one with issues and loads of baggage. Issues that Garrett thinks he can fix and baggage he thinks he can carry. But he can't. It always blows

79

up in his face, leaving emotional destruction and financial damage in its wake.

"Dad, she's just coming over for brunch," Garrett says. "We're not getting married, not moving in together. It's just a meal."

I guess I should be happy that my son wants me to meet his girlfriends, that he wants me involved in his personal life. As a father, I always work hard to maintain a close relationship with both of my sons. I always make sure I spend one-on-one time with each of them every week. Since the accident at least. Before then, I spent my life at the office. I'd come home and sometimes be surprised at how tall Caleb was or that Garrett was already in high school. It was like I'd spend a day at the office, and in the meantime, years would pass. I missed out on taking them to get ice cream or to a batting cage. If I could do it again, I'd make an effort. I'd take them somewhere every week, somewhere we could talk—never to the movies or to a loud arcade. But I can't get those years back.

Today, I go golfing with my boys. Twice a week I leave the office early—Tuesdays with Caleb, Thursdays with Garrett—and we spend the afternoon on the green together, just the two of us. It's where Caleb first told me that he was thinking of proposing to his now wife, Caroline, and where Garrett confided in me about his previous girlfriends' issues. Mostly, we talk about work; projects we're working on, future investment plans, but what I value most is when we talk about their personal lives.

"Whatever you say," I tell Garrett. "What's her name again? Marie?"

"Mara," he responds. "She's different. I think you will like her." I'm pretty sure he has told me that before.

Chapter 11
Mara

I've been kidnapped. I open my eyes and I don't know where I am. I jerk my head up off the white pillow and look around. There's a clock next to me, bright red numbers warning me that it is 7:14. The room is sterile, like a hospital. There is a window covered with tan drapes and a tall wooden dresser beside it. My eyes drift around the bare walls and reach a flat screen TV mounted on the wall. My eyes keep turning and then I jump. Next to me is a naked man—my kidnapper—sleeping with his face sunken into the pillow. Alarms in my head start to go off. A siren, flashing red wails at me. *GET OUT OF HERE!* The voice is screaming. *GET OUT WHILE YOU CAN!* But I'm paralyzed. Maybe the kidnapper drugged me and that's why I can't move. The siren is getting louder and louder and I fear the naked man may start to hear it. I'm perched on the bed, hovering over the naked man when he blinks his eyes open.

"Good morning," he says, lifting his hand and gently brushing it up my arm. The touch sends electric shocks through me, further paralyzing me in my captivity. "Did you sleep OK?" I stare at him, my mouth agape. I'm unable to respond, the electric shock seems to have paralyzed all the muscles in my face. He moves closer to me, putting his hand on my lower back. His hand is warm, transmitting heat through my skin. I'm suddenly aware that I'm naked too, at least the top half of me is. He lifts his head to kiss my shoulder and then plops it back down on the pillow. "You don't sleep in on weekends?" he asks, drawing circles into my lower pack with his fingers. I focus on the sensation. The rhythm reminds me of my sister and a game we used to play. We would draw pictures with our fingers on each other's backs and try to guess what it was. *A HOUSE! A FLOWER!* We would scream when we got it right. This man is just drawing circles, round and round and round and round and round, but it brings me back and I realize it's Garrett. I lower myself back down on my pillow facing him.

"Good morning," I finally respond to him, the details of the night before starting to fill in the blanks in my mind. We went out to dinner. Had ice cream. Then he invited me over for a drink at his place. He had promised to make mojitos for us, but after he fiddled with the blender for a few minutes, I grabbed a couple beers from his fridge and told him to come to the couch. He followed, leaving the mojito ingredients strewn over the counter. When he sat down, I kissed him. I knew what the invitation to his place meant. I didn't come for the drinks. I moved on top of him, straddling him sitting on his black leather couch, and continued kissing him, harder and harder, my arms holding the back of his neck. At first, his response was gentle. His lips playing the back-and-forth with mine and his arms holding my back. But, as I kissed him harder, he started to grasp at my waist. His lips started to plunge into mine and he stood up, still holding me around his waist. He carried me into the bedroom without missing a beat with his tongue and smoothly placed me down on the bed. He paused for a moment and pulled back, looking down at me with a wide smile. Then, I pulled him down on top of me. He was sweet, considerate, tender, while I swallowed him up inside me. Then, we both fell asleep. Shame isn't the right word to describe how I feel about last night. It's more like confusion—how did it happen—and embarrassment—what must he think of me now?

"Do you want some coffee?" he asks. His voice is starting to sound more awake. "Or we could continue sleeping." He's smiling at me.

"You can continue sleeping," I say. "I'm going to get up." I can't stay in bed any longer, but I make no moves to get out.

"I'll get up with you," he says, lifting his head. "I can make coffee, I have a French press here. Or we can go out for coffee if you prefer something else."

"No, it's fine," I say. I roll over and sit up on the edge of the bed. I hold my arms in front of my chest, a small grasp for modesty. I see my bra, underwear and dress on the floor. I slide down to grab them and hold them in front of me as I run to the bathroom and shut the door behind me. The bathroom is clean and organized. A white counter with one cup on it holding a toothbrush that looks brand new and a tube of whitening toothpaste. I throw on my clothes and splash some water on my face.

"Mara? You OK?" Garrett knocks gently on the other side of the door.

"Fine!" I say, trying my hardest to sound just that. I look at myself in the mirror, black smeared around my eyes. My hair is frizzy and knotted and I pull it back using the rubber band I have around my wrist. I splash more water on my face, rubbing my eyes with my fingers, trying to clean away the remnants from last night.

When I open the door, I see Garrett in a pair of black boxers. He's picking up the two opened but full bottles of beer that are sitting on the coffee table next to my purse and a pile of magazines. "I made coffee," he says, carrying the bottles into the kitchen. "It'll be ready in a few minutes. You can sit down, I'll bring you some."

I follow orders and sit down on the couch, careful not to sit in the same spot as last night. My eyes drift to the magazines on the coffee table. *California Real Estate. Homes & Land. Forbes. The Economist.* His name and address are printed above the barcode. *Garrett Derby.* The name is mocking me. I don't think I know anyone else under the age of sixty who subscribes to magazines, but I guess I also just don't know that many people. Garrett reappears with two mugs of coffee, which he places on the coffee table in front of me. "One sec, I'll bring milk and sugar," he says. "I don't know how you like your coffee, so you can add them yourself." A few moments later, he's back, placing a carton of milk and a paper bag of sugar on the counter. He hands me a spoon and waits for me to fix my coffee. I lean forward and grab the milk, pouring enough into my mug to turn the dark liquid into the creamy color of caramel. Then I mix it with the spoon and lean back and take a sip. "Lots of milk, no sugar—noted," Garrett says with a smile. Then he adds a spoonful of sugar and a splash of milk to his own coffee.

"So, I guess I should warn you a little about my family," he says abruptly, as though he were getting ready to teach me how to use his alarm or his stereo system. "They're really nice, but sometimes they come off a little... detached." He emphasizes the last word as though he had thought a lot about what to say. "But don't worry, they'll like you."

I wasn't at all worried about that. I hadn't even thought about whether or not they would like me. I had only thought about whether I could actually go through with it and meet them. When Garrett first asked me to, I told him I needed to think about it. After talking to my grandma, I agreed to meet them, even though I hadn't really committed to it myself. I could always cancel. Pretend to be sick, or just stop answering any of Garrett's calls or texts until he gave up. I still am not sure if I can go through with it.

"Thanks for the warning," I say. "I won't take it personally when they act *detached*." I make quotations with my fingers when I say the last word. Garrett smiles at me. He seems satisfied with his warning and ready to move on to a new topic. The voice in my head is laughing, because really, I am the one who should be coming with a warning about meeting his parents. That I already know his dad from the courtroom. I know how he pinched the bridge of his nose whenever the victims—my family—were mentioned and how his posture became unnaturally straight when he was acquitted of manslaughter.

I finish my coffee and reach for my purse, which I hold tight to my side. I need to go home and shower. And decide whether I will go through with meeting Garrett's family in a few hours. He offers to drive me home and I let him because I don't want to pay for a cab. When we get to my home, he turns off the car and opens his door.

"Don't," I say to him. "You don't have to. I can make it to my door by myself."

He smiles at me and closes his door. Then he leans over to give me a kiss. I lean forward, allowing his lips to touch mine. "I'll pick you up at 11:00," he says. "Be hungry."

"OK," I respond and slide out of the car, slamming the door behind me. I walk up to the front door of my house without looking back at him. I can feel that he is still there, waiting for me to get inside before he drives away.

Once I'm inside, I breathe. It's like a layer of Styrofoam padding around me disappears. I drop my purse on the floor and go straight into the bathroom. I turn on the shower, getting inside with my clothes still on. The water is cold. It always takes a long time to heat up. Shannon used to turn the water on and then brush her teeth before getting in. My mom would complain we were wasting water, but Shannon would just roll her eyes. Slowly the water becomes warmer. It continues to heat up until it starts to scald my skin. I peel off my wet clothes and slather myself with soap. I stay under the water. It feels nice. The pounding on my shoulders, the burning of my skin. After some time, the water starts to get cold again and I turn it off. I can hear my phone ringing from the living room, but I ignore it. When I get out, my skin is red and splotchy, sore where I've scalded myself. I dry off and go to my bedroom where I curl up on my twin bed and close my eyes. When I'm sleeping, I think I may hear someone banging on the door. I tell myself it's part of the dream. The bad dream I always have where he comes to get me. To finish me off like what happened to my parents. I keep my eyes shut, trying hard to ignore the banging. Until I no longer can.

Chapter 12
Mara

"It's time, Mara," Shannon said. "We can't keep living like we're little girls anymore. It's time to grow up. For me, at least. You too, probably." Shannon closed the top drawer of her dresser, opened the one under it and started throwing the clothes into the box on the floor. "And you can always come stay with us, whenever you want."

I snorted and sat on my bed, watching her pack. I had just moved back home after graduation and had been looking forward to sharing a room together again. It would be like old times. We'd stay up late talking, sharing candy bars and pretending to be asleep when our parents knocked. Shannon had been living at home since she graduated college, but suddenly she was acting like she would suffocate if she stayed for another minute. It was like the moment I came home, she decided there wasn't enough space in our old room for both of us together.

"You know, Paul really is a good guy, if you would just give him a chance," Shannon said without looking at me. Again, I snorted. She and Paul had been together for six months, but they acted like they didn't remember life before they met. They were one of those couples who stopped using pronouns like 'I' and 'me' and instead always talked with 'we' and 'us.' *We love that restaurant! We had fun. We want to live together.*

I had just met Paul a few months ago. I was home for a weekend, trying to escape the buzz of the dorms at school. The buzz had been getting louder, so loud that I was sure the bees would come and sting me. I started wearing long sleeves and gloves even though it was April and most of the girls on campus were wearing miniskirts and boots, a trend I could never understand. The buzzing followed me everywhere, to class, to the bathroom, and always got louder in my bed. So I needed to escape and I was sure Shannon would know how to stop the buzzing. I arrived on a Friday afternoon and sat myself down on my bed, waiting for Shannon to come home from work.

"Do you want to have dinner with us?" my mom had asked, peeking her head through the doorway. I shook my head, I'd wait for Shannon. By 8:00 she hadn't come in. Was she working so late on a Friday? I decided to call her, to surprise her that I came home to visit. I opened my phone and scrolled to her number, trying to remember the last time I had called her. It was that one time when she was writing an article for the paper about some event at UCLA and she told me to meet her afterwards. I showed up at the crowded hall she was supposed to be in, but I couldn't find her. I called, she didn't answer. I called again, and she texted me to wait a few minutes. I waited what felt like hours and then she finally called me back. She had been interviewing a famous professor about his research. She didn't think she was going to be lucky enough to catch him, so she couldn't interrupt their talk with my call. She was sorry, but she had to get back and type up the article. *Could we raincheck?* Sure, I told her. That was months ago. Since then, we'd just texted a few times.

I dialed Shannon's number, my heart racing as the phone rang. Would she pick up? "Mara? Hey!" She said in a tone that was half confused, half excited. I could hear loud noises in the background. People shouting, a base booming. "How's it going?" She shouted into the phone.

"Shannon? Where are you?" I questioned, suddenly realizing that Shannon's whereabouts was something I rarely knew anything about.

"Out with friends! What's up?"

"I'm home! I came to visit you," I said as though my visit was planned for her, instead of mostly for me. "When are you coming home?" I heard her muffled voice in the background. "What?" I shouted, mirroring her tone.

"I'll be home soon," she responded hurriedly before hanging up the phone. I waited in our room until I heard the front door open and giggles spilling inside. I got up and walked to the living room, where she was standing with a tall, thick man wearing a polo shirt that stretched over his chest. My first instinct was alarm, was Shannon being followed? Should I wake up dad?

"Mara," Shannon said as she walked slowly toward me to give me a hug. "What are you doing here?"

"I told you, I came to visit you." I was annoyed that she hadn't seemed more excited.

"You should have told me," she responded. "I had plans." She looked to the tall man who was still standing by the front door, his hands folded in front of his chest. "This is Paul," Shannon introduced him. "My boyfriend."

"Nice to meet you," he said, lunging at me with his hand. I stepped back and looked at Shannon. Questions sprouted in my head, swirling up and escaping through my ears. They were escaping so fast that I didn't have time to catch and ask them. Instead, the questions just floated around the room, until they turned into smoke and disappeared. I looked at Paul, his eyes holding that somewhat annoyed, somewhat smug look to them.

"Anyways, Mara, we're going to Paul's place," Shannon said. "I'll be over in the morning and we can get breakfast or something." Then she and Paul disappeared. In the morning, she called to tell me to come outside, she was taking me out to breakfast. I was excited, finally some time with Shannon! But when I walked outside, I saw her sitting in the passenger seat of a car I didn't recognize with Paul driving. I slipped into the back as they drove me to a diner, talking the entire way about a movie they had just watched. I hadn't seen the movie and sat quietly in the back.

"What should I order?" Shannon asked while browsing the menu. Her favorite breakfast food was French toast. I knew this from years of

Saturdays sitting at home in front of the television and making breakfast together.

"I think you'd like eggs benedict," Paul said to her, pointing it out on the menu. No, I wanted to scream. Shannon does not like mayonnaise. How could Paul not know that? I wanted to roll my eyes at him, but when the waiter came, Shannon ordered the eggs benedict and she ate the entire thing. It was then I realized that Paul had changed Shannon.

Now, Shannon and Paul were moving in together. They had found a nice one-bedroom, near both of their jobs. Our parents couldn't have been happier. Apparently, they actually liked Paul and were happy Shannon was finally leaving the nest. I knew she was making a big mistake.

"Do you want to have dinner with us tonight?" Shannon asked as she continued packing. "We can get takeout in the new apartment."

I shook my head. I had had dinner with them before. Paul chose what they ordered and spent the evening pretending that his tastes were superior to all. *I never order chicken in restaurants,* he had once said. *The chefs just put that there for people who are not adventurous eaters. Are you sure you want that dish? There is no meat in it, you won't be full afterward.* No, I definitely did not want to have dinner with them.

I continued watching Shannon pack. Suddenly I heard heavy footsteps clomping down the hall and then Paul poked his head in our room. He kissed Shannon on the lips in a way that should never happen in someone's childhood bedroom that they share with their sister and then he started grabbing boxes and walking with them out the door.

"What about the flowers?" I asked when the boxes had been moved out. "Are you going to bring them to your new apartment?"

Shannon looked at her wall, where dried flowers were still tacked upside down. I walked to her desk and opened the drawer where she stacked her laminated flowers. I grabbed a few and held them out to her. "No," she said, looking at the laminated flowers in my hand. "I'll leave these here." Maybe that was when the old Shannon was really gone.

Dear diary,

I'm being pulled in two directions, like always. On one hand, I finally met someone who understands me. Someone who takes away the loneliness I feel. When I'm with him, I'm not alone. I feel like I'm a part of something, like together, we're more than we would be apart. But on the other hand, the closer I get to him, the farther I get from her. It's not her fault. She's always needed me. Maybe it's my fault for always being there for her. Every time. And I mean that. No matter what, if she needed me, I was there. I would drop everything for her, like I did that one time she called me when I was in the middle of a date. I felt so bad leaving that guy with my barely touched cocktail. He wouldn't even let me pay for it. But that's who I am, I'm always there for her. Would she do that for me? I'm not sure. I've never tested it. And I probably never will.

I need to get out, for me. Leaving our old bedroom, moving in with Paul, it will be good for me. I'll be able to focus on myself and my own wellbeing for once. She'll just have to learn to understand. Of course, I'll always still be there for her, but things will be different.

Chapter 13
Mara

The buzz of the doorbell wakes me up. I didn't realize I was sleeping until I felt the shock of being startled in the middle of a deep sleep. I'm still naked, curled up on top of the messy sheets on my bed. Then there is a gentle knock on the door and I hear the muffled voice of someone outside.

"Mara? Are you ready?"

It's Garrett. It seems like only minutes ago he dropped me off, but now he's back, as promised, to pick me up for brunch with his family. I slide out of the bed and pull a short summery dress over my head, not bothering to put on a bra or underwear underneath. I glance at the mirror as I walk out to answer the door. My hair is matted and still damp from my shower. There is a flat spot where I was sleeping on it and a bump on the top. I run my hands through it and give my head a little shake as I approach the front door. He rings the doorbell again.

"Hey," I say as I answer the door. "Sorry, still getting ready." He leans in to kiss me, but I turn around and walk back to my room, leaving him standing in the open doorway. I hear the click of the door being closed and his footsteps as he enters the house. I'm back in front of my mirror. My hair looks a little better, but not good enough to leave it as it is. I gather the brown waves into a ponytail at the nape of my neck and slide a hair tie around them. Then I wrap a pink ribbon around my head, tying it below the ponytail. It covers the frizz. I pat my face with foundation and brush eyeliner and eyeshadow around my eyes. A few swipes of mascara and I am happy enough with how I look. I dab on some lip gloss and go back to the living room where Garrett is sitting still on the couch.

"You look beautiful," he says as he stands up and kisses me on the cheek. This time, I let him. Then, I grab my purse, which is still on the floor next to the front door. "You ready?"

It feels like a loaded question. I'm definitely not ready. I still feel like I haven't decided whether or not I want to meet his family, but instead I'm just flowing with waves of the sea which are carrying me in that direction and I don't fight back. I pause for a moment, thinking about the gun locked in the safe in my parents' room. I debate for a moment whether to go get it, but I can't think of an excuse to tell Garrett as I disappear again, so I forget about it. Next time.

"Yup," I say as I open the front door and lead him out. He opens the passenger door of his BMW for me and gently closes it after I sit down. The top is down and a cool breeze is playing with the ponytail between my shoulder blades. Garrett walks around the front of the car, smiling at me, and gets in the driver's side.

"Let me know if the wind bothers you," he says as he starts the engine and pulls away from the curb. The wind whips at my face, bringing curls around my neck which get stuck in my lip gloss. But it feels nice. It doesn't bother me. "How are you feeling this morning?" While driving, he keeps looking at me, like he expects a magic trick to happen any moment and he is afraid to miss it.

"Fine," I say, realizing I need to respond with more than one word. "A little tired, if you know what I mean." I give him a smile and a wink that seems to jump off my face to his. He fiddles with the radio, raising the volume as a Taylor Swift song starts to come through and he hums along. I'm staring at him, wondering what he is doing. Why someone like him has put in so much effort into dating someone like me. Why he's taken me out on nice dates and consistently been a gentleman, even when I've been volatile and unsettling. But he seems to calm me. His presence is soothing, making me feel less awkward and manic when I'm around him. While others often look at me like a water balloon about to explode on their dry-clean only clothes, he looks at me like he is actually seeing me. He looks at me with intrigue. No judgment or fear.

As we drive, it begins to dawn on me that time is running out before my imminent meeting with my family's murderer. I'm trapped in this car that feels like it's heading straight towards doom. I see a shadow of the man who haunts me, shaking his head at me. He's angry, yelling at me for not holding up my end of the bargain.

As we get closer, it gets hotter. So hot, that I can feel the sweat starting to pool on my lower back and between my thighs. The thumping in my chest is becoming spastic and I can feel a pulsing in my forehead as the blood rushes through my brain and tries to escape through my pores. Garrett continues humming along the radio. He seems calm, unnerved by the two of us sitting side by side without saying a word. I feel compelled to say something, start a conversation so he won't hear the noises my blood and heart are making. But on the other hand, I wish he would do it. Why should I be the one responsible for conversation when he is the one so obviously comfortable in his surroundings?

"Do you eat eggs?" He asks, as though he suddenly understood it's his job to make conversation. Even a dull one at that. "I guess I should have asked before, because our brunches usually revolve around eggs."

In my head I start to picture a table of people spinning around a pot of eggs, like they are sitting in the teacups at Disneyland, turning faster and faster until the eggs in the middle start to fly off. The image makes me laugh. "Don't worry, I eat eggs," I say. "These brunches your family has, do they happen every weekend? Or is this a special occasion?"

"We try to do brunch at least once a month, sometimes more often," he responds. "We started after my dad had that accident. You know, the one he talked about at the CADD fundraiser? After the accident, he became obsessed with family time. All the time, he wanted us to do things together. And he always told us how important family is because you never know when it could be gone. It's like he saw his own mortality then. But I guess you understand that more than anyone."

"Yeah," I nod to him.

"But to answer your question, today is a special occasion, because I wanted them to meet you." Suddenly he turns into a driveway framed with two statues that look like chess pieces on either side. The paved driveway curves through a row of trees that block the view of where we're going. After several turns back and forth, we pull up to a three-story house with a fountain in front that looks like it belongs in Rome. Garrett parks in the circular driveway between the fountain and the front door that's tall enough for Goliath to enter without bending his head.

"This is your parents' house?" I ask, my eyes are racing up and down around the house from the stained glass windows on the sides of the front door to the second-floor balcony that has a telescope and a jacuzzi on it.

"I know," he responds. "It's ridiculous." He opens my door and gives me a hand to help me out of the car. He holds my hand tight as he leads me up the stairs to the giant doors. Where the lock should be, there is a small gray square that Garrett presses his thumb against and the doors become alive, slowly swinging open to reveal the foyer, where a large crystal chandelier is hanging above the wooden floor. Garrett leads me in, still holding my hand. He walks me through the foyer, past a large room with bookcases and a red blush couch, to the back of the house, which has floor to ceiling windows. Outside, the grass is an unrealistic shade of green and trees shaped like mushrooms line the edge. On one side is a rose garden, with red and yellow flowers tangled with each other. On the other side is a marble bar, where a couple is standing with champagne glasses in their hands. For some reason, I'm startled by the people, even though I knew we were meeting his family here. The sight of them makes me start panting, as though I just walked up Everest without a Sherpa.

"Don't worry, everyone is really nice," Garrett says. He stopped walking and is facing me. My hand inside his is clammy and my fingers feel brittle. "Do you want to go outside? Or we can stay in here for a few minutes if you want. Do you want some water?"

I shake my head. Waiting any longer just makes it harder. Garrett continues walking outside and when the couple notices us, they smile and turn their bodies to face ours.

"Always late," the man says to Garrett, shaking his head with a smile. Then he turns to me. "He can't help it, it's part of his genes."

"If it were part of his genes why are you always on time?" the woman says to the man, as she takes a swig from her glass.

"I got that gene from mom, Garrett got the late gene from dad," the man says. "I'm Caleb, by the way." He reaches out his hand to shake mine. "Garrett's big brother, in case he hasn't told you about me. And this is my wife Caroline."

"Nice to meet you," Caroline says to me. She reaches in for a slight hug and taps her cheek against mine while blowing a kiss. "You'll get used to the Derby family," she whispers in my ear. "They aren't as intimidating as they look."

"You, of course, must be Mara," Caleb says. "Garrett's told us a lot about you. He says you want to be a writer, that's interesting."

I still haven't said a word and am not sure when I will be able to. A moment later I hear the glass door of the house slide open and there he is. My family's murderer, wearing polo shorts and a Ralph Lauren t-shirt as though he had the nerve to enjoy the day.

"We didn't hear you come in!" the murderer says, raising his arms as he approaches Garrett, looking ready to smother him. *Of course you didn't hear*, the voice in my head tells him, *your house is too damn big*. He's followed by his wife, wearing a white tennis outfit, complete with the visor and white tennis shoes that look like they just came out of the box. Both of them hug Garrett, holding the hug a little longer than seems necessary.

"And you must be Mara," the murderer says as he turns to me. "Welcome to our home. I'm Robert." He reaches out his arms as though he wants to strangle me, but I step back almost tripping on the grass. He clasps my hand, holding it in both of his and giving it a warm squeeze. "Thank you so much for coming."

I open my mouth to say something to him, but there is nothing to say. I suddenly feel my eyes blinking rapidly and unsynchronized. I want to pull my hand from his, but I can't. I'm paralyzed. After an eternity, he lets go and Garrett's mother gently grabs my hand. "I'm Bonnie. Lovely to meet you, Dear," she says. "I hope you're hungry."

She lets go and Garrett ushers me around the side of the house where a large wooden table is set with a white tablecloth and plates around the perimeter. Garrett motions me to sit down and then he sits down next to me. Caleb and Caroline sit across from us. Robert takes a pitcher and starts to fill each one of our glasses while Bonnie disappears inside the house.

"Mara, do you drink alcohol?" he says when he gets to my glass. I nod and smile, still not sure where my voice is. "Wonderful. These mimosas are just delicious." He pours me a glass. Moments later, Bonnie appears carrying a tray that is almost as wide as she is tall. She's followed by a waiter dressed in black, carrying an equally large tray. She empties the contents onto the table. A frittata the size of a pizza; a tray of bacon that looks like it is shivering; crispy potatoes; a fruit and cheese platter; a basket of artisanal breads; a tray with different spreads like butter, jam, and honey.

When everything is on the table, Garrett stands up and puts a little of everything on my plate. "Let me know if you want more of something," he whispers in my ear and kisses me on the cheek. I push the food around on my plate. My hand is too shaky to stab anything with the fork and bring it to my mouth. I can hear the rumble of chatter, laughs sprinkled through, but I can't understand what everyone is saying. It's like they all just decided to switch over to speaking Latin and I'm the only one who doesn't know the language. The static in my head starts to take over.

"Mara?" Caroline says leaning forward towards me. She has a big smile covered in orange lipstick and curly hair the color of autumn pinned up in a bun on the top of her head. "Garrett says you work in publishing. How do you like that?" The words are somehow preserved through all the Latin and the static and I am able to understand them.

"I'm just a receptionist," I respond, still moving my fork in circles around my plate.

"For now," Garrett adds. "One day she'll be an author and all those editors at her company will be sorry." I grunt. *Probably not,* the voice says.

"What do you want to write about?" Caroline asks. I can feel the spotlight shining down on me.

"My sister," I say. It's the first thing that comes to mind. Suddenly the waiter reappears carrying a tray full of seafood, which he places in the middle of the table.

"Mom! It's too much!" Caleb yells, while grabbing a lobster and putting it on his plate.

"It was no trouble at all," Bonnie responds, lifting her shoulders to her ears. It's like she wants recognition for her effort, but everyone knows all she did was order the food from catering. Garrett asks if I want any, and I shake my head. He helps himself to some of the calamari. The chatter continues, everyone talking to each other as though I'm not there. I manage to take a few bites of the frittata and Garrett squeezes my knee under the table. Soon the waiter returns to clear the plates and Bonnie takes coffee orders. "Garrett and Robert, you want an espresso? Caleb, a macchiato with extra foam? Caroline, a cappuccino?" Everyone nods when their drink is mentioned. "Mara, what can I get you?"

"Cappuccino," I manage to blurt out. Bonnie then disappears and returns a few minutes later with the waiter, bringing out the coffees and a few cakes. Garrett slices me a small piece of each and the conversation above me continues. When it's finally over, Garrett stands up.

"Well, Mara and I need to get going," he says. "Thanks so much for brunch." I nod, trying to express my thank you as I stand up, but my eyes are feeling dry and stuck open.

"Of course, Dear," Bonnie says as she stands up to hug her son goodbye. After hugging him, she gives me a quick squeeze and then Robert stands up. He gives his son a hug and then wraps his arms around me.

"I hope you enjoyed yourself," he says with his arms still around me. He's squeezing the life out of me and I am unable to breathe. The arms of my family's murderer are wrapped around me and I feel compelled to wrap mine around him. How can I do this? How can I hug the man who took everything from me?

Chapter 14
Garrett

"Well if it isn't Jesus, the savior," Caleb says as I approach our table. He and Caroline already look like they need a refill. I give my mom a kiss on the cheek and squeeze my dad's shoulders before I sit down.

"What's on the menu tonight?" I ask, trying to ignore Caleb's comment as I grab the printed menu sitting on my plate and start reading.

"So you found another soul to save," Caleb jabs again, a big smile on his face as he takes his empty whiskey glass and brings it to his lips. "Where did you find that one?"

"Can we just have a nice dinner together, without you picking on my girlfriend?" I ask, still reading the menu. We're at the Club for Sunday dinner. Every week the Club creates a special four-course menu for members and our family never misses it. Tonight the first course is an amuse-bouche of carpaccio with figs and parmesan, the second course is a blue cheese salad, followed by a surf and turf and a crème brûlée for dessert.

"I just have to know," Caleb continues. "Is there like a bank of girls who need saviors where you go when you want to start dating someone?"

"Caleb," I say, my voice raised just slightly so the next table over won't hear. "Stop."

"She wasn't even wearing a bra," he continues.

My mother snorts. "A bra? She wasn't wearing panties! Can you imagine going to brunch without panties? What kind of person does that?"

"Mom," I shoot her a look. "I know she wasn't her best yesterday, OK. Can you give her the benefit of the doubt? Not judge her so quickly."

"It's quite difficult not to, Dear," my mother says. "Especially when she shows up like that to meet our family."

After brunch, I led Mara back to my car. The instant I started driving she burst into tears. "I'm so sorry, I'm so sorry!" she kept screaming over and over between sobs. "I shouldn't have come, it was a mistake."

"It's okay," I tried to console her, one hand on the steering wheel, the other on her shoulder. "My family is intimidating. You don't have to see them ever again if you don't want to. It will be just us." She cried the entire drive home and when we got to her house, I followed her inside, holding her curled up on her twin bed for hours as she continued to convulse with tears. It must be hard for her, I thought, seeing a whole family together when she lost hers. I hadn't thought of that before convincing her to come. I felt responsible for her tears, for throwing it in her face that my family is still whole while hers is buried under the ground. When she started to calm down, she rolled over in her bed to face me and kissed me on the lips. My arms were still around her and I kissed her back as she pressed her body into mine. We made love for the second time there in her twin bed. The sex was like therapy, she expressed out her sadness, her fear, and I tried to take it over, carry the weight of the burden she was trying to shake off. When we finished she gave me a soft smile and snuggled into the crook of my arm. As I held her, I couldn't help myself from looking around the room. On the other side was a second twin bed, made with pillows and a comforter as though it's owner would be tucking in there later. On the wall above it, were dead flowers pinned upside down to the wall. I couldn't tell if the dead flowers held a purpose, or if they were the remnants of some memorial, never cleaned up after their lives had ended. Better not mention them, I thought, and forced my eyes back to Mara's side of the room.

In the evening, we ordered pizza and watched the Food Network on her couch. "How do you like this brioche with tomato coulis with mozzarella tuile?" she joked, making fun of how the contestants on the cooking competition would describe a pizza.

"The flavors are very accurate," I joked back pretending to think very hard as I chewed the pizza in my mouth. "I think you definitely have what it takes to be the next Food Network Star." She was a different person then, the person who I had first met at the fundraiser. The one with the electric personality, sharp wit, and fatal smile.

"Give her a break," I say to the table. "She hasn't had an easy life. It was hard for her to see our family all happy together."

"I can imagine," Caleb says sarcastically. "Really hard to see your boyfriend is super rich and if you marry him, you'll never have to work a day in your life again. Like Caroline, here." He laughs and nudges Caroline's arm.

"Just because I don't get paid doesn't mean I don't work, Caleb," she responds. "I actually work much harder than you do." Caroline volunteered with several different charities, including CADD, where she did bookkeeping and helped organize events. She was also head of their daughter's school's PTA, even though the nanny did most of the job raising their child.

"Oh Garrett," my mother says. "You don't want to date someone who only wants your money. That girl Mara is obviously not part of our class. Could you imagine bringing her here to the club? Or to one of our galas? What would people think!"

"Actually, that's the funny thing," I say. "I met her at the CADD fundraiser last month."

"Really?" my mother asks as though I just told her that Mara was really an Indian princess who rode an elephant to work.

"Was she wearing panties then?" Caleb says, bursting with laughter. Caroline also giggles as she places a hand on Caleb's arm.

"Garrett, Dear, what's wrong with Ainsley?" my mother says. "When can you stop with all this dating nonsense and start dating the right type of woman. Someone who fits in with us."

I look over to my father, who has been silent through all of this carping. He's holding his whiskey glass, focusing on the typed menu sitting on his plate. He looks up and catches my eyes.

"Mara seems like a very nice girl," he says. "You say you met her at the CADD fundraiser? She's one of our supporters?"

"Dad! Are you serious?" Caleb exclaims. "You're usually the first to harp on Garrett's girlfriends. You can't seriously think Mara is normal."

"You know, if the tower of Pisa were straight, no one would look twice at it," my father says.

"Yeah, she is a supporter of CADD," I say. "She was at the gala."

"Interesting," my father says. He scrunches his eyebrows hard as though trying to remember something. "I don't recognize her name from the list of attendees. Does she volunteer with us?"

"Dad, how could you remember all the names on the list of attendees?" I say. "I don't think she volunteers. Just likes the cause."

"Oh, well if she is a CADD supporter, of course dad likes her," Caleb remarks. "Does she have any money she can donate?"

"Caleb, I think that's enough," my father says. "Why don't we try to enjoy our dinner."

As if in cue, the waiter comes bringing us the amuse-bouche that starts our four-course dinner. The dish is a bite size and looks more like a figurine that would sit on a mantlepiece than something you're supposed to eat. I slip the bite

111

into my mouth. It's delicious, living up to its French name that means "mouth amusement." I think about what Mara would say if she were here eating one. "Like eating a firework," I imagine her saying while daintily slipping the bite into her mouth with two fingers.

The waiter brings over a bottle of wine—compliments from the chef—and pours each of us a tall glass before clearing the plates from the amuse-bouche.

"So what are the goals for the week?" my father says, opening up our usual Sunday dinner conversation. "Can we expect to close on 762 Hamilton?"

Chapter 15
Robert

The alarm rings at 7:00 am and I reach over to turn it off. Rays of light are spilling in around the window shades, lighting the room enough for me to sit up, slip my feet into my slippers and walk to the bathroom. I shave, brush my teeth, and put on my suit, quietly not to wake my wife.

I walk through the house, my footsteps echoing against the empty halls, and make my way into the garage. I slip into the Porsche and start driving down the winding driveway to the road. There is dew on the trees that line the driveway, like a blanket coating them as they try to sleep in for the last few moments before the day becomes chaotic. I try to focus on the silence, but it's cut by a buzzing in my pocket that leads to a number showing up on the dashboard.

"Robert speaking," I say after answering the call.

"Hey, how was your weekend?" Sylvia says, but it's just a formality, I'm not really supposed to answer.

"Fine, yours?" I say as I stop my car by the mailbox. I get out, dreading getting another anonymous letter because now I fear I know who they're from.

"Same. Yesterday our first ad ran on national television," Sylvia says.

"Yes, I remember. During the evening news." I open the box and the white envelope is staring me in the face.

"Well, since then, we've gotten more than a thousand emails and calls at the office. Also, the driver hotline blew up."

"Great," I respond, as I open the letter. *The countdown has begun.* My heart skips a beat. These letters are about to explode into something else. The question is, what are we counting down from? Do I have ten? 100? How much time do I have?

"Not great. We can't handle this much traffic right now. It's just me and Jamie and we're already swamped as it is," Sylvia said. "And TeleVoice is angry. Our contract with them doesn't allow for that many calls in a night." She pauses. "And we still haven't paid them."

I hold the letter in my hands, searching it for another clue. Anything that might prove my recent theory.

"Robert? Hello?" Sylvia reminds me she's still on the phone.

"I'll pay them today out of pocket," I say, trying not to voice the frustration I feel at having to invest even more of my personal money to keep this charity afloat. I guess we jumped the gun on the national ad campaign. Our first national commercial was focused on trying to get a national base of volunteers. The charity relies on volunteers who agree to drive people home when they are unable to drive themselves. TeleVoice runs our driver hotline, where inebriated customers call to request rides and the requests are routed to active volunteers.

"Robert, we're drowning," Sylvia says. "Even if you pay them, we need to renegotiate the contract now that the charity is going national. And Jamie needs to get the online orientation ready so all the new volunteers can start driving."

"What do you need from me?" I get back my focus, putting the letter in my pocket and getting back in the car.

"I don't know. We're in over our heads," Sylvia says. "This is too much work for two people to keep up with. There is only so much time in the day."

"You always manage."

She's quiet on the other end of the line. "We'll figure it out." Then she hangs up.

When I arrive at the Derby Ventures office, I park my car and head up the elevators to the forty-ninth floor. I walk through the glass lobby, greeting the receptionist, and walk back to my office. As I walk down the hall, I see Garrett sitting at his desk, squeezing a red stress relief ball in his right hand.

"'Morning," I say as I walk in and take a seat across from him. He smiles at me and leans back in his chair. "How are you doing?"

"I'm all right," he says with a big exhale. "Just crunching the numbers on 762 Hamilton."

"How's it looking?"

"Something is off, I'm not sure. I'll find it."

"I'm sure you will." He smiles at me, the smile that children give their parents when they want you to understand something without having to say it. I wish I could read his mind, but after children pass the age of five, it's almost impossible. "Everything OK, after the weekend?" I ask. As a father, I want what's best for my sons, even if I don't understand or agree with their choices. I try to listen, try not to scold when offering advice even when I know better.

"Fine," he responds with another exhale, like he wants to say something but isn't sure what.

"Did Mara enjoy brunch?" I try to say something on level ground, that won't sound judgmental or concerning. Of course I was concerned when meeting Mara in my home. There was something unsettling about seeing her, seeing how my son doted on her. And I'm not sure where this is going, so I must stay alert. Garrett lowers his chin and raises his eyebrows at me, but doesn't say a word.

"You said she works at a publishing company?" Suddenly an idea pops into my head. An idea that can simultaneously solve two of my biggest problems.

"Yeah," he responds, squeezing the stress relief ball at intermittent intervals.

"Does she like it?"

"Not really."

"Do you think she would be interested in coming to work for CADD? You said she was a supporter," I say. If she came to work at CADD, I could keep a closer eye on her. Well, at least I can have Sylvia keep a close eye on her. "We need extra hands right now, with the national ad campaign that launched yesterday."

Garrett stares at me silently.

"She wouldn't have to talk to me, she could work only with Sylvia and Jamie," I respond. "Whatever she's making right now, I'll give her a 30% raise."

Garrett looks at me like there is a maze on my face he is trying to solve. I smile at him, trying to convey that there is nothing here except goodwill.

"Why don't you just ask her," I say, trying to sound like it doesn't matter to me, either way.

"Can you even afford another employee?"

"Of course we can," I say, although he is right—I'll need to take out more equity on the house soon to pay TeleVoice and salaries for Sylvia, Jamie, and now Mara.

"I'll ask her," he responds, leaning forward in his chair towards his computer.

"Let me know," I say as I get up from the chair and head to my office at the end of the hall. I close the door and sit down in my large leather chair and turn it around to face the window. I sigh as I pinch the bridge of my nose. Who knew being rich was so expensive? The more money I make, the more I spend. I'm hemorrhaging money with every step. A new investment, means contractors, consultants, permits; I hemorrhage hundreds of thousands and then it can be years before I make it back. This charity was supposed to need just one investment to get the ball rolling, but that hole never healed and no bandage can stop the hemorrhaging. And not to mention the amount spent to keep up the appearances of being rich. Club membership, car maintenance, house maintenance, my wife's donations to other trending charities, as well as her investments in Chanel, Burberry, and Hermes—investments, she calls them, since well kept clothes can become vintage and sold on consignment—I just can't keep up.

I look out the window of my office at the other skyscrapers around me. Each window is another person sitting at a desk, working away at their computer, and for what? For money? It's not worth it, I want to yell across to the other skyscrapers. The more money you make, the less you have. I make hundreds of thousands a month, but my bank account is in the red and I'm constantly begging the bank for help.

It didn't used to be like this. When I was young, having just finished my MBA at USC, I got a job at Monrollo Capital, a large real estate investment company. I made a decent salary, most of which I saved. I met Bonnie at a USC alumni event, she had a Master's in Occupational Therapy and was working at a small practice with several other therapists. We both came from middle-class families—we didn't consider ourselves rich, but had never wanted for anything. After several years of both of us working and getting frustrated with our bosses, jobs, and office politics, we decided to make a change.

We did our research and developed a twenty-slide PowerPoint presentation to show our parents, or as we called them, our potential investors. It detailed a property we had found that we wanted to buy and our plan for turning it around and selling it at a profit. We presented our plan to our potential investors, who agreed to give us the money. Bonnie and I worked on the project together, learning the entire business of renovating and flipping commercial properties. When we successfully sold the property at a higher premium than even we expected, we quit our day jobs and asked our parents for another investment for a second property. Soon, other family members wanted to invest with us. We started growing and flipping multiple properties at a time. We hired employees and started working with more investors who were begging us to take their money. Within ten years, Derby Ventures had become bigger than we could have ever imagined. By the time we were thirty-five, we were multi-millionaires, managing almost 500 million in assets. We built our dream house and had two young boys who would never have to think about money for a day in their lives. Bonnie started getting busy with lunches and tennis matches and different clubs, until one day she stopped working completely. It didn't matter though, we had enough employees to do everything we needed. That's when Bonnie and I started fighting. Everything became about money—I had thought being rich would stop the fighting about money, but it only made it worse. Much worse. How could we fight so much about something we had in such abundance?

Our forties were spent schmoozing with the top echelons of society—the people who flew private jets to Paris for dinner or hired the Backstreet Boys to be the entertainment at their children's birthday parties. We were those people, until the accident. Just one second hesitation, and our world was shattered. It was an accident, one that could have happened to anyone. An innocent mistake that led to unimaginable consequences. It was like the luck that followed us for the last twenty something years just up and went away. Our investments went sour, our friends turned away. Bonnie would never forgive me for that, but for some reason, that's when the fighting stopped. She stayed with me, when it would have been a thousand times easier to leave.

I've spent the last two years trying to get that luck back. I founded CADD, spent every waking moment trying to protect my family, when really, how much can I be blamed? It was dark, the stoplight wasn't visible, the other car was speeding, why is the universe still punishing me?

A knock on my door startles me and I turn around. It's Garrett, holding his cell phone in his hand. I motion to him through the glass door to come in. He opens the door and says, "She said yes."

"What?" I can't remember what he is talking about. I'm not as sharp as I used to be.

"Mara," he says, with a little annoyance. "She said she'll take the job at CADD."

Chapter 16
Mara

"It was an accident!" Shannon laughed while sitting on her couch. I had finally agreed to come visit her at her new apartment that she shared with Paul. She rested her leg on the coffee table in front of us and had a bag of ice sitting on top. "Can you just make sure the ice doesn't drip on the table? Paul would get annoyed if I ruined the table with watermarks already." I nodded and already started wiping the table around her foot.

I had agreed to come visit on condition: it would be just us. Shannon had sighed heavily when I said that, but confirmed that Paul had plans with his friends that evening. When I showed up, Shannon had hobbled to the door to let me in before repositioning herself on the couch with ice on her foot. I looked at her foot and then slowly up to her face. She had a few small round bruises on her left bicep and a small scratch on her cheek.

"Are you sure?" I asked, wondering if I was really supposed to believe it was an accident. Shannon explained everything to me when I walked in. The night before, she and Paul had gone to a salsa dancing class.

"You know I have two left feet," she said. But no, I didn't know. I had always thought Shannon was such a graceful dancer. But then again, when had I ever seen her dancing before with a man? "So I stepped front when I was supposed to step back and Paul, he stepped front like he was supposed to, but since I'm an idiot, he stepped right on my foot. I tried to pull my foot back, but then I lost balance and Paul grabbed my arm to catch me." She pointed to the bruises on her bicep.

"And the scratch on your face?" I asked.

"Oh, I don't know where that came from," She responded. "I probably scratched myself with one of my rings or something." Shannon often wore a few bands on her fingers. We used to have matching ones that had a heart on top and said sisters on the inside, but I noticed that she wasn't wearing that one then.

"Want to order takeout?" she asked. "Usually I'd cook for us, but I don't feel like standing up in the kitchen now." Shannon laughed at herself. We ordered Chinese food and sat awkwardly in her living room while we waited for it to arrive. Shannon sat with her phone at her side, and she was constantly checking it, picking it up and putting it back down. I stayed focused on wiping the drops from the ice bag off the table the moment they fell. I had never felt awkward around my sister before. It was a strange feeling. Before I came over, I had thought we would sit around talking about everything like we always had. I wanted to complain to her about what it was like living at home without her. Our parents were always nagging! They wanted me to eat with them, to know whether I needed anything from the store, if I wanted to go with them to the store. They asked me when I was going to find a job, whether I had decided what I wanted to do now that I graduated. I didn't know what I wanted to do, I didn't even know what kind of job I was qualified for with a psychology degree or where I should apply. I wanted to ask Shannon what she thought. Whether she had friends with psychology degrees and what they had done after graduation. I also thought we would talk about Paul. Maybe she would tell me that things weren't as serious as they appeared to be, and that she didn't think it would last.

But instead, I found myself looking around the apartment. The walls were beige and had a few pieces of art made from iron wire hanging on them. My eyes got stuck on one, the black cable was twisted into what looked like it could be the trunk of a tree with roots spilling out the bottom. The couches were light blue and hard like they hadn't been sat on much before. In one corner of the room was a tall bookshelf, filled with books and a few picture frames with Shannon's and Paul's smiling faces inside. A large television hung on the wall directly in front of the couch.

When the doorbell rang, I got up and picked up the food and brought it back to the living room. I started opening the boxes on the coffee table, careful not to get too close to Shannon's foot. "Try not to make a mess," Shannon said. "Soy sauce stains." Shannon had never been so conscientious of cleanliness before. Her bed at home was always full of crumbs and spots where she dropped chocolate or cranberry juice. Maybe this was what happened to people when they moved out, I thought.

The awkwardness continued, but at least we found something to talk about. Shannon had run into one of her old friends earlier that day at the grocery store, she told me. "She was pregnant!" Shannon exclaimed as if that were as unusual as bringing an elephant on a leash to the grocery store. "I'm pretty sure she got married right after high school. Crazy how different people become!" I couldn't help but agree.

Later that evening, when we were discussing some Netflix show that Shannon insisted I just had to watch, her phone buzzed. Like all the previous times it came alive, Shannon jumped for it. "Paul's on the way home!" she said with eager excitement. She suddenly sat up straighter and grabbed the ice from her ankle. "He didn't have dinner yet," she said, getting up to limp towards their little kitchen. "I'm going to throw him something together." I watched as Shannon shuffled to the kitchen, careful not to put weight on her injured foot. She threw the ice in the sink. It hit with a loud clunk that echoed through my ears and bounced off the metal fixtures on the walls, making them vibrate at different frequencies. I could almost see the vibrations if I looked close enough, the wires shook violently as though they were about to tear open the walls behind them.

"How long do you plan on staying here?" Shannon called from the kitchen. "Not that I'm trying to kick you out or anything, but you know, Paul likes some quiet time when he gets home."

I took that as my cue and stood up from the couch, piling the empty cartons of Chinese food back into the paper bag. "Oh yea, can you take that out when you go?" Shannon called as I got up. "The smell really stinks up the whole place." It was like Shannon wanted to erase any evidence that I was there that night. Like she was hiding it from Paul. I tried to tell myself I was being paranoid. Often I felt like I was.

When I stopped in the kitchen to say goodbye, carrying the bag of empty takeout cartons, Shannon was busy chopping an onion. Her eyes were red and she sniffled. "These onions," she said with a smile. I wanted to believe it was the onion, but there was a desperate look in her eye that I was sure I didn't imagine. Or maybe I did, it was hard to tell with the echo of the ice dropping in the sink still bouncing around in my head like a pinball machine.

Dear diary,

I hate lying, but was I lying? Sometimes things seem so blurred that it's hard to know what really happened. I find myself second guessing myself a lot lately. I can't trust my own reading of reality. Did that happen? Did it not? Did I read the situation wrong? Paul would tell me I probably did. He's good at seeing things from above. Seeing the big picture and understanding things. Not like me.

Then why do I feel like such a liar? Why do I feel so guilty about what I did? It's funny, the older I get, the more complicated life becomes. In high school, I couldn't imagine it getting harder. Then I went to college. And now...now I'm afraid to grow up. I'm afraid I won't be able to handle it. I'll be as clueless as my parents! Oh diary, you were supposed to hold me accountable to that! To not being clueless, but that is unreasonable! Every day I feel more and more clueless. Every day I feel like I understand less and less. And that's why I hold on to Paul. I just have to listen to him, he just seems to know what he's talking about. He understands more than I do.

Chapter 17
Mara

They say keep your friends close and your enemies closer. My biggest enemy is already inside my head, but with everyone else, I don't know which are which anymore, I think to myself as I take the elevator down to the lobby. I just finished my first week working at CADD, the organization that was founded on the graves of my family. On my first day, I arrived at the small office space nudged on the sixth floor of an old office building. I navigated the halls, lined with fluorescent lights and closed beige doors, until I found the one numbered sixty-four. Under the number was a small white plaque with the charity's logo—the four letters followed by a cartoon taxi.

I knocked and the door was answered by a woman with boy-short curly hair and big turquoise earrings that brushed her shoulders. "I'm Sylvia," she reached her hand out to shake mine before ushering me into the office. Compared to the publishing house I had just left, this space could barely be called an office. It looked more like the publishing house's storage area. The main room had a second-hand felt couch, a folding table covered in piles of papers, and a bookshelf stacked with binders and papers that looked like the end of a game of Jenga.

Around the main room, were three doors, two leading to offices with wooden desks squeezed inside and the third—the only room with a window—had a small round table and TV mounted on the wall. Sylvia gave me a tour of the office like she was leading me through the canals of Venice and was afraid I may get lost. "That's Jamie," she said when we approached the second office door. "She's in charge of volunteer outreach. You're going to help her out." Jamie smiled and waved at me, before Sylvia continued the tour to the third room; the conference room, although I couldn't imagine having a conference in there. At the publishing house, the conference room had a table the size of a humpback whale, with swivel chairs evenly spaced around, and large glass windows that made the room look like an aquarium. "You can sit in here for now," Sylvia said. "Jamie will come by in a few minutes."

I sat quietly, my heart beating through my chest, and picked at my fingernails. When I told my boss I was quitting my receptionist job, she smiled politely. "No need to give two weeks' notice," she had said. "We'll call the temp agency and get someone to take over right away. Good luck!" I took a couple days off to sleep at home, and then there I was sitting in the CADD office. As I waited for Jamie, I noticed a hangnail on the middle finger on my right hand and I enlisted my teeth to resolve it. I bit down and started pulling it off my finger. My nail bed filled with blood just as Jamie entered the room. She was blonde with a body like a can of soup, round and square at the same time. Her smile dimmed when she saw me sucking on my finger, but she continued shimmying into the conference room and sat down next to me, placing a dusty laptop on the table.

"Did Sylvia explain what you're going to be helping with?" I shook my head and Jamie smiled patiently. "We just released a national ad campaign to recruit volunteers around the US. We got a ton of responses and now we need to organize all the people and get them to take the orientation so they can start driving for us." She explained exactly how the program works—volunteers take the orientation and have a background check. The orientation includes four one-hour online classes. The first class explains how the program works, the second discusses alcohol safety, the third talks about how to deal with rowdy and drunk callers, and the fourth gives basic first-aid information and tips. Once someone completes the orientation and passes the background check, they sign up for shifts when they will be on call to drive people home. When someone calls the hotline in need of a ride, the call center enlists a driver—based on the driver's rating, proximity to the caller and the number of rides the driver had already given that shift. The driver then is given the address and a keyword by which to identify the caller and picks them up and safely drops them off at home. Drivers are only allowed to take callers to their homes—no dropping off at bars or parties—and they agree to wait until the caller is in the house before they leave. They are not allowed to go inside the caller's house and they must report in the CADD app that the caller has been safely dropped off at home before they can take another ride. Drivers also have to give callers a pamphlet about alcohol safety and what to do in cases of emergencies. Drivers are reimbursed for gas, based on their mileage, and thanked for their time. The next day, all callers are requested to give feedback about their ride home, but most can't remember much or don't bother to respond. Callers are also asked if they'd like to make a donation to CADD, but of course, very few do.

After the explanation, Jamie left me to watch the online orientation on the dusty laptop. "I'll be in my office if you need anything," she said with a tap on the door frame. I sat back and watched the orientation in which Jamie goes through a detailed PowerPoint presentation, sprinkled with short movie clips. Sometime during the day, I heard the office door open and the muffled voice of a man. My heart jumped and twisted into a knot when I realized who it was.

"Do you want to say hi to Mara?" Sylvia asked. "She's in the conference room."

"No, I won't bother her," Robert responded. "Just wanted to drop off these checks and get back to work." The front door clicked closed and my heart strings released.

The first week went by fast. After watching the orientation, Jamie had me respond to emails from potential volunteers—a job that took days due to the response from the national ad campaign. Then she had me organizing lists of volunteers for background checks and setting up the ones who passed to start taking callers. Robert hadn't come in again during the week, but his presence seemed to linger in the office like a ghost haunting the place where it had died.

Now, my first week is over and Garrett is picking me up to celebrate. When I leave the office building, Garrett is waiting outside, leaning against his illegally parked car in front of the doors. He smiles when he sees me, his arms unfold in front of his chest and he leans forward to kiss me. I wrap my arms around his neck and kiss him hard, releasing the pressure I feel building up inside me. He opens the passenger door for me to get in and then closes it gently as I put my seatbelt on. I watch him walk in front of the car, grinning at him as he runs his hand through his hair—a small movement that looks unintentional but choreographed at the same time. He gets in and starts the car, the weekend feeling blanketing us as we drive.

"My dad says you're doing a great job at CADD so far," Garrett says, taking intermittent looks in my direction.

"Really? I haven't even seen him around," I respond. I suddenly feel like I'm naked and Garrett had just told me that his father noticed my lack of clothing at the office. I cross my arms in front of my chest.

"Probably Sylvia told him. They talk all the time." Garrett smiles at me and opens the convertible top of the car. The wind gets wrapped up in my hair, whipping it in all directions. I shake my head, loving the feeling. He takes me to a bar where he orders an expensive bottle of wine and tequila shots. Hours later, Garrett does the look with eyes that mean it's time to go.

"I have an idea," I say, bursting with excitement while trying to sound collected and mysterious. Garrett's smile widens so that it looks like it could split his face in half. "Let's call CADD! We can get a ride home."

Garrett thinks a moment. "Yes!" he slams his fists on the table. "This is perfect. You will be like undercover to get the full experience!"

"Yes, this is purely for research purposes, so that I can better perform my job." I giggle as I pull out my cellphone and call the hotline. The line rings once and then clicks as it is transferred to an agent.

"Thanks for calling CADD! This is Mandy, how can I help you?" Mandy sounds chipper, like answering the CADD hotline were her true calling.

"Hi Mandy," I say, stifling my giggles. "I need a ride home."

"No problem! Can you tell me your name and location?"

"Yes, my name is..." I hesitate a moment, deciding whether to give my real name. "Bethany Anderson. I'm at The Three Monkeys downtown."

"Thanks Bethany," Mandy says. "And the phone number you are calling from is the best way to reach you?"

"Yes, ma'am." I cover the phone as I try not to laugh. Garrett's lips are pursed and he is shaking his head as though I just did something really impressive like a backflip while balancing an empty wine bottle on my head.

"One moment please," Mandy says. "OK, we have a driver ready for you. His ETA is seven minutes. Your keyword is 'pineapple.' Please say this to the driver before getting into the car. Get home safe!"

"You too!" I roar into the phone before hanging up. Garrett starts clapping, like I just did a second backflip. "Come on!" I grab his hand and start pulling him up from the table. "We have to go." I lead him out of the bar where a line has started to form. There are girls in short skirts and high heels taking selfies and texting away on their cellphones. Cabs are pulling up and dropping off more girls and men in wrinkled shirts. "PINEAPPLE!" I shout into the air, trying not to laugh. "PINEAPPLE!"

"What are you doing?" Garrett pulls on my arm that is still attached to his, a look of confusion plastered on his face.

"It's the keyword," I say, assuming that explains it all. But Garrett still doesn't seem to understand. "Don't you know how CADD works?" He shrugs his shoulders, a move that absolves him of his lack of knowledge without him having to admit it. I suddenly feel like I have the upper hand and I clear my throat before explaining the keyword to him. I feel professional, like my first week at CADD was a huge accomplishment, all for this moment. When I finish, he yells out: "PINEAPPLE!" We both start laughing.

"Over here!" a driver in a silver Camry shouts. "Pineapple!" Garrett and I look at each other, and simultaneously lean in for a kiss. I feel like a magician and our magic word turned the pineapple into a carriage. We stuff ourselves into the backseat of the car and give the driver Garrett's address. Garrett has his arm around me and he is nuzzling my neck. I watch the driver who nervously looks back at us through the rearview mirror as though he were transporting explosives that could detonate at any moment. I do sort of feel like that's possible.

When we arrive at Garrett's apartment building the driver turns around and hands Garrett the pamphlet. It's yellow and says *Thanks for calling CADD* on the front, exactly like the pamphlets I saw in the office. We say thanks and goodnight and head up the elevator to Garrett's apartment.

"So CADD works well!" Garrett says as he presses his body against mine. "You must be doing a great job at work."

"Oh yes, that was all my doing," I respond sarcastically. "The charity simply could not function without me."

"I can't function without you," Garrett says as he starts kissing my neck and chest. How incredibly cheesy, I think to myself. But isn't that what we're all looking for? Someone who says the cheesiest things, but really means them? I put my hands on his cheeks and pull his head up towards my face. He leans in to kiss my lips but I hold him back, staring into his eyes. The elevator dings and the doors open to his floor. He walks backwards out of the elevator, his hands holding onto mine, and opens his front door. Inside, I let him kiss my lips and I snake my arms around him, pulling his white collared shirt out from his pants. He takes me into the bedroom and for one night, it seems like everything is going to be OK.

Chapter 18
Mara

RING RING! I'm startled awake by my cellphone screaming on the nightstand. I reach my hand from under the pillow to grab it and bring it to my face. When I don't recognize the number, my heart stops. *He found me,* is my first thought. I should ignore it, but I am compelled to answer. "Hello?" My voice cracks.

"Thanks for using CADD!" An automated message starts. "We're happy to hear you got home safely and wanted to know how you would rate your experience. Please use your keypad to select a number one through nine to rate your ride home—one being the worst, nine being the best." I bring the phone to my face and press nine. No wonder very few callers rate their experience, I think to myself. It's way too early for a hungover person to function. "Thanks for your rating! If you were happy with your experience, we'd like to invite you to make a donation to CADD. Donations help us to continue providing a safe way home for others. To make a donation, please press one." I hang up the phone and toss it on the nightstand. The phone hits the table's corner and bounces to the floor.

"Who was that?" Garrett mumbles next to me without moving. He's lying on his stomach facing me.

"No one," I respond and inch my body closer to his. I'm naked under the covers and I squirm my body around so that I'm curled up on Garrett's side. I kiss his cheek and then close my eyes. He moans.

"Good morning to you," he says, wrapping his arm around me. The phone rings again. I roll over and look at my phone on the floor, but the screen is black. Then I look up and see Garrett's phone wiggling on the nightstand next to him. I can see it's his dad calling.

"It's yours." I nudge Garrett, but I'm hoping he just turns off the phone. Even naked in bed, I can't get away from my family's murderer. Garrett opens his eyes and turns over. He squints as he picks up the phone and answers.

"Hi Dad," he says. I can hear his dad's muffled voice through the phone. I hear a few words and phrases: *CADD... the hotline... driver reported...* "Dad," Garrett says, but I can still hear Robert talking through the phone. *Address...you can't...how it looks...* "Dad, let's talk about this later," Garrett mumbles. There is silence on the other side. The next sentence I hear loud and clear. *Are you with her?*

"Dad, I can't talk now," Garrett says. "I'll call you later." He hangs up the phone and rolls back over to me. He wraps his arm around me and closes his eyes as he snuggles his face into his pillow. The sirens in my head start to ring. Flashing lights go off, red, yellow, orange warnings. *Are you with her?* I keep hearing

Robert saying that over and over: *Are you with HER? Are you WITH her? Are YOU with her?* The meaning of the sentence starts to ramble in my head. Did I make a mistake? Am I going to be fired? Has Robert figured out who I am? I feel trapped. Garrett's arm is on top of me, like a lead pole holding me down underwater. I can't breathe, I need air. I'm drowning. I tilt my head so I can see Garrett's face. His eyes are closed and he is breathing peacefully. But how can he, when the sirens are so loud? I try to lift his arm, but it's heavy. So heavy, I start to sweat. I'm panting as I use all my strength to free myself from his grasp. He must feel my fretting, because his arm lifts and I am able to dash from the room to the bathroom. I turn on the cold water in the shower and step inside, trying to freeze out the sirens. The water pounds my skin and I force myself to stay under the stream even though every instinct is telling me to get out. I'm shivering now.

I grab the towel hanging outside the shower and wrap it around me, but the water is still on and in moments the towel is soaked. But I stand still, holding the heavy towel around my head and body. The sirens have been replaced by the pounding of the water. I stay there, focusing on the rhythm until I hear the door opening.

"Mara? Everything OK?" Garrett asks. He's wearing boxers and his blonde hair is messy and matted in places. He's looking at me through the glass door of the shower, his eyes moving up and down. Then he reaches his hand inside and turns off the water. "Let me get you a new towel." He disappears for a moment and then comes back with a folded white towel that he hands me. I drop the wet towel to my feet and wrap the dry one around me. He rubs his hands up and down my arms as though trying to dry me off.

"What did your dad say?" I ask.

"The driver reported that he dropped us off at my address. Somehow it was flagged and made its way to my dad," Garrett says. The right side of his lips curl up. "He said I shouldn't be using CADD and wasting their minimal resources. That I should just call a cab next time. It's no big deal." He's still rubbing my arms. "Are you OK?"

"Just a little hungover," I say and start moving out of the shower. "Your dad's going to fire me now, huh?"

"No, it's no big deal," Garrett says.

"He must hate me."

"Why would you think that?"

"Why wouldn't he?" I stare into Garrett's eyes, like I'm challenging him.

"No, he doesn't..." Garrett looks around the bathroom with his hands on the back of his neck like he's hoping to find the words somewhere between the rug and the toilet. I leave the bathroom and start collecting my clothes from the floor of the bedroom. My underwear is rolled up under the bed. My bra is hanging over the top of the headboard. My dress is on the floor. I put it all back on and grab my phone that's still lying next to the nightstand.

"I have to go," I say. Garrett is standing in the doorway of his bedroom. I can't help notice his abs and the faint line of hair from his belly button into his boxers.

"What about coffee? Breakfast?" He asks.

"Don't you have a family brunch to get to?"

"I don't have to go. We could stay here."

I shake my head. I need to go see my grandma. She will be able to calm me down, to help me figure out what I am feeling. Besides, I haven't visited her in a few weeks.

"Let me call you a cab, at least," Garrett says, grabbing his phone. He orders a taxi and then we sit down on the couch to wait for it.

"Can I come over tonight?" he asks, like a puppy who isn't sure why he is being punished for peeing in the house. I start to shake my head, but then his phone rings. It's the cab driver who is downstairs. Garrett kisses me as I leave. He waits in his doorway until the elevator doors close behind me. I have to end it with him. When I look at him, I see his father. His father's deep blue eyes, his father's sharp chin, his thick blonde hair. How did I not notice that at the CADD fundraiser? I also see his father's bloody hands, the scar on his eyebrow, and my dead family at his feet. I tell myself that this is the last time I will see Garrett as his girlfriend. If I see him again, it will be because I've gathered up the courage to take my revenge.

I get in the cab and take it straight to my grandma's house. I pay the driver and walk from the sidewalk to the front door. All the windows are closed, which is unusual for my grandma. She likes the fresh air, the sounds of the birds outside. I knock on the door and notice the dry flowers in the pot on the porch. I knock again and when she doesn't answer I dig into my purse to pull out her house key. Even though I have a key to her house, I prefer not to use it. I like the way my grandma opens the door for me, like she's been expecting me to come.

I insert the key into the lock and turn it, opening the door. The air in the house smells stale, like it has already been breathed and exhaled. The floor creaks as I walk through the living room to the kitchen. "Grandma?" I call out, but she doesn't answer. I turn down the hall to her bedroom. The door is ajar and I peek inside. She's in bed, totally still. "Grandma?" I ask again, afraid of entering the bedroom. When she doesn't answer, I force myself inside and approach her. She's lying on her back; her eyes closed, her arms folded in front of her chest. As I get closer, I'm hit with a smell and I force myself not to think what I am thinking. I get closer and grab her hand which is cold and stiff like a plank of wood. "Grandma!" I yell this time, but I already know she won't answer. The tears start to escape my eyes and I shake her hand in mine. "Grandma!" I yell again as I fall to the floor. I start pounding the ground and screaming. This can't be happening. She was so healthy, so alive. She was the only person I had left. I pull myself up to look at her again. Her face is tranquil, her lips are soft and curled up slightly like she's holding in a secret. "Grandma," I say one more time quietly, begging her to release that secret to me.

I kneel down on the side of her bed and wait. For what, I am not sure, but there is nothing else to do. I came here to visit my grandma and that's what I will do. "Grandma, I need you more than ever right now," I say to her. I wait for a response, but of course there is none. "I don't know what to do." I stay by her side quietly, and I start to imagine what she would say to me. *Do you love him?* She would ask me. I hear the words aloud as though she is sitting up next to me instead of lying lifeless in the bed.

"I don't know," I say. "I like being with him. He's so nice to me. Too nice, even."

There is no such thing as too nice. She would have said it with a click of her tongue. *Does he make you happy? Does he help you feel whole?*

"He does, Grandma. He calms me."

So what's the problem, Dear?

I start to cry. "Grandma, the problem is his father."

Nobody likes their in-laws. Let me tell you about your grandfather's parents! They would have done anything to get rid of me! She would have grunted.

I smile and wipe a tear that has slid down to my chin. I'm still kneeling and I stay quiet for a few more moments, even though I know what I have to do. I grab my phone and I call him, because who else is there?

Chapter 19
Garrett

I have my arm around Mara's shoulders as we stand above the grave. It's just us, a funeral director and a few other people—two ladies who look like they are in their eighties and go to funerals as often as they have lunch, and a couple that looks about my parents' age wearing suits and holding their cellphones in their hands. Mara feels limp as she leans into me.

The funeral director is speaking into the air, as no one seems to be listening. The old ladies are talking loudly to each other as though they have forgotten how to whisper and the couple is fighting the urge to look at their cellphones. Mara is somewhere else and I am focusing on holding her up.

"Would you like to say a few words?" The funeral director says to me. He must think I am the grandson since I organized the funeral. I had to. When Mara called me that day, hours after she left, I hadn't answered. I was already at my parents' home guzzling mimosas and putting on the mini green in our backyard with Caleb who was complaining about how his three-year-old daughter couldn't even read yet. *Can you believe that? He said to me. We're paying $20,000 a year for preschool. The least they could do was teach her how to read!* I nodded and tried to sympathize with him, but the truth is I have no idea when kids are supposed to learn how to read.

In the afternoon, when I saw the missed call from Mara, a pit grew in my stomach. It was just one missed call with no voice message, no text message, but it was so unexpected that I knew something was wrong. Up to that point, I was always the one who had called her, I always texted first.

I called her back and she answered on the first ring. Her voice was sultry and crackled when she said hello and told me about her grandma and that she needed my help. On one hand, I felt honored and giddy that she wanted my help. On the other, I felt guilty that her pain made me excited to take care of her. I had rushed over to her grandma's while calling a funeral home on the way over. The funeral director took down the address and organized to have the body collected and prepped for burial.

When I arrived, Mara was sitting on the floor next to her grandma's bed. For a moment, I was afraid that Mara was as lifeless as the body above her, but then she flinched. I picked her up in my arms and carried her to the living room. She didn't say a word as we waited for the funeral director to arrive. She just sat on the couch biting her nails as I rubbed her shoulders and felt good about myself for being there for her.

Soon, the funeral director arrived with a crew to collect the body. He handed me a death certificate to sign, which I tried to give to Mara, but when she looked right through it, I took it and signed my name. When the body was gone, I picked up Mara, put her in my car and drove to my place. For the next two days she stayed in bed without eating or drinking, while I arranged the funeral. Luckily, her grandma already had a burial plot waiting for her next to her late husband. I just needed to order flowers and put a notice in the local paper. I asked Mara if there was anyone I could call to invite them to the funeral, but she just shook her head.

The morning of the funeral I drove Mara to her house and found a black dress in her closet. I helped her in the shower and gently pulled the dress on over her head the way I had seen Caroline dress my niece. Mara was more cooperative than the three-year-old and she even put on a little makeup once the dress was on.

When we arrived at the cemetery, the parking lot was full and droves of people in black were walking towards the entrance. At first I was surprised, thinking that my notice in the paper was rather successful, but it turned out there was another funeral going on at the same time several rows over. At ours, there was just the seven of us.

"Would you like to say a few words?" the funeral director repeats to me, as though he thought I hadn't heard him. I look at Mara who is still staring off somewhere and then back at the funeral director. I clear my throat.

"Grandma Ruth was a very loving person," I start. "She had a hard life, but managed to be kind and take care of those around her." I try to think about what Mara had told me about her grandma, but it wasn't much. "She spent a lot of time with her granddaughter Mara, and helped her get through some difficult times. She will always be loved and in our hearts." I nod to the funeral director as a signal that I had finished. He smiles politely and continues talking.

When the service ends, the couple approaches Mara and me. "So sorry for your loss," the woman says. "Susan and I were friends when we were younger. Your grandmother would always give us cookies after school. When I saw the notice in the paper, I just wanted to come and share my condolences." Her husband stands silently next to her.

"Thank you for coming," I respond, although I don't know who Susan is. I should feel awkward or uncomfortable taking charge when I wasn't even related to Ruth, but I feel fortunate that I can do this for Mara. Then the old ladies come up to us.

"We played bridge with Ruth," one of them says. "She was quite a good player."

"We'll need to find a fourth now," the other says stretching her lips and looking around as though she may find that fourth right here.

"Thank you for coming," I say.

"We're happy to see Mara found someone," the first says. "Ruth was always so worried." She's speaking to me as though Mara isn't still leaning into my shoulder.

"And someone as handsome as you!" the second woman says. "Ruth must have loved you! But it's strange she never mentioned you to us. We just saw her last Thursday."

I smile and raise my eyebrows. "I guess she was saving the news for next time." I feel ashamed that I never met Ruth and don't want to reveal that secret to her friends.

"Oh well," the first one sighs. "You get used to these things when you're our age. Everyone's just dropping like flies."

I can see the women want to stay and continue talking, but suddenly Mara pulls away and starts walking. She's walking like a zombie being drawn toward its energy source, like she has no control over the movements of her legs steadily carrying her. I politely excuse us from the women and follow her, staying a couple steps behind. I don't want to crowd her, but I want to be there when she needs me. She walks down the row of graves and turns down a small hill that leads deeper into the cemetery. Then she starts zigzagging until she stops in front of three matching gravestones. She stands still, her arms stretched down by her sides and her head bowed. I'm still a few paces behind her and can't decide whether to approach. I'm afraid she'll spook and run away. My eyes move to the gravestones. *Mark Sanders September 1, 1972—June 5, 2017; Susan Sanders May 6, 1975— June 5, 2017; Shannon Sanders January 16, 1993—June 5, 2017.*

Something strikes me about the date June 5, 2017, the date that's repeated on all three gravestones, like it's a holiday I'm supposed to remember, but I brush that thought aside. I do recognize the last name Sanders, it's Mara's. I slowly start to get closer to her and gently put my hands on her shoulders. She doesn't even flinch. I squeeze tight, letting her know I am here. She's swaying slightly, like the breeze is controlling her and she is just flowing wherever it takes her, then she falls back into me.

"I'm so sorry," I say, wrapping my arms around her neck and kissing her cheek from behind. Mara never told me how her parents died. She never told me anything about them, aside from the fact that they were no longer alive. I start to wonder about them and about the third grave in the row—Shannon. Based on the years under her name, I guess she was Mara's older sister. Thoughts start swirling in my head—maybe they all died in a fire, in some freak accident that Mara somehow escaped. My lips are burning to ask the questions my brain is starting to formulate, but I just can't do it. I don't want to cause her more pain.

We stand there silently for what feels like hours, but I don't move my arms to check. When the shadows of the gravestones start to stretch back onto the row of graves behind them, Mara leans forward. "Let's go," she says and already she is walking towards the cemetery entrance. She navigates as though in the dark with her eyes closed, like she knows every pebble, every turn by memory. Like she's walked this way many times before.

I drive her back to her house and follow her inside. She's silent, indifferent to my presence, but I don't want her to be alone. I wish I could understand what she is feeling, could try to sympathize with her, but I know I can't. The closest thing I've experienced to the loss of a family member is when Baxter died when I was eight. My little Jack Russell terrier who I had spent my childhood playing with in the yard was fourteen years old and one morning he just didn't wake up. Caleb and I cried, but soon forgot about him when our parents bought us matching electric motocross bikes. One afternoon of riding them up and down the driveway and Baxter was a distant memory. I wish I could give something like that to Mara, to ease her pain, but I know that is a naïve thought. No toy could distract her from her loss.

Mara pulls off her dress and goes into her bedroom, motioning me to follow. When I'm in the doorway, she violently grabs my hand and leads me to her bed where she pulls me on top of her and tugs at my belt. She uses her feet to kick down my pants and she starts biting my lower lip. It takes me by surprise, but I tell myself that everyone grieves in their own way and my job here is to help Mara anyway I can. So I clutch her waist and toss her farther up on the bed. Then I hold her hands above her head and push myself inside her. She squirms under me, biting my lips harder until they start to bleed, but I continue.

When we finish, she rolls over and falls asleep. I stay next to her, grabbing a tissue off her nightstand to wipe my lips, which are swollen and probably bruised. I start looking around her room—I know I've been in here before, but it all seems new to me. My eyes drift up to the wall above the bed. There is a painting of two hands reaching for each other, like in the Creation of Adam in the Sistine Chapel, but these hands are feminine and covered in bracelets. Next to the painting is a quote that was drawn on the walls with a sharpie: *"At every moment of our lives, we all have one foot in a fairy tale and the other in the abyss."*

My eyes slide over to the other side of the room, where a twin bed is resting in the corner, mirroring the one we're in. The bed is made, but the pillow is half propped up on the wall behind it and the top of the comforter is a little crooked. Above the bed, pictures of smiling girls are taped to the wall. The pictures are cut up around the people in them and taped over each other like the collage is growing from an epicenter in the middle. I'm too far to see if I recognize anyone in the pictures, but from where I am, I can see the girls are happy. There are pictures taken at the beach, around campfires, on bikes. There are closeups on faces, and silhouettes of girls dancing in the sunset. I start to wonder whether these are Shannon's pictures, waiting for the collage to grow as the story continues. But the story won't continue. There will be no more pictures. My eyes are again drawn to the dead flowers hanging upside down on the walls. It seems like there are more now, like the dead flowers are somehow reproducing on the wall. I avert my eyes.

I roll onto my side and wrap my arms around Mara. I hope that one day, she'll tell me about the smiling girls in the pictures. I hope she'll tell me about Shannon and her parents, and about the dead flowers hanging upside down. Maybe one day she'll even tell me what happened on June 5, 2017.

Chapter 20
Mara

"It's my birthday!" I screamed to Shannon on the phone. "For one evening, can't you just think about me? And not just about yourself all the time?" I heard Shannon huffing on the other side.

"I just don't understand the problem," she said. She was trying to sound mature and pragmatic, but it came off condescending and mean. "You're acting like I am trying to bring your arch nemesis to your birthday dinner. It's just Paul! He's family!"

"He's not family!" I screamed back. "It's my birthday and I want just us, just our family! If I had a boyfriend and you asked that of me, I would do it for you! Paul will survive one evening without you!"

Shannon and I had been arguing about this for a week already. My 21st birthday was a few days away and we had been planning it since I was 16. Shannon promised that when I turned 21, we would have a nice dinner with our parents where we would be classy and drink wine with them. After dinner, our parents would go home, and the two of us would party like we were in the movies. We'd go to a club and find boys to buy us drinks. We'd dance and get free shots all night! I'd been looking forward to that for years, but it seemed Shannon had forgotten all about that. All she wanted was for Paul to come to dinner with us. And I knew that meant there would be no afterparty. No dancing, no boys buying us drinks, no pretending like we were in the movies.

"You're being dramatic," Shannon said, her voice still calm, but showing the slight quiver of annoyance. "It's just dinner. There is no difference if Paul is there or not."

Maybe to Shannon it made no difference. To me it did. I had only seen her twice without Paul since I came home from school—once when she was packing up her things and the second when I visited her that evening at her apartment when she was icing her ankle she hurt from 'salsa dancing.' Since then, every time Shannon was around, Paul was too. They came over a few times for dinner, always sitting next to each other and feeding off each other's sentences. When I asked Shannon to come help me work on job applications, she had said "Paul is great at this! We'll be over soon!" Why was Paul so great at job applications? Because he had a job? The two of them had come over and criticized every line in my resume and cover letter, making me feel even less confident about ever finding employment. I ended up submitting no applications.

"So maybe you shouldn't come either!" I yelled, although that also was not what I wanted. I was starting to feel the anger taking control. Any rationality I had in my brain was backing away into a dark crevice to hibernate, letting the anger take over. The anger grabbed the steering wheel in my head and veered left, so far left that I felt my whole body swerving and heading down the wrong direction—down a road I didn't want to go on, but couldn't stop myself from pedaling through farther and farther from where I wanted to be. "You know what Shannon," the anger continued talking, masking itself in my rational voice. "I think it would be better for everyone if you didn't come. You and Paul can stay home by yourselves and I will go to dinner with our parents. Everyone's happy."

"Don't be ridiculous," Shannon said, this time the frustration coming through her tone. "Nobody is happy. You're not happy, I am not happy, our parents are not happy. Paul's not happy. Paul *wants* to celebrate with you. He sees *you* as family. But you know what, if that is what you really want, then fine. I'm tired of always having to defend myself and Paul to you. You don't even realize everything I've done for you—everything I do for you! Last week, I basically rewrote your resume! So you can just celebrate without me and one day you'll realize how selfish you are being."

"I think, *you'll* realize how selfish *you're* being," the anger retorted, still sounding eerily tranquil. "You know where to find me when you want to apologize." The anger hung up the phone, leaving me alone with it in my room. But once off the phone, the anger dissipated, as though bored with my solitude. What was there for the anger to do, without a target around? So it left me, being replaced by loneliness, which was even stronger than the anger. The loneliness surrounded me like a wet blanket, heavy and cold. I started shivering and dove into my bed to try to stay warm. The bed creaked as I landed and the noise vibrated in my ears, turning into static that roared against the walls. I looked at Shannon's side of the room. Empty except the pictures and drying flowers she left behind. I wanted to rip them down, tear them into a million pieces. But I knew I couldn't. Those flowers were the only things that could bring Shannon back. The only things that could remind her of who she used to be. Who *we* used to be.

The static shook through my brain, making the lamp and the pens on my desk tremble. I held onto the bed, afraid that I could fall off. An earthquake had ruptured with me at the epicenter and I watched as the room flowed back and forth, shaking everything inside like a snowglobe. I held on tight, the static still loud in my ears and the flowing of the room making me dizzy. So dizzy, until suddenly everything went black.

Dear diary,

I think I've just about had enough. I don't know what to do any more. I'm so torn. Paul says one thing, but my instincts say another. When I talk, I find myself going with what Paul says, even though I am not sure if he is right anymore. These last few weeks with him... they've been, I don't know, hard. I just don't know what's happening, if I'm doing something wrong. I can't keep feeling like this, like I'm walking on eggshells with everyone. If I do this, Paul is upset. If I do that, Mara is. It's too much, all of it.

Does everyone feel this way? Torn between their boyfriend and their sister? I'd hoped they'd get along, that Mara would be able to see what I see in him and then I would be sure he was right for me. But she doesn't. And sometimes, I'm not sure anymore. I'm not sure about anything anymore. I'm only sure that I can't go on like this. Something has to change.

Chapter 21
Mara

Life rolls on like waves crashing on the sand. Some reach farther than others, ferociously destroying sandcastles and soaking into the sand to suffocate anything underneath, while others are smooth and gentle, barely reaching far enough to leave their mark. I'm just floating, going with the tide, landing wherever the waves take me. Sometimes I flow in and out and sometimes I find myself washed up on the sand.

The room is already bright when I wake up. The sheer curtains are fluttering in front of the open window that's letting in a symphony of birds chirping and car engines. Garrett is still asleep next to me. He's on his back, one hand over his heart on his bare chest and the other hanging off the side of the bed. His breathing is harmonious with the sounds from outside.

It's Sunday, meaning we'll probably spend most of the day relaxing in bed, maybe get up for lunch or to go for a walk somewhere and then he'll take me home before he goes to dinner at the club with his family. He's never pressured me to come to Sunday dinner or Saturday brunch. In fact, he's done more than never pressured me, he's actively avoided inviting me or making any indication that I should join. It makes things easier for both of us.

I always wake up first. I try to lie quietly in bed without waking him, but somehow, the heat of my stare usually wakes him up. He looks so calm, his whole face relaxed, his chest rising and falling with his breaths. Every morning, I am surprised to wake up next to him. There's a part of me that always believes he will get up and leave in the middle of the night. It's a silly thought, especially since we are at his apartment, but the thought persists. It haunts me when we go to sleep, when he goes to work or the bathroom. I'm sure one day he will and I will be totally alone.

After my grandma's funeral, I gave in to Garrett's arms. I let him hold me, feed me, bathe me. I had no strength to protest, and frankly, it was nice to be cared for. He took time off work to stay with me, convinced Sylvia in the CADD office not to fire me after I didn't show up for a week, and slowly he started moving me into his apartment. It started with a duffel bag so I would have clean things to wear, but then every time I went home, the clothes never came back with me and new duffel bags started to fill up. Now, most of my things are here. Sometimes I go weeks without going to my house. Sometimes I even call this apartment home.

Garrett's head slowly turns and falls to the other side. He's breathing rhythmically, the veil of sleep still covering him. I keep my head resting on my pillow, facing him. I don't want to move, don't want to disturb him.

In the last six months, I've seen Garrett's father three and a half times. Two times were at the CADD office when he hosted board meetings. There were four board members who crammed inside the conference room where I had laid out cookies and refreshments. I came into the meeting to ask who wanted coffee and came back with five boiling drinks that I placed in front of each person. I had fantasized briefly about throwing Robert's double espresso in his face, but what would that have accomplished? A small burn on his already blemished face? It would have been the weakest possible revenge and have made any real attempts at revenge impossible. Instead, I smiled while avoiding eye contact as I placed the glass shot glass in front of him. The third time I saw him was at an event Jamie had planned for volunteers. Every volunteer who had driven more than one hundred miles was invited for an open bar event. Robert showed up to shake hands and say thank you, but rushed off before he would have needed to actually speak with anyone.

The half time I saw him, I didn't really see him. I was in Garrett's bed when Robert showed up at the apartment. Garrett let him in and had coffee with him in the kitchen while I pretended I wasn't feeling well. The thought of sitting in my pajamas and having coffee with him really did make me want to vomit, so it wasn't exactly pretending. I tried to eavesdrop, getting bits of the conversation. Robert asked about how I was doing, how Garrett was doing, whether he would be bringing me to the club any time soon. When

Robert left, Garrett came back to the bedroom with fresh coffee for me. "My dad hopes you feel better soon," Garrett said as though inviting me to a conversation. I didn't take the bait. I just responded with a simple "thank you," and drank my hot coffee.

"Good morning," he mumbles with his eyes still closed. I'm sure he feels the burn from my irises on him. He rolls over onto his side and gently drops his arm over me. "How'd you sleep?"

"Fine," I respond, but it's a lie. I didn't sleep fine. In fact I haven't slept fine in ages. I thought sleep would become easier for me over time. That nightmares would fade, but they didn't. The nightmares just morph into new ones, each as scary as the last. In every nightmare I force myself awake and stare at the dark ceiling until I succumb to the next one. Only light brings relief.

"Coffee?" he asks, his eyes still shut. He looks asleep, and if I didn't know any better, I would think he still was, talking through a romantic dream that included a beautiful woman in his bed. But Garrett never talks in his sleep.

"I can make it," I offer and try to slide out from under his arm, but his arm is heavy and he doesn't budge to let me through.

"No, I'll get it," he says, suddenly becoming alert. "I want you to just stay in bed and relax." I can't argue. I never do. There is something consoling in letting someone else make your decisions for you. Garrett almost jumps out of the bed, wearing his white boxers which fall a little low on his waist. I pretend not to look and focus on his face where a smile has already formed. He disappears from the bedroom and I can hear him in the kitchen. First, I hear the faucet running as he fills a kettle with water to boil. Then the pop of the coffee can, and rattle of the grinds as he scoops them into the French press. Then there is some more rustling around, drawers opening, mugs chiming as they are placed on the counter, more drawers sliding in and out of their rails. I zero in on the sounds. It helps me focus, helps me avoid the static in my head. A few minutes later there's the whistle of the kettle and the water pouring into the French press. I hear Garrett placing everything on a small tray and then moments later he appears in the bedroom doorway smothered in the smell of coffee. I smile at him and sit up as he gently places the tray in the middle of the bed. Something inside me tells me this is a bad idea—I suddenly imagine myself making a sudden movement and the French press toppling over, spilling all over the cream colored sheets—but I hold my breath and move very carefully to grab my mug—already poured, half coffee half milk.

On the tray also sits a small plate with slices of an orange cake we bought the previous day and a small, inconspicuous brown box. I grab a slice of cake and bite into it, watching the crumbs fall onto the sheets in front of me. I immediately try to pick each crumb up, but as I do more fall.

"Aren't you interested in the little box?" Garrett asks. He's sitting next to me, smiling at me in anticipation. I notice that he hasn't touched his coffee yet. My eyes drift to the box. It's leather and has small gold lining around the sides. My heart starts to drum when I look at it. I know I don't want to open it, but I can tell from Garrett's face that I have to. I pick it up and gently pull the top up, revealing a small white gold ring with a single square diamond on top. My eyes get caught on the ring, like fabric snagged on one of the sharp corners and if I pull away I might unravel. My heart goes silent, the drumming stops and it becomes so still that I fear it's no longer pumping blood to my brain.

Garrett gently picks up the ring with his fingers and slides it on my left ring finger. My eyes follow, and suddenly my hand looks like it belongs to somebody else. "What do you think?" Garrett asks. "Marry me?"

Chapter 22
Robert

"I'm sorry, but the bank won't allow you to pull anymore equity out of your home," Steve says to me. He's sitting behind his desk in his corner office where I've sat across from him hundreds of times before. I sat here when we got our first commercial loan from the bank. The first time we refinanced one of our properties. When we paid off the mortgage of our home. When we took out a second mortgage on our home to pay the legal expenses after the accident.

"But last time, you extended the line of credit," I recall. It was a few months ago, when CADD needed another $40,000, to pay salaries and close up a few gaps. Things are actually starting to go well there, now that the organization has gone national. We have hordes of volunteers signing up and doing our online orientation. Local organizations have even started hosting fundraisers for us and becoming advocates for our cause. Many of these local organizations had been founded due to their own drunk driving related tragedies—and I always take the time to hear each and every one of their stories. One mother told me the story of how her son was killed by a car going the wrong way on the highway. Another told me about her two children who were in their church's youth group bus when it was hit by an inebriated truck driver. I rubbed my scar upon hearing each story. It was like the stories opened the gash anew on my forehead, making my head ache and my skin burn. I often spent time researching what happened to these drunk drivers who caused so much pain. Some died themselves, others were serving time in prison for manslaughter. It made me nauseous thinking that I had gotten off so easily.

But these local fundraisers, and plethora of volunteers, also brought in more callers needing designated drivers. We need more money to reimburse drivers, fund our insurance policies and our call centers—we now have three located in different corners of the country. The bigger CADD got, the more of a money drain it became.

"I only drew once on that new line of credit," I remind Steve. I remember being conservative at the time, thinking that I could use the line of credit again if I needed it.

"That's not what I see here," Steve says. "Last week, $120,000 was drawn. That was the last of it. I can't extend it further."

That just wasn't possible. I would remember drawing that amount of money. And last month had been good. We had been almost in the black. "Please check again," I ask Steve. Something wasn't adding up.

"Yup, it says right here, Mrs. Derby took out the credit," Steve responded, turning his computer screen to show my wife's signature at the end of the withdrawal slip. "Maybe she forgot to mention it."

I sigh and stand up to leave. There isn't much I can do here, I can't argue with the signature staring back at me. It is so obviously Bonnie's. The large curves of the letters, drawn like bubbles traveling through water.

"You actually need to start making payments back," Steve says, as he notices me starting to leave. "Under the line of credit, you agreed that once the full amount was drawn, you would begin making interest-only payments. So the first was due last week."

I laugh. Pay the interest with what? I pull out my check book and write a check to the bank, tossing it over to Steve. I'm not sure what will happen when they cash it, all my liquid funds—if there are any left—are here at this bank already anyway.

Back in my car, I am not sure where to go. I'm needed at the office. We are having a problem with 803 Riesling, a project we just sold for $64 million. The sale was a huge relief for us. It gave us capital to cover some of our recent failings plus more that could be used for future investments. But now the buyer was trying to back out, saying that we lied about the conditions of the building. He was asserting that he found asbestos in the ceiling and termites in the foundation—two absurd allegations. We had had the property checked both before we bought it and before we effectuated the sale. But the buyer was threatening to sue if we didn't let him out of the contract and give a full refund. Normally I'd tell him to sue, but luck hadn't been on my side lately and frankly, we didn't have the capital for a lengthy legal battle. On the other hand, the money from the sale was already tied up. We paid for damages on 523 Heirbloom, our project with the fire, and had put down a deposit on 6 Lincoln, a rundown office building in a soon-to-be gentrified neighborhood. Six Lincoln will turn Derby Ventures around, I am sure of it. According to Garrett's calculations, it is poised to be our most profitable project yet. I can't let it get away. And I can't lose the $15 million deposit.

I turn on the car and find myself driving home. The office will wait. I have to talk to Bonnie about the money she withdrew. My phone rings while I drive and I press the speaker button on my dash to answer.

"We need a bigger office," Sylvia says without saying hello. "Everyone is stepping on everyone's toes. Yesterday Mara ran out in a fit while some of the volunteers were arguing in the conference room. Jamie had to get her and calm her down. Sometimes I don't know what is with her. Some days she's super helpful and useful and others, she's more of a drain on us than anything else." Sylvia paused. "I know you're against this, but Jamie and I both think we should let her go. There are plenty of people who can do her job."

"No," I respond instinctively. "You can't fire her."

"Won't she be too busy to work soon anyway? Isn't that what happens to women in your family?" I know Sylvia isn't meaning to be condescending but that's exactly how it sounds. Like she thinks that the Derby's think they are above everyone else. That the Derby's are elitists where women don't work and instead spend their whole days planning parties and drinking tequila. It offends me that people think this about my family, but then I think about Bonnie and Caroline and I see where the assumption comes from.

"I'm not sure Mara's like that," I respond. My words have many different meanings. I don't think Mara fits in with the women in my family. I am not even sure if I believe she really will become a Derby. "Have you spoken with her about the engagement?" I ask Sylvia, fishing for any information. "Did she say anything?"

"She didn't have to," Sylvia responds. "She just blinded everyone with that ring when she came in."

"Sylvia," I say softly, taking in a deep breath. "Is there anything unusual about Mara? I mean, aside from her fits. Does she say anything worrisome?"

"What do you mean?"

"Has she ever mentioned me?" I ask. I didn't want to be so forward, but I need an answer. "Or said anything threatening about Garrett? Even as a joke?"

"What are you getting at, Rob?" Sylvia sounds annoyed. She's always all business. If it isn't related to CADD, discussions never get very far.

"Nothing, just trying to learn more about my future daughter-in-law," I respond. I know I'm not getting anywhere.

A few days ago, Garrett had broken the news at Sunday dinner at the club.

"She said yes!" he exclaimed after ordering a bottle of champagne from the waiter.

"Of course she did, Dear," Bonnie said, downing her cocktail and motioning the waiter for a new one. "Congratulations to you both." Her words were poised yet unenthusiastic.

"What happened?" I had asked. I felt like I had missed part of the conversation, even though I had been sitting there since before Garrett arrived. "Who said yes? Yes to what?"

"Mara, Dear," Bonnie said. "Garrett proposed." Then she turned to Garrett. "If you're sure that's what you want, Dear." Again she paused, looking around the club. "Oh look! What a surprise!"

I looked to the direction Bonnie was staring and saw Ainsley Worthington walking into the club with her parents. The three of them were all wearing beige, as though their outfits were planned and Ainsley's blonde hair shone bright down her shoulders. Her lips were painted red, a dark contrast to her beige look.

"Deborah, Dear!" Bonnie called out to Mrs. Worthington. "What a surprise! Why don't we all have dinner together?" Bonnie motioned to a waiter who reseated us at a larger table where Bonnie insisted that Garrett and Ainsley sit next to each other. "You two must have so much to catch up on!" she exclaimed while the waiter poured champagne for everyone.

We sat through a theatrical dinner, where any mention of Mara or Garrett's new engagement was quickly dismissed and Deborah and Bonnie set an infinite amount of future plans together. *We'll do lunch! Let's check out that museum gallery! I've been meaning to find someone to help me plan the club's charity gala. How lovely it will be to work together!*

I watched Garrett as he politely engaged with Ainsley, who looked so composed and graceful that it seemed her every move had been perfectly choreographed and practiced as though it were part of a ballet. A stark difference from how Mara looked the one time she had sat down with our family.

I hang up the phone with Sylvia, promising to look into canceling CADD's lease to get a bigger office, just as I pull into the driveway at home. There's an envelope sticking out of the mailbox. Not again, I sigh as I pinch the bridge of my nose. I stop the car and get out, grabbing the letter. *See you soon.* The same unmarked envelope, same typed letter. Maybe I do need to go back to the police. The letters are getting worse and if my theory is right, the sender is going to follow through soon.

I get back in the car and continue driving up to the house. There is a big white truck parked and a couple vans behind it. Men are unloading something from the truck and carrying whatever it is around to the back of the house. I park and jump out of the car, jogging around the men to the yard where Bonnie is standing with a clipboard talking to a woman in a pressed white blouse.

"What's going on here?" I ask.

"The engagement party, Dear," Bonnie said. "It will be this weekend. There is so much to do!"

I vaguely remember Bonnie mentioning an engagement party that night after we returned from the club. But based on her tone and the sentences she said when she mentioned those words, I didn't believe it would actually be happening.

"Please put the bar over there," Bonnie yelled to a few men carrying what must have been a bar setup.

"Bonnie, did you draw from our line of credit?" I ask her. I would have preferred to speak to her privately about this, but I can see that's not happening. When Bonnie is focused on something like party planning and organizing, there is no pivoting her.

"Yes, Dear, these parties are expensive," she responds without looking at me. "The small tables over there!" She yells to more men bringing in things.

"$120,000?" I ask.

Bonnie laughs. "What do you think these things cost? If Garrett really is going to go through with this, then we need to support him, exactly like we did for Caroline and Caleb. Those chairs over there! Don't worry not all the money is going to the party. I also gave some to Saul to work on a prenup. I gave him extra to make sure the prenup is rock solid. And of course, I gave some to Garrett so he could buy Mara something to wear. She can't show up to this in one of her Forever21 dresses. I offered to take her shopping myself, but Garrett said she wasn't interested. What nerve to turn down your mother-in-law! Isn't it? Oh well, I wouldn't have anything to say to that girl anyway. But like I said, supporting Garrett!"

I pinch the bridge of my nose as the men start setting up white tables and chairs in the backyard. Of course I want to support Garrett. He's smart, he's a good person. He deserves the best and I always want what's best for him. But based on what I know, I am not sure if Mara is that. I stuff my hand in my pocket, crinkling the letter inside.

Chapter 23
Garrett

"No parties!" I yell to my mother on the phone, but I know it's too late. A caterer has already been hired, tables and linens delivered. We can still change the cake flavor if Mara and I want to stop by the bakery today for a tasting, my mother offers. I tell mother she can choose the flavor. The party is for her, after all.

About a month ago, I decided to propose. Mara had been living with me for a few months already and things were going smoothly. She *needed* me. She needed me to get up in the morning, to shower, to make sure she was eating and getting to work. I brought balance and stability to her life. And me, I like feeling needed. I like making sure she gets up, showers and taking care of everything. Things were going so perfectly.

I first told mother about my plans. I could see she wasn't thrilled, but I knew that was only because she didn't really know Mara. She didn't know what a funny, smart and deep person she is. Mother only knew the shy, sad woman who showed up to brunch that one time forgetting to put on her underwear. "Things will change," I promised my mother and I knew they would. Giving Mara the family she was missing would help her heal. She wouldn't feel so alone anymore once we got married. It was a perfect solution.

Mother took me to her jeweler who helped me pick out a classic ring. Mother preferred the rings with multiple diamonds or with rocks as big as paperweights, but I knew that Mara wouldn't want those. I wanted something clean, small, something that wouldn't grab too much attention. I found the perfect ring—mother scoffed, but agreed it was dainty, like Mara herself. That was the biggest endorsement I had gotten from mother as of yet. Father, on the other hand, had been more supportive. Aside from hiring Mara at CADD, he continually asked about Mara's wellbeing. Sometimes he asked too much, to the point where it felt like prying, but I quickly let my father know when he overstepped his boundaries. Like when he asked about Mara's family. Honestly, there wasn't much I could have told him anyway, as Mara preferred not to talk about them. Every once in a while she let something about them slip. I knew her sister was a journalist and had some scumbag boyfriend. I knew she and her sister used to sit together on their roof sometimes. Her father was a cop and her mother, a teacher. Her grandma baked pies and her mother liked to cook. But I still know nothing about how they died. I'm sure Mara will tell me when she is ready.

When I gave Mara the ring, I thought she was going to faint. Her face became whiter than my sheets and she sat as still as a statue. But she let me slip the ring on her finger. And she let me kiss her as she stared at it, her eyes open wide. I can't remember if she actually said the word "yes" or not, but afterwards we made love with the ring still on her finger. We spent the day at home relaxing together in bed, admiring the beautiful stone on her hand. It looked perfect on her, like it was designed especially for her. Sometime midday, she seemed to warm up to it. *Oh future husband!* She called to me while I prepared breakfast. *What do you think of the name Mara Derby? It sounds like a horse's name. Maybe let's both change our last names. It can be something like Thon! I can be Mara Thon, get it?? But Garrett Thon sounds weird. Oh well, you will deal!* Her wit and sarcastic humor are two of the things I love most about her.

That evening, I went to the club for family dinner. I wanted to ask Mara to join, but I knew it was better for me to break the news without her there. I still wasn't sure how my family would react. And that was a smart decision, since we ended up having dinner with Ainsley's family.

When I told my family about the engagement, mother looked unsurprised. Father looked concerned and lost. Caleb and Caroline could barely stop the giggles between them. They tried to stop laughing, when really they should have been happy for me. Why wasn't anyone acting like they were happy for me? I love Mara, I really do. We're perfect for each other, giving each other exactly what the other needs. Why can't my family see that?

When the reactions couldn't have made me feel any worse, mother invited the Worthington's to eat with us, forcing me and Ainsley to sit right next to each other. I hadn't seen Ainsley in years and she was as beautiful as always. Her long blonde hair shining as it brushed her shoulders, her lips thick and so red they looked poisonous. She was wearing a classic beige cocktail dress, showing her white chest and deep collar bones that led into her thin neck. Yes, Ainsley was beautiful in that magazine portrait way. But that wasn't what I was attracted to. It wasn't like Mara's rawness that broke every convention to create the most beautiful creature possible. Ainsley and I spoke politely about our lives. She mentioned how she and her friend had just started a luxury travel agency—they had been flying all over the world for free with companies that wanted to be promoted. She had just returned from Brazil, she said, where she stayed in a wonderful hotel. She asked how the investments were going. It was a polite question that deserved a polite answer with no details whatsoever. By the end of the meal, I realized I hadn't mentioned Mara to her. Not that I was hiding her, it just didn't come up. We left the club waiting for our mothers to finalize their lunch plans while we stood at the side aching to check our phones. She gave me a quick smile and eye roll the fifth time our mothers hugged and I couldn't stop myself from returning the gesture. I immediately felt guilty after and excused myself. Who knew how many more hugs there would be.

Now, my mother had just called to tell me about the engagement party at their home on Saturday. "Please get Mara a new dress! I've wired you the money. Make sure to get her something appropriate with the necessary undergarments!" my mother pleads with me on the phone. I roll my eyes, but understand. I remember Caleb's engagement party. There were hundreds of guests. If you added up the costs of everyone's wardrobe, you could have funded an entire country in Africa for at least a year.

"Garrett, Dear, you know how important this party is," my mother continues. I know what she means and it has nothing to do with Mara and me. My parents will be inviting every professional contact they have: investors of Derby Ventures, CADD donors. The better the party, the more money people are willing to hand you for unrelated activities.

"Don't worry, Mother," I try to console her, but I am also worried. Worried that Mara will get spooked somehow and run away. Worried that she'll change her mind. But then I remember the day we met, at the fundraiser. How calm she looked standing in her long black dress. She looked so comfortable, so in her element. I'm sure that Mara is still around somewhere. I just need to figure out how to bring that one back.

Chapter 24
Mara

I slid into the office building wearing a brand-new outfit that my mother had bought me the previous day. A black pencil skirt and a white feminine blouse with ruffles around the collar and sleeves; and a black blazer that forced me to sit up straight as a redwood. "I don't understand why people wear these things," I had said to my mother in the fitting room. "What's wrong with t-shirts? They're hiring me for my brain not my looks."

"Oh, Sweetheart, you're right," my mother had said. "But they won't even consider your brains if you don't make a good impression."

She must have been right, because everyone sitting in the office lobby was wearing the same black and white uniform that I was. Only everyone else looked a little less uncomfortable. Somehow, I had gotten a job interview to be a researcher at a marketing firm. The interview was at 5:00 p.m. on my birthday and I stepped into the office right on time. My parents had made reservations for the three of us at a fancy restaurant nearby and they promised to meet me there at 6:30 for my birthday celebration. I hadn't spoken to Shannon since our fight on the phone. She had tried to call a couple times, but I ignored her. I didn't have the strength to argue and I figured that if she felt bad enough, she knew where to find me.

"Mara Sanders?" A woman standing in the doorway of the lobby said. The woman was tall and also wearing a blouse and pencil skirt. It made me wonder how everyone in the world knew they needed to be wearing this today. How my mom knew and why I was the only person who felt so restrained in these clothing. I stood up and approached the woman. She smiled at me, watching me sashay through the lobby. It made me uncomfortable—I didn't know where to place my eyes. Should I look back at her? Would that come off as creepy? Should I look around the room? Would I then look aloof? I settled by looking down at the floor, even though I knew this was also wrong. "Thanks for coming in," the woman said when I reached the door. "I'm Evelyn Lane, I'm the manager of the department you are interviewing to join."

"Nice to meet you," I said, still unsure where to put my eyes. I jutted out a hand to shake hers, which she promptly grabbed and shook with enough force to down a small tree. My hand ached slightly from the shake, but I pretended not to notice. She continued with small talk as she led me through the office to a small conference room in the back. *Did I find parking? Am I familiar with this area?* I wasn't sure if these questions were part of the interview—was difficulty finding parking a sign that someone wasn't right for the job? Thankfully I had found a spot nearby.

She stretched out her arm to offer me a seat around the table, where a pitcher of water and two glasses stood. She promptly poured the water into the glasses and slid one over to me. "So Mara, tell me about yourself," she said as she crossed her legs and clasped her hands in front of her.

My mouth opened like it was ready to answer the question, but my brain had not yet figured out what to say. What could I tell her about myself? I felt like I barely knew myself, like I needed this job so that when someone asked me that question, I could say *I am a researcher at a marketing firm.* "It's my birthday," my lips finally said. "I'm 21." I guessed that if someone wants to know about me I should start from the beginning, the day I was born—21 years ago.

"Oh, well, happy birthday!" she said. "How nice of you to come in on your special day. What can you tell me about why you are right for this job?"

Again, I had no answer, other than that I knew I was supposed to get a job. That's what people did when they graduated. There weren't even other options. The interview continued with questions that I couldn't answer in any honest way, making me trip over my words and wish I had never shown up. But finally it ended and Evelyn dismissed me, promising that she would get back to me within a week. I thanked her and shook her hand again—this time bracing myself when she jolted my arm almost out of its socket.

In my car, I cried. I wanted to call Shannon and tell her about the interview and how horrible it went. I wanted to hear her tell me it was OK and that maybe that job wasn't right for me anyway.

She would have known what to say. She would have known how to make me feel better, instead of feeling like a waste of breath and an expensive college education. But I couldn't call her, I was still mad at her. And I wouldn't call her like this—crying on my birthday, needing her help. Instead, I curled up in the backseat and cried. I dug my nails into my arms, leaving bright red smiles everywhere until the tears dried up. Then I climbed to the front seat and drove to the restaurant.

I was late. My parents should have been there already, sitting at a table with the menus all around. But they weren't there. The hostess led me to our reserved table, seating me in a room full of diners where I was the only person who was alone. I pulled out my phone to see a text from my dad: *Sorry kiddo! Running late because we're picking up a surprise! See you soon.*

The text made me angry. *How could they do this to me on my birthday? Why couldn't they pick up the surprise earlier?* I just wanted them there with me, so I wasn't sitting alone at a big table on my birthday. I waited. Eventually I ordered a bottle of wine—it was good to air wine out, right? I would have the wine fully aerated when they arrived. I poured myself a glass and drank it as I held my phone in front of my face, waiting for an update. I called my mom and then my dad. No answer. After an hour, I was still drinking my one glass of wine, not wanting to drink anymore before my parents came.

By then, I was fuming. Steam was coming out of my ears, I was so angry. I paid for the bottle of wine and left the restaurant, planning how I would tell my parents what horrible people they were for doing that to me on my birthday. I would make them feel terrible; like they made me feel. On my way out of the restaurant, my phone rang. *Finally*! I thought, before looking at it and seeing that I didn't recognize the number. Maybe this had something to do with their surprise.

"Mara Sanders?" A serious man said through the phone. "This is Officer Hicks. I'm calling to tell you that your parents and sister were in an accident."

That's when I realized the surprise they were picking up was Shannon.

Dear diary,

Is it possible I made a huge mistake? With my entire life? Could I have ruined my life? Is it possible to go back now? I think I finally have some clarity and I understand what I have to do. As soon as I realized it, I called my parents. They're on the way to get me now, and hopefully it's not too late to rectify this situation.

It's funny how all these years I felt so clueless and then in one sudden moment, there's clarity. It happened in the car, we were just driving and I looked at the small bruise on my wrist. It's from when I almost fell down the stairs, but then Paul caught me. He saved me from my fall, but his grip left a mark. That's what happened, the alternative just doesn't make sense. Feeling the bruise in the car, I suddenly knew I had to fix things. That's what sisters do. What older sisters do. I have to do the right thing. Paul was angry, but I'll deal with him later. Maybe I'll even ask Mara if it's OK for me to stay with her for the night. It could be like old times, when life was much less complicated. When I felt sure about what to do. It will be good for me to get away for a night, I need to decide what to do.

Chapter 25
Mara

"You're stunning," Garrett says as he slips his hands around my waist. I'm standing in front of the full-length mirror in his closet—our closet, I'm supposed to call it now. I'm wearing the beige dress we bought yesterday. It has thick straps, a square-cut neck and falls straight down to my shins. A thin row of lace lines the bottom and the outside of the shoulder straps. There's no arguing, it is a beautiful dress. A perfect dress for a bride-to-be. But in it, I look like a little girl playing dress up in my mother's closet. But like every girl who tries on their mother's clothes, I pretend that it's fitting. I stand up straight and stare at myself in the mirror, telling myself that this is me now. At least it's the me I am pretending to be. *The me I want to be?*

I love Garrett. I really do. I love the way he reads my emotions. How he notices if I am uncomfortable or need something. I love his calming presence, and his desire to take care of me. I love that he is smart and cares about his family, and that he never pressures me to see them. Until now, I have somehow been able to forget that Garrett is a Derby. That Garrett's father is the reason I am alone in this world. That I wanted and still sometimes want revenge on his father. The feeling comes whenever I am reminded about my family. When I see a police car rolling by and I imagine my dad in the driver's seat; or when I see the newspaper my sister worked for and I remember the first time she had an article on the front page. I still believe Garrett's father deserves to feel the pain I felt, no matter what he has done to try to make amends. There is no amending, no changing the past. Some sins can only be atoned for in suffering.

I know today I will have to see Robert Derby. I will have to see him smiling and enjoying this party with his family. I will probably have to greet him and hug him, pretending how wonderful it will be for us to be family. But I don't intend for us to ever be family. I'm still figuring out how I can keep Garrett while ridding us of his evil father. I haven't figured it out yet. The man's voice in my head is spitting out all kinds of ideas, but none I can accept. I have to find a way to rid myself of that voice.

"No one will be able to take their eyes off you!" Garrett is kissing my neck. I turn around in his arms and kiss him back. The kissing gives me the confidence to move forward. I can do this. I can go to this party and face my family's murderer. It will be like the CADD fundraiser, I just have to remember to play that Mara, the one who can charm anyone. I think about whether I should bring my dad's gun with me. It's hiding in one of the drawers Garrett cleared for me in his closet. Once when I was bringing stuff over from my house, I brought it. Just in case. Sometimes I carry it with me in my purse, just in case. But I have to be careful. Garrett doesn't know I have a gun.

A limousine arrives to drive us to the party. Bonnie insisted we arrive this way, especially so both of us could enjoy the mimosas without worrying about driving home. They are so extra cautious about drinking and driving it makes me livid. It feels so forced and disingenuous.

When we arrive, the party has already begun. The limousine drops us off in the front and Garrett holds my hand as we walk around the house to the lawn where white tables and chairs checker the grass. A bar sits on one side with tall tables surrounded by people drinking colorful cocktails and wearing equally colorful wide brimmed hats. Soon, Bonnie approaches, carrying two different cocktails in her hands.

"Welcome my dears!" she yells to us as she skips our way. "What would you like to drink? We have two specialty cocktails created for you! This is the *Marett*." Bonnie holds up a tall glass that is yellow on the bottom and orange on top. "Get it, Mara and Garrett. It's a mixture of pineapple and raspberry with rum. Very delicious! We also have the *Something Blue*." Bonnie held up the cocktail in her other hand. "It's a Blue Curacao lemonade with vodka. Which would you like?"

Garrett looks at me to choose and I grab the *Marett*. Bonnie hands the *Something Blue* to Garrett, who taps his glass against mine and says "Cheers" before taking a sip. I also place my lips around the straw. The drink is sweet and tangy with no trace of the rum that is supposed to be in it.

"Come now, Mara," Bonnie says, gently clasping her hand around mine. "There are so many people I need you to meet! Everyone is just dying to get to know you and you look marvelous! I'm so glad you used the money I sent to buy such a perfect dress!" Bonnie's enthusiasm would make it appear we were already friendly, even though we had only met that one time. But I play along and smile at her, letting her drag me away from Garrett and into the lion's den of women wearing white gloves and designer labels. I look back to see Garrett's eyes on me, a questioning look as though he isn't sure how to react. His eyes are asking if I am OK, and I try to smile at him to tell him yes, I can do this. With Bonnie, I can do this. She continues to flutter me around the lawn introducing me to her friends from tennis, from the club, from an organization she works with, Derby Venture investors, CADD donors. I smile and make small talk with everyone. I'm so smooth I even surprise myself. If only I could always be this Mara, life would be so simple. I could fit in anywhere.

I keep looking around the lawn for him, but I don't see him. I see countless men in polos and V-neck sweaters looking like they are ready to golf, but not Robert. His presence is not easy to miss; I remember from the CADD fundraiser, he is tall and people gravitate to him, always seeming to become shorter in his presence. I see Garrett standing in a group of men around his age. He's switched his blue Curacao for a whiskey and is laughing. He looks so comfortable standing there with his peers, all equally well dressed, with dignified postures. I watch him as a tall blonde woman comes up from behind him and places her hand on his shoulder. He turns around and hugs her gently as she kisses his cheek. They stand there in conversation, their bodies square to each other and arms still lingering from the hug. It looks so natural, like Barbie and Ken, a perfect couple that was molded to be together.

"Would you like that, Mara?" I'm suddenly awoken from my trance by the puffy-cheeked woman standing in front of me. Bonnie had just introduced us; her name was Trudy or Tracy or something like that. I see Bonnie and the puffy-cheeked woman both looking at me with expectant expressions and I know what I am supposed to say.

"Why yes, I'd love that," I say, even though I am not sure what I agreed to. But the woman seems overjoyed, her smile growing, as are her already puffy cheeks.

"Lovely, Darling!" the woman says. "I'll have a car come get you tomorrow morning. It will just be so much fun! I can't wait for us all to get to know each other better!"

I look back to Garrett and the blonde woman is gone. Then I see him. He puts his hand on Garrett's shoulder and uses his other hand to greet the other men in the circle. Everyone is smiling at him as though they love and admire him. How easy it is for people to forget when it's convenient. Robert then pulls Garrett away from the group and they start walking. The two of them are talking quietly to each other, while stopping every so often to shake hands and smile at someone. They keep walking and then I realize it's me they are approaching.

"You'll have so many options, really," the puffy-cheeked woman says. "It's funny, you never realize how many different color whites there are until you are a bride!" She and Bonnie are laughing, both looking for my laugh to join. I give a small chuckle, but my throat is starting to tighten as Robert gets closer. I'm worried I won't be able to continue breathing much longer, I could pass out any minute now. I'm starting to feel dizzy and then Garrett grabs my arm.

"Mind if I steal Mara for a moment?" Garrett asks. "I'm sure she will be happy to visit your boutique, Terry." Terry! That was the puffy-cheeked woman's name. Bonnie and Terry politely excuse themselves, leaving me with Garrett and Robert. I can feel energy passing from Garrett's hand through my arm. It's keeping me conscious, keeping me standing while I face the murderer. Somehow, I have strength to smile.

"Mara," Robert says. "I just wanted to give you my best wishes and tell you I am very happy for you." It sounds endearing, but there is a threatening undertone. Or maybe that's just my imagination.

"Thank you." My voice croaks, but I maintain the smile on my face. The next moment, Robert is pulled away by another man in a V-neck sweater and the two of them walk toward the bar.

"How are you doing?" Garrett asks. I can see the concern in his eyes and it makes me love him even more. "If you want to go, we can leave whenever you want."

"I'm fine," I respond. "Thank you. I'm really OK." Garrett looks relieved. "I'm just going to step inside a moment and find a bathroom."

"Do you need help?"

"No, really, I'm fine. Go have fun!" I say to him. I really need a moment alone to catch my breath so I can continue being here and being the person I am supposed to be. I step inside the house and start to wander upstairs. The wooden staircase is covered in a red carpet and the railing is intricately carved with images of leaves. It's beautiful and I run my hand up the railing feeling every indention until I get upstairs. I wander into the first room, which looks like a library. The walls are fully covered in bookshelves holding an endless amount of colorful books. I walk around the room admiring it until I reach the far side where a door is leading out to a balcony. I step outside. There is a breeze up here on the second floor and the air feels refreshing on my face. I look out to see the driveway of the house, full of parked cars, without a person in sight. What a perfect place to get away for a moment, I think, enjoying my solitude until I hear the balcony door creak.

"Mara? Is everything OK?"

I turn to the doorway and see Robert standing there. He steps outside and approaches me at the railing. I suddenly feel trapped, like the murderer has cornered me and is about to push me over the edge. I look down at the cars below. He could push me and no one would see it. No one would be there to see me fall. He could get away with it! But then I think, what if the tables were turned. What if I pushed him over the railing with no one there to see it happen?

"Hi, Mr. Derby," I say, my voice fluttering but I try hard to keep a straight face.

"Garrett really loves you and I hope you really love my son," Robert says. He's standing an arm's length in front of me, leaning on the railing. I could easily step forward and push him with all my might and he would topple over.

"I do, of course," I say.

"And that you don't have some hidden agenda here," Robert continues. He looks at me, his arms folded across his chest, like he's accusing me of something. But really, I should be accusing him. I've done nothing wrong—yet.

"I'm not sure what you mean," I respond.

"Do you think I don't know who you are? Do you think I don't know what you're doing?" Robert says. "I recognized you at the CADD fundraiser. I knew exactly who you were the moment my son mentioned he was dating you. Do you think I would ever forget your name? Your face?"

191

Robert continues. "And I know it's you, putting those letters in my mailbox. At first, I wasn't sure. But now it all makes sense."

My mouth drops open, but I have nothing to say.

"Listen, I am very sorry about your family," Robert continues. "I don't want to make more trouble for you, which I easily could with those letters. You're young, and you're probably not thinking through your actions. So why don't you just disappear? Do you want money? I'll give you whatever you want. Just don't bring my son into this."

"Money!?" I exclaim. "You think money can change what you did?"

"Of course not, but neither can threatening me, or trying to punish my son," Robert says. There is something hostile in his eyes. "I've done everything I can to atone for what I did. I founded CADD, I paid the lawsuit settlement, I hired you so you could have a better job, what else can I do?"

I shake my head. Rage is born in my head and suddenly screaming out from all directions.

Robert continues talking. "I'm not going to stand by when you do whatever it is you're trying to do to my son. I'm going to tell him who you are. And I'm going to make sure you don't hurt him. That won't bring your family back."

The rage comes out of my ears, my nose, my pores. There is so much rage that I think I won't even have to push Robert, the rage will do it for me. The rage will get my revenge, ending Robert's life so that I can continue living on happily with Garrett, relieved of my family's murderer. The rage is getting ready for the revenge, but then another figure steps out on the balcony.

"Mara? Dad? Everything all right?"

The rage makes a run for it, jumping off the balcony edge and leaving the three of us still standing. I'm disappointed at the lost opportunity, but seeing Garrett also brings relief.

"Mom wants to bring out the cake and she wants everyone there for it," Garrett says. "I came to find you two. Having an interesting chat?" I sense his confusion. After seeing me avoid his father for all this time to find me alone with him on a balcony must look strange.

"Just getting to know each other better," Robert says, smiling at his son. His expression shows no remnants of the previous moments. "We better get down, we don't want to miss the cake."

Robert steps past Garrett who kisses my cheek and puts an arm around my waist to guide me back into the library. I'm suddenly hot, so hot that sweat starts to leak out from my forehead and down my back. I can feel a pulse in my right eyelid and the cool Mara is slipping away. I'm weak and as I step over the ledge into the library, my knees buckle.

Chapter 26
Mara

The sky was overcast and gray and haze blanketed the ground. I stood on the soft grass listening as the preacher spoke. My grandma's arm hugged my shoulders, keeping me from falling over. I looked down at the ground, three brown rectangles cut into the lawn. They looked so fresh, like a new beginning, a blank canvas, but really, they signified the end. The end of life, for my family and for me. I couldn't imagine my life going on. This was it, if my life continued, it would be as a ghost, or a monument to my family.

When the preacher finished, he invited the police chief to speak. "Mark Sander was a pillar in this community. Not only was he a fair and hardworking officer who made this town a safer place, he was also a leader in our squad. New officers always looked up to him and he always had time to provide advice, counsel, or any other help they needed.

"I remember one time at the station, when he was doing a late shift. And Mark rarely did late shifts, he liked to be home in the evenings with his family. He was a family man, with pictures of his wife and beautiful daughters on his desk. He was so proud of them. Anyway, this particular late shift, a couple officers had just come back after a domestic abuse call. Those domestic abuse calls are always hard to come back from, especially when you see an abused woman trying to protect her man. Anyway, this was a particularly difficult call. The officers had arrived at the scene to see a woman with a black eye and cut up cheek. She had insisted nothing happened, forcing the officers to leave the scene. When the officers arrived at the station, they told Mark about it. He suggested they go back for a surprise check in, which they did, to find the man slapping his wife around. Mark saved that woman's life. He saved many people's lives. I just wish we could have saved his." The police chief stood stoically and notified the preacher he had finished. Then my mom's friend Marie stood forward.

"I've known Susan for about twenty years now," Marie started. "We met because Mara and Thomas were in the same daycare. Our children never became friends, they don't really do that at such a young age, but Susan and I, we clicked. And we stayed in touch even though our children ended up at different schools. Susan was such a sweet and kind person, and she was so thoughtful. When my husband was sick, she used to bake us casseroles every week. She didn't need to, but Thomas and Henry just loved those casseroles. They looked forward to getting some home cooked food, better than what their mom could make. That wasn't what made Susan thoughtful though. She used to remember things. If I mentioned Henry had a doctor's appointment or Thomas had a recital, she would remember and she'd always ask about it. And she was genuinely interested in the answer. Anytime you spoke with her, you were left with a good feeling inside you. Like the world was a good place.

"And Susan was so proud of her girls. She was a supermom, the kind that baked cookies and had dinner ready at 6:00. I always envied her, how she did that and also always seemed so put together all the time. She acted like being a mother was easy, even when she had two teenagers storming around. It's such a shame the world has lost such a wonderful person. Not just for her daughters, but for all of us who were touched by Susan."

When Marie finished, the preacher looked to me to see if I wanted to say something. I didn't. I couldn't stand there and talk about what wonderful people my parents or sister were. All I could think about was how horrible and unfair this world was. How much I hated everyone who could have let this happen.

When I didn't step forward, someone else did. His tall frame was conspicuous among the crowd. He towered over everyone, with his broad shoulders and sinister gaze. "I'd like to say a few words," Paul said, unfolding a piece of paper with his fingers like he was untangling a knot.

"For those of you who don't know me, I'm Paul, I was Shannon's boyfriend. I loved Shannon more than I ever loved anyone. She was beautiful and smart and just an amazing person. We had just moved in together a few weeks ago actually and what she didn't know was that I was planning to propose. I already bought the ring; I don't know what I'll do with it now. I'm sure I'll never meet anyone else like her. The thing about Shannon was that she loved her little sister. She loved her so much, even more than she loved me. And in the end, that's what killed her. You hear that, Mara, you killed her—" The preacher placed one hand over the white paper that Paul was holding in front of his eyes and his other on Paul's shoulder. My grandma's arm tightens around my shoulder.

"Thank you, Paul, I think that's enough," the preacher said. "It's no one's fault when these things happen. It's all part of God's plan, even if we can't understand that now."

I wanted to laugh when I heard that. No one's fault? What about the drunk driver who hit them? He isn't at fault? I pulled myself out of my grandma's grasp and started to run away. I ran through the graveyard, without even being careful to stay on the path. I ran as far as I could until I was out of breath and couldn't even see those three ugly rectangles in the ground. Paul's words somehow followed me. *You killed her! YOU killed her. You KILLED her. You killed HER. You... You... You...*

The words attacked me from all directions like vultures nipping at a carcass that's not yet dead. I raised my arms to try to bat them away, but I wasn't strong enough. They bit harder, more aggressively, until I felt them pulling the flesh from my bones. They ate my skin, my blood and they were getting into my brain. I couldn't fight them anymore, I fell to the ground; a corpse they could finish off until I was just a pile of bones.

Chapter 27
Garrett

I have always had the instincts to catch. Whether a ball, a cold, or a woman fainting, my body instantly reacts. I catch Mara before her head could have hit the wooden floor of the library. "Mara!" I yell, my arms under her back like a stretcher. I lift her up and bring her to a couch in the corner of the library. One that no one had probably sat on in years. My father is in the doorway looking back like he isn't sure what to do.

"Should I call an ambulance?" he asks. I shake my head. "I'll tell Bonnie to cut the cake without you." Then he disappears from the library. I rub my hand along Mara's cheek and softly call her name until her eyes flutter open.

"Did I fall?" she asks. I shake my head, unsure what she means. She suddenly looks scared, like a child waking from a nightmare. She looks like a completely different person than the one I arrived at the party with hours ago. I help her up and take her through the front door of the house so we can avoid all the guests in the back. When we get home, I get her a warm washcloth to put on her forehead. She's quiet, hasn't said a word since we left the library at my parent's home. I haven't said anything either, except for asking if she wants tea or coffee or anything to help her feel better.

We're sitting on the couch next to each other, my hand on her knee. I move my fingers back and forth, trying to show some comfort, but what I really want to know is what happened. How did Mara do a complete one-eighty so quickly at the party? What was it about my father that caused this change?

"Are you sure you don't want coffee?" I ask again. I'm good at being useful. I'm not good at sitting around. I like to solve things by doing something. Like making coffee, cleaning up a mess, organizing. I feel useless sitting there with my hand on her knee.

She shakes her head without moving her eyes which are transfixed on something intangible in front of her. It's like she's staring at a ghost that's not there or at least one that I cannot see. She's so focused that it makes me sure there is something there in front of her.

"Did my father say something to you?"

She shakes her head again.

"Did he *do* something?" Fear starts to bubble inside me as possibilities start to parade through my mind. Is it possible my father isn't who I thought him to be? Today with everything going on with the Me Too movement, you can never be too sure. It seems like every rich and successful man has done something wrong, has harassed someone to some extent. Is my father just like everyone else? Could he possibly have harassed Mara there on the balcony? Or worse! He's been harassing her this entire time she worked at

CADD! My heart starts pounding out of my chest. "Mara, please tell me, no matter what, it's OK. I'll take care of you. I promise. I love you. I'm here for you no matter what. You can tell me anything!" I'm dying to know. No matter what Mara tells me, it would be better than not knowing.

Mara stays silent and still. She doesn't shake her head this time, making the fear inside me start to burrow deeper. I can't believe it. I simply cannot believe my father would do something to Mara. "He *did* do something to you, didn't he?" I yell out. My voice is frantic. "Did he touch you? Did he say something? You can tell me anything, Mara! Please."

"Your father," she says slowly then stops. I'm holding my breath, waiting for the next word, but it doesn't come. It's like the words are stuck somewhere and Mara can't reach them. I want to be able to reach them for her, to pull them out of hiding and help her continue, but I can't. I'm helpless.

"Mara, please," I say. "No matter what it is, you can tell me."

She's still looking at that invisible ghost in front of her. "Your father killed my family." If the words weren't hanging in the air in front of me, I would have thought I misheard. I was prepared for her to say many different things, like maybe my father had hit on her, or said something inappropriate. Maybe he tried to bribe her to leave me (it wouldn't have been the first time), but I never would have expected to hear what she said.

"What?"

"Your father killed—"

"I heard you, but I don't understand."

"He's a murderer," she says and I want to tell her she must be mistaken. Not my father, he would never hurt anyone. He's the kind of person who gets woozy from a papercut and hates violence in movies. He would never murder someone.

"Mara," is the only thing I can say. Maybe he hurt her so badly, she's afraid to tell me the truth? "Your family died a few years ago, before we even met..." But then everything starts rushing back to me. The accident. Seeing Mara at the CADD fundraisers. The gravestones for Mark, Susan, and Shannon Sanders. June 5, 2017. It was her family in the car that night. Her family that was speeding through the intersection when my father ran the red light. "Why didn't you tell me from the beginning?"

"Because in the beginning, I wanted to kill you."

Chapter 28
Robert

For the rest of the party, the honored guests are nowhere to be found. After I leave the library, I tell Bonnie to bring out the cake without them. Her eyes cut into me like daggers, blaming me as though I ruined this party. She may be right, but what she doesn't realize is that ruining the party may save our son's life. She smiles at the guests as they eat square pieces of the white cake covered in big red frosting roses, trying to pretend that it's totally normal to be celebrating an engagement without the couple around.

I'm not sure why I confronted Mara here at the party. When Garrett first started dating her, I was sure it wouldn't go very far. Soon enough they would realize their connection and then they would surely part ways. There was no way—in my mind at least—that they would want to be together. To each other, they would both be reminders of pain and loss.

After a few months I realized that Mara must have known that Garrett was my son from the beginning. I started to wonder if maybe she was targeting him for some reason. Trying to get close to me, or seek revenge. That's when I knew the letters were from her. I did what I could to try to placate her, offering her a job and trying to support Garrett in this relationship that would never work.

I remember the first time I saw Mara. She was sitting across from me at the plaintiff's table. The criminal case against me after the accident had ended and the civil case had just begun. I had been so elated at that point—my acquittal of criminal charges saved me from jail time and allowed me to go back to my family and move on. Yes, my license was limited for a year, but it didn't matter. It was nothing compared to where I could have been: locked up behind bars with real criminals who killed with intent.

When the civil case started, I sat in the courtroom with my team of lawyers filling up half the pews behind me. Mara sat with one lawyer, a woman who looked like she had a million other things on her mind. Mara sat at the plaintiff table with her head bowed, her curly brown hair covering most of her face. She looked so young, I thought. Looking at her made my scar hurt, it caused pain to shoot through my forehead, down my eyelids, giving me a crushing migraine that took days to go away. When the judge came in and everyone stood, I finally saw Mara's eyes. They were dark blue, big and sad. I realized that when this was all over, I would go home to my family, but she wouldn't. I could move on, but she couldn't. I whispered to my lawyer that we should just settle the civil suit, pay whatever they wanted and move on. Saul winked at me and told the court we would begin settlement discussions. I didn't have to be around for those. All I had to do was sign the check when everything was done.

I thought about Mara a lot that first year. How young she was to be alone. I wanted to reach out, but that would have violated the settlement agreement. When I started CADD, I wanted to notify her about it, to see if she wanted to be involved. But I didn't want to dig up old wounds or cause her further pain. When I saw her at the fundraiser some time ago, I was happy. I didn't say hi or try to talk to her, I figured she wanted her anonymity, but I was hoping that her presence was the first step towards forgiveness. That it meant that she no longer hated me for the mistake I made. But now, I am sure I must have been wrong.

I continue mingling at the engagement party; sharing drinks with Derby Ventures investors, CADD donors, and others in our societal circle. I watch guests dump half-eaten hors d'oeuvres on the linen tablecloths and think about how much money is being thrown in the trash. Money that could have gone to advancing CADD's mission. But maybe I'm thinking about this all wrong. If a few people decide to become donors after attending this party, then maybe the investment was worth it. I try to think optimistically and steer my conversations toward CADD.

"We're actually looking for sponsors," I tell an old colleague of mine who works at his own investment fund. "We'll put the sponsors' names on the back of the volunteers' t-shirts and our brochures." My colleague nods and smiles and asks if I'd tried the salmon tartare that was being passed around.

Later I find myself standing with Kent Worthington. He asks where Garrett is and starts telling me about Ainsley's new travel agency. He invested $500,000 in her new business to get her started and already it was paying off. "Maybe Ainsley can help the couple plan their honeymoon," he offers. "Or maybe you should speak with her, you look like you need some time off." I smile and imagine what it would be like if this party were for Garrett and Ainsley instead of Garrett and Mara. Maybe I wouldn't look like I was so desperate to escape.

When the part is finally over, the yard is packed up and cleaned as though the party never happened. I find Bonnie sitting on the couch in our living room, holding a large glass of red wine. Bonnie is still beautiful, but her beauty has evolved over the years. When we first met, she was naturally beautiful, with blonde hair, blue eyes, a wide smile, and an athletic body. Today she is more superficially beautiful. She's had Botox, facelifts, spends hours rubbing creams around her eyes and painting her cheekbones. Sometimes, when she thinks no one is watching, the younger, natural Bonnie peeks through. Watching her sit on the couch, I see the remnants of her old self coming through in the way she is scrunching her brow and tightening her lips. She's still wearing her dress from the party, a teal V-neck that wraps her body to her knees. It is a beautiful color on her.

Twenty years ago, I would have told her that. I would have said to her that teal makes her eyes pop and her skin radiate. But today I know my opinion means nothing. She looks to the label to tell her if she is beautiful. The label's name and size says it all.

I see the open wine bottle breathing on the end table next to her. I grab myself a glass, sit down by her side and place my hand on her knee.

"What a disaster," she says, taking a swig of her wine. "I should have known. Garrett hadn't wanted the party in the first place. Now everyone is probably talking about how dysfunctional we are again."

"Don't worry," I tell her. "Everyone was drunk by the time they disappeared anyway."

"Have you heard from Garrett? I tried calling him, but he isn't answering." Bonnie looks at me as though begging for an answer.

I shake my head. "I'm sure they just wanted some privacy, that's all. You know Mara isn't very sociable." Although, in my head, I am also worried.

"But she was doing so great in the beginning!" Bonnie continues. "She was so friendly and everyone just loved her! I barely recognized her myself."

"I guess there is still a lot we don't know about her," I say, my voice trailing off at the end. The pit in my stomach growing as I wonder what happened after I left the library. Did my confrontation ignite Mara? Is she planning something against my son? Should I race over to Garrett's to tell him everything? Is it possible for me to save him?

Chapter 29
Mara

You'd expect that some admissions are unforgivable. That some things can never be taken back or forgotten. That a simple sentence can elicit fear, hate, and confusion all at the same time. Was that the expected response to my admission? I hadn't anticipated any response. I hadn't anticipated saying what I said.

I couldn't stop the words from tumbling out of my mouth. The words had been forming in my throat as I sat there on the couch listening to Garrett's pleas. I could feel them coming together, each syllable building on top of the previous. I tried to wreck them with my tongue, grind them with my teeth, but the words were strong. If only I could have swallowed them, sending them deep into my stomach where they would be digested and never let loose, but I wasn't strong enough. The words sprang out, like a cannonball from its barrel.

"Because in the beginning, I wanted to kill you."

Garrett is sitting next to me, his hand on my leg. He wrinkles his brow and his bottom lip drops slightly, showing the deep black hole in his mouth. There are no words forming in there. No response building itself to meet my statement.

"I mean..." I start saying, without knowing how to continue. What did I mean? The statement's meaning was hardly ambiguous. I look down at his hand on my knee, his fingers suddenly stop drawing circles. Garrett's knuckles are white as his hand starts to clamp up. He doesn't move. The silence continues, layering on thicker between us as we both try to figure out what to say. How to dig through this silence that is covering us like an avalanche. "I didn't—"

"I get it," Garrett says at the same time that I started speaking. I'm glad he spoke, because I don't know where my sentence was going. "I guess I'd want to kill me too. It must have been so hard on you to lose your family. And you must have been so angry."

I nod, realizing that Garrett didn't understand the depth of the statement. That killing him was actually an option, not just a figure of speech. I open my mouth to explain, maybe I should tell him about the plans when I came to the CADD fundraiser, about my revenge and how I wanted his father to suffer like I suffered, by losing his whole family. Maybe I should tell him about the man who haunts me, who won't get out of my head. He's the one who wanted me to do it. Maybe I should tell Garrett that I didn't carry out the plan because he spoke to me. His friendly smile and cool demeanor saved his life, and mine. I open my mouth to start telling him all this, but he lifts his hands.

"You don't need to explain anything, really," he says. "I will always do everything I can to help make things better." He hugs me, nuzzling his nose into my hair. "And now I understand why you don't get along so well with my father." I wrap my arms around his neck and feel the calm wash over me. Then, we stand up and both go to the bedroom, where we strip ourselves of the clothes from our engagement party. It's like peeling off the top layer of my skin, and I feel exposed. Garrett looks at me and it's like this is the first time he sees me—the real me. I catch his eyes for a moment, but the gaze is too difficult for me to keep. My eyes drop and I try to cover myself.

"It's OK," Garrett says, placing his hand under my chin. "This doesn't change anything between us. We'll work through this together. Everything is going to be OK."

I want to believe him, but then I think about Robert and what he said to me at the party. *I'm not going to stand by when you do whatever it is you're trying to do to my son.* As though he hasn't taken enough away from me already, he now wants to take this away from me too.

Garrett slowly moves me toward the bed and gently kisses my neck. We make love slowly and calmly, our eyes glued together as though communicating in a new language for the first time. While we've made love many times before, this is a totally new experience for me. I melt into him and let him take over. Each moment I become more and more sure that Garrett and I are meant to be together, that our love is real and has the ability to heal. I need his love to heal me. I need him to save me, but I know as long as his father is around, there will always be someone there trying to stop me from healing. Robert will always be a constant reminder of pain and he will continue trying to rip open my wounds, no matter how hard Garrett tries to seal them. And I know in that moment, that I can't let Robert continue haunting me.

Chapter 30
Garrett

I kiss Mara on the cheek and tell her I'll be home in a few hours. It's Sunday evening and I'm expected for family dinner at the club as usual. I had been hoping that after the engagement, Mara would join, but now I know that milestone is still far off. I have to figure out what I can do so that she can be around my father without him reminding her of what she lost. I need to show Mara what a wonderful person my father is, that he is more than the mistakes he made. That he is a good man, an attentive father and loving person. It won't be easy for Mara to see these things, but I will spend my life working on this. One day, she will hug him and appreciate the man he is. One day, he will also become her family.

I pull up a few minutes late and leave my car with the valet. Inside, I see our table, with one seat open for me. Caleb and Caroline are laughing as usual, and my parents smile at them fondly. Sometimes I'm jealous of my brother and his wife. Everything seems so easy to them. They're always smiling, laughing, making fun of things. It's like they've never seen the real world where people struggle and experience setbacks. Their biggest setback was when the wedding venue they wanted was all booked up. Poor Caroline thought the world would end, but they found a new venue and no one spoke of the previous ever again. I sigh as I approach the table and put a big smile on my face.

"Well if it isn't the invisible groom!" Caleb jokes as I sit down, sending Caroline into a new spurt of laughter. "Did you bring your invisibility cloak to dinner? Maybe Mara is here hiding underneath it! Should we bring up another chair for her?"

"Hilarious, Caleb, really," I respond. "I'll never understand why you didn't go for a career as a comedian."

"Too many late nights in that profession," Caleb responds. "No one goes to see comedians during working hours."

"Garrett, Dear, is everything all right?" My mother asks. "I was so worried! Shirley sends her regards, she wanted to say goodbye to you before she left yesterday, but she couldn't find you. So did Cynthia and Marilyn. I told them all you were celebrating with your friends. Is that where you were, Dear?"

I nod. "Yup," I lie. "Mara and I got caught up with some of my buddies." I catch my father's eyes as the words leave my lips.

"Well, I'm glad you had fun," my mother responds. By her tone, I can tell she knows I'm lying, but I also know she would prefer to believe the lie than to know the truth. "Now, shall we start with the wedding planning? I think we should have it in the spring. It will be nice weather and that gives us plenty of time to plan. I can talk to

Eric. You remember Eric? He can start searching for the right venue."

Eric was Caleb and Caroline's wedding planner. He spent a year ushering the couple around to napkin conventions and themed exhibits for how to decorate. He had almost convinced them to bring a pair of lions to lay at the entrance. Caleb was onboard, but Caroline vetoed that. "We cannot offend people who care about animal rights!" she had said. "They drug the lions so they don't bite anyone! Surely, we'll end up with PETA protesting our wedding!"

"I think we're going for something a little more lowkey," I respond.

"Of course," my mother says. "Eric can handle that. He can plan something intimate and classy at the same time."

I shake my head knowing that in the end I will have no choice. I'm going to spend the next year arguing with Eric over color schemes when, really, I couldn't care less whether the tablecloths would match the drapes in the venue.

We're served our first-course: a poached-quail egg sitting atop of a slice of sashimi tuna. It's delicious and I try to focus on eating rather than on my mother starting to relive all the wonders about Caleb and Caroline's wedding. Caroline's dress was specially designed by some French designer whom they flew in monthly for fittings ("He was such a funny man!" my mother laughs). Each napkin was embroidered with their initials CC on the bottom ("The handiwork was so beautiful!"). At their entrance was an ice sculpture of the two of them dancing ("By the end of the night, no one could tell what that was! Good thing the photographer captured it before Caroline's nose was in her brassiere!"). Everyone seemed to enjoy this trot down memory lane, so I smile and nod, going along with the reminiscing. "Remember dad's speech?" I ask. "I'm pretty sure you put a few people to sleep! You'll need to work on that more this time!" Everyone, except my father, laughs.

When dinner ends, we all get up to go. My father places his hand on my shoulder. "Garrett, let's get a drink at the bar," he says. It's a command, not a request, and I kiss my mother's cheek before following my father to the club's bar. We sit next to each other on the high stools in front of the wooden bar. My father orders two whiskeys on the rocks and sits silently until the drinks arrive.

"Congrats on your engagement," he says, raising the glass to me. I lift my glass and gently clink it against his before putting it to my mouth. "Listen, there is something I need to tell you. It won't be easy to hear, but you need to remember that I love you and I always want what's best for you. It may be hard to hear what I am saying, but in a few years, when you have some clarity, you will thank me."

"I know, Dad," I say.

My father smiles at me with his lips closed together and puts one hand on my shoulder. With his free arm, he is swirling the whiskey glass around. "Listen, Mara isn't who you think she is."

"No, Dad, *I know*," I say. "I know what you're going to tell me."

"You do?"

"Yes, she told me everything after the party yesterday," I say. "I know it was her family in the car that night." We try to avoid the words *accident* or *killed* when we talk about what happened. Those words just couldn't be used to describe something my father did. My father's mouth drops open. I'm sure he had a whole speech planned, but my statement ruined it. He no longer needed to give me that speech that he probably rehearsed over and over in his head.

"It's just one of those crazy coincidences, Dad," I continue. "I know it makes things hard on her and on you. I'm sure it's hard for both of you to see each other, but time will heal. Things will change. One day you'll be able to see her like I do."

"Do you really think it's a coincidence?" my father asks.

"Of course! She didn't know you were my father when we started dating," I say, although I am not sure if this is true. I mean, I didn't introduce myself to her with my last name or anything. And besides, I was the one who asked her out, and I certainly had no idea who she was. It was definitely a coincidence, I convince myself.

"Garrett, I don't know," my father says, taking his hand from my shoulder to pinch the bridge of his nose. "Something doesn't feel right to me about this. I think she's hiding something and I'm worried about you."

"You're being paranoid," I respond and with every breath I feel more assured that this is the case. "Really, not everyone I date is out to get me, or our money, or whatever. Mara is a good person. It's just serendipity." While I'm feeling lighter every moment, I can see the weight piling onto my father's shoulders. He is struggling to sit up straight, his fingers pinch his nose harder, he scrunches his eyes.

"Garrett," he says. "Look, I'm saying this because I care about you, OK? You can't marry Mara. I don't think it was a coincidence."

"Dad—"

"Garrett, I'm serious. You met her at the CADD fundraiser. What was she doing there? Why did she register under a fake name? Out of everyone there, all the beautiful women and young men, how did it happen that you two met? Trust me, Garrett, for once. I know you always like to see the good in people, but sometimes you have to be a little more guarded. Not everyone is who they seem."

He's calling me naïve. It's not the first time we've had this talk. We had it about Carmen and Brittany, my two ex-girlfriends who I'll never hear the end of. OK, so I've made mistakes dating the past. But this time is different. Mara is different. She isn't like those other girls who took advantage of my kindness, my money. No, Mara is with me for me.

"Dad—"

"Garrett, it's not just that, there's more. She's planning something—"

"I wish you would just get to know her, Dad," I respond, stopping my father from continuing. "Then maybe you would see how ridiculous you sound."

"I think I do know a little bit about her. Another reason I'm worried, Son. Are you going to spend the rest of your life splitting your life between your wife and your family? Does that sound logical to you? Mara doesn't want to be a part of this family. That should raise a red flag for you right away."

I shake my head and roll my eyes. "That's because of you! You make her uncomfortable! You think that what happened doesn't matter anymore because you founded some big organization that you pour a ton of money into. You think that because you paid your dues that it's over, but it's not! For Mara, it's not! She lives with it every day! She's trying, you know. She's trying really hard to move on, so that she can embrace our family, but it's not easy! Especially when you're here accusing her of... of... I don't even know what you're accusing her of!" The more I speak, the angrier I'm getting. "Maybe you don't like seeing her because she reminds you of what you did, but that's not her fault! Think about how it feels for her to see you! All happy with your happy little family!" I'm tired of defending Mara all the time. I'm tired of defending myself and my choices. I finish my whiskey and stand up.

"Garrett, Son, please listen—"

"No, Dad, you listen," I retort. "Mara and I are getting married. You have two choices. You can accept that and embrace her into this family and try to make her feel as comfortable as possible, or you can leave us alone and we'll be a family without you. It's up to you." I slam my glass down on the bar and turn around, leaving my father sitting there alone. I'm still getting angrier with every step as I leave the bar. After everything that Mara's been through, why can't my father be a little more understanding? Why is he being so selfish!?

Chapter 31
Mara

I didn't need to knock because I had the key. It was in the tiny black purse I was given at the hospital, along with her cellphone, wallet, a tube of lipstick, a pack of gum, and a bunch of old receipts that were completely illegible. I tried reading all the receipts, looking for some clue, but there was none. Her keychain had just three keys on it, but twice as many keychains. I recognized all of them – there was the mini Eiffel tower, the pink pompom, the plastic piece of toast with eyes on it, a crocheted starfish, a heart made of newsprint, and a metal chip engraved with her name: Shannon.

It was impossible to stop the jingling of the keychain as I approached the apartment door and slipped in the key. As soon as I opened the door, I could smell the thick air beckoning me to open a window. I felt like I was breathing in dust as I walked into the living room. The blue couch sat undisturbed just as it had the last time I'd seen it. There were no indentions signaling whether anyone had ever sat on it before. The coffee table sat in front of it looking rigid and clean with a couple books piled on it neatly as though positioned perfectly for a magazine photo. The apartment was silent, despite the ominous metal hangings on the wall that look like they should be screaming. I gently placed the keys into my bag and walked through the living room to the bedroom. I'd never been inside before, so I slowly pushed open the bedroom, not knowing what to expect.

Inside there was a double bed, the sheets were twisted with sweat stains on them. The pillows were scrunched up in the middle, as though someone couldn't figure out where they were supposed to go. On each side of the bed was a small wooden table and I instantly recognized which side was Shannon's. On her side sat a small digital clock—the same one she used to use at home. In front of it sat her glasses case and a small diary and pen. Shannon would always write in her diary before bed. Sometimes in the mornings she would open it up to scribble in her dreams. I instantly dove for the diary and threw it in the duffel bag I brought, hiding it as though it were exposed out there on the bedside table. I'd never read it, I thought to myself, but I needed to make sure no one else would either, especially not Paul. I took her glasses case and the glasses inside as well. Then I started walking around the room looking for other things that belonged to Shannon. Her jewelry box was on the dresser. I opened it up to find it neatly organized with little compartments inside. There is a compartment with earrings tucked into the plush cushions, another compartment with rings and in the middle necklaces are lined up, side by side. I recognized the sisters ring that we both had—the one she hadn't been wearing recently. I also saw a necklace that once belonged to our mother. Her favorite necklace wasn't there because she was wearing it during the accident. They also gave me that at the hospital; with dried blood crusting on the chain. I closed the jewelry box and gently placed the whole thing into my bag. There was a light click and at first I thought it must have been the jewelry box hitting the glasses case, but then I realized the noise came from the living room. There was another click and then footsteps thumping around. I held my breath, listening to the sound of a glass hitting a counter, and the gurgle of liquid being poured. Then the footsteps continued and suddenly darkness filled the bedroom doorway.

"What the fuck?" Paul said when he saw me. "What the fuck are you doing here?"

"Leaving," I tried to say confidently. My hands were sweating and I tightened my grip on the duffel bag. I marched toward Paul, planning to slip under his arm, but when I got to the doorway, I was pushed backwards.

"How did you get in here?" The smell of alcohol puffed like smoke from Paul's mouth.

"The front door," I responded as confidently as I could, but my voice still creaked. "Let me pass."

"Who the fuck do you think you are?" Paul shoved me again and I stepped back to brace myself from falling. A third push and I was up against the edge of the bed. "Huh? What are you doing in my bedroom?" Paul leaned his face inches in front of mine and the heat from his breathing burned my skin. "Do you have some sort of weird fantasy about me? Is that what this is? Now that your sister's gone, you want me?" He shoved me back again and I fell onto the bed.

"You're a sick person, Mara!" He yelled. "After everything you did to your sister! She was fucking perfect, you understand? Except one thing! She was always worried about you! It always got in the way! Because of you, she died! You understand? And after all that, you sneak in here like this." His face got redder with each word. Then he climbed on top of me and grabbed my wrists with his hands. "Is this what you want? Huh? He slammed his body on top of mine. "You sick fucker."

I tried to scream but no sound would come out. I wriggled my body, but I was no match for someone the size of Paul. He continued screaming at me until I spit in his face. The spit had such force that it somehow pushed Paul off of me. "Get the fuck out of here!" he screamed. "I never want to see your face again, you understand?"

I clutched the duffel bag and ran as fast as I could out of the apartment, down the stairs and to the street. When I got home, I ran into my parents' room and opened the safe where my father's guns were stored. I threw Shannon's diary, glasses case and jewelry box into the safe. I was about to slam it shut, but then I pulled out the gun. I held it in my hand, thinking about the power that it contained.

"Holding a weapon is a big responsibility," my dad had always said. "You need to realize that you hold the power for life and death with that thing. It can never be taken lightly." I felt the weight of his statement in my hands as I held the gun, thinking of what I would do with this responsibility. Then I replaced the gun and slammed the safe shut.

Chapter 32
Mara

It's too much, I think to myself as I look in the mirror. I scan my body, which is wrapped in white silk and lace that make me look like a cupcake. There are feathers tucked in around the waist and beads causing the dress to sparkle when I move. I'm not sure how I ended up here, standing on a pedestal, surrounded by mirrors and women with expectant eyes. Bonnie and Caroline are sipping champagne with little red berries floating in the flutes and Terry—who I met at the engagement party—is standing at my feet with pins in her mouth.

"So avant garde," Bonnie says. "Are you sure this is the new trend?"

"Bonnie!" Caroline screeches. "Didn't you see the Donatello bridal line at fashion week? This look is what everyone is going for now. It's daring, sort of shabby-chic, very memorable!" Caroline turns to me. "And Mara, you have the body to pull it off! Most women can't, but you have that model figure that these dresses were built for!"

Her compliment makes me self-conscious of my curveless body; my small chest, and how my waist goes straight into my thighs. It's a body that does better in light summer dresses, plain garments that don't call too much attention. A body that should never be wrapped in feathers and beads.

"Maybe something more classic," Bonnie says to Terry. "Just something straight from satin. I have a feeling that's more Mara's type." I can't help but smile at Bonnie, surprised at her intuition. Since we arrived at the bridal boutique—which feels like hours ago—I've been slipped in and out of more dresses than I can count; none of which were chosen by me. Immediately upon entering the boutique, Caroline took the reins and started barking orders at Terry about what we were looking for. Terry nodded and added her own suggestions. Bonnie browsed the dresses, humming to herself while sipping champagne. No one asked me what I wanted, but even if they did, I wouldn't have been able to answer. A wedding dress is just not something I've ever thought about; and Caroline's authoritativeness gives me the jitters.

"This wedding could make the tabloids!" Caroline says. "We need to give them something to talk about with regards to the dress. You don't want the reporters thinking 'oh just another lifeless gown' when they write, do you?" I'm not sure who Caroline is asking.

"Let's just try something," Bonnie responds. "That's all I ask."

Terry pulls another tent-like thing off one of the many racks in the boutique and ushers me into the dressing room where she begins to unpin the dress on me. I finally feel like I can breathe.

"Did you like any of the dresses so far?" Terry says quietly so that only I can hear. I look at her, a little stunned to be asked my opinion after what I had experienced over the last few hours. I shake my head. "It's OK," she says, lifting the heavy gown over my head. "Not everyone feels like they fit in a wedding dress. Maybe you'd feel more comfortable shopping with your own mother. Bonnie and Caroline can be, how should I put this, overbearing." I'm not sure if it's her words or one of the pins, but something stabs me in the chest. I let out a small yelp, causing Terry to jump. "Oh, did I nick you? So sorry! You may like this next dress better. It's much cleaner."

I'm not sure I can handle trying on any more dresses. They are all too tight. All too much for me. I cross my arms in front of my bare chest and shake my head vigorously. "No," I plead. "I'm done."

"One more," Terry encourages me. "You'll like this one, I have a good feeling." I loosen up and let her slip it over my head. I feel like she is fastening a straightjacket around me, constraining me with ropes and ties so I can't hurt anyone. It makes me want to rip it off.

But then, I catch a glance in the mirror. At first I don't recognize the woman in there. She's taller than I am, with light skin and sandy brown hair feathered around her face. She has a tear rolling down her cheek and I can't read her expression. She looks afraid, maybe even a little distressed. It's my mother. I feel like she is trying to tell me something, but I can't understand her.

"You look darling," Terry says as she sticks the last pin in the back of the dress. "I think this one is it."

I'm still looking in the mirror, but my mother has disappeared and in her place is Shannon. She's standing with her arms crossed, shaking her head at me. "What?" I snap at the mirror.

"Oh, I just said I think this dress is perfect," Terry says, as though questioning her own judgment. "What do you think? Take a look in the mirror before we step outside."

I can't look at the mirror anymore. It's full of disappointment, I decide. They are disappointed in me for what I am doing. For moving on with my life. For marrying their killer's son. For allowing the Derby family to throw their money at me like it fixes things. *Don't worry*, I say quietly in my head. *I promise I'll fix things somehow. I promise.* I lift my head to the mirror again and this time I'm alone. The strapless dress is tight to the waist and then loosens up around the legs. There are no feathers, no beads, nothing except the shining fabric around me.

"We can shorten it to your ankles if you like, and get rid of the train," Terry says. "It will make it feel less formal."

I'm still looking at myself in the mirror and I wish my mother and Shannon were still there. Even if they are disappointed in me, at least I wouldn't be so alone.

"Let's show Bonnie and Caroline," Terry says, beckoning me out of the dressing room, back to the pedestal. I hold my breath and step outside where the two of them are sitting with their cell phones out.

"That's beautiful!" Bonnie exclaims. "Caroline? What do you think? Classic! A dress that would never go out of style!"

"Well that's true," Caroline responds as though that is a negative attribute. "It's nice, I guess."

"It seems we're settled then." Bonnie claps as she speaks. "Terry, this is the one. Let's start scheduling the fittings."

I return to the dressing room with Terry who frees me from the dress and then exits to schedule with Bonnie. I'm left alone to put on my clothes, feeling relieved that the experience is over. I realize that as much as I don't feel connected to Bonnie and Caroline, they must feel the same about me. I'm being forced upon them as much as they are being forced upon me. I'm sure we'd both be better off—and happier—if we didn't need to see each other and pretend we could be family. I could never be a part of their family. All of them are as guilty as Robert for thinking what happened was no big deal. As I slip into my clothes, I feel more and more convinced that I need to do something to separate Garrett and me from them. Garrett's not like them, he feels pain. He can see past the tip of his own nose. He'd also be better off without them.

When we leave the boutique my eyes drift to a figure standing across the street. It's a big tall man leaning against the building. I avert my eyes and try to stand between Bonnie and Caroline, hoping the man doesn't see me. *I'm imagining him*, I try to tell myself, but even I don't believe it. I'm being followed and I know there is only one way to make the haunting stop.

Chapter 33
Robert

I pull up exactly on time, but I sit in the car a few moments still deciding whether to go in. Going in means accepting the situation and giving up. But not going means giving in and making everything easier for her. When I'm sitting in the car, my phone buzzes.

They signed, says the text message from Caleb. I sigh with relief, knowing he is talking about the buyers for a building we just sold. I had high hopes for 910 Juniper. I was sure we'd fix that place up quickly and sell it with a huge profit. But after infusing almost $200,000 into repairs the property sat on the market for months with no offers. We finally got an offer just under what we had originally paid for it. Under normal circumstances, I would never have agreed to that. I would have kept the property on the market for as long as it took to get a good offer, enjoying the small rental income in the meantime, but this time, I didn't have a choice. We needed the cash. I am paying back the line of equity on the house, Garrett's wedding expenses are already exploding, and CADD still needs my help. Selling 910 Juniper will keep us afloat until the next deal comes. I'm sure of it.

There are three dots bouncing on my phone's screen under the last message from Caleb. *Where are you?* Suddenly pops up on the screen. I turn off the car and open the door. *Coming,* I respond. *Be there in two minutes.*

I walk from the parking lot to the entrance of the Grand Banquet Club, where we are doing a food tasting for the wedding. Bonnie had been taking Garrett and Mara to venues for the last couple weeks and they chose a few they liked. Now, we'll be doing tastings at all of them to decide which will be the one. I still don't believe the wedding will actually happen. Something inside me says it won't, that something will happen between now and then that will open Garrett's eyes or worse, a disaster as promised from the letters will force the wedding off. The latter seems more likely to me, but I pray for the former.

Inside the big banquet hall is empty except for one table organized in the middle. From the entrance, I can see the table is decorated for a wedding, with a shining tablecloth and centerpiece with candles and white flowers. With just one table inside, the room looks huge, like it could fit an Olympic stadium. Near the table, Bonnie is standing with Garrett, Mara, Caleb and Caroline, who are all looking at a petit man in a tuxedo talking to them with his hands pressed in front of his chest.

"There he is!" Bonnie exclaims when she hears my footsteps. "We're all famished!"

"I'm right on time," I respond, looking at my watch. I'm five minutes late, but does five minutes really make such a difference? I know it does. Seconds can make a difference. But I try not to think about that.

"We can get started," Bonnie says to the man in the tuxedo who motions all of us to sit down around the table. On top of every plate is a small printed menu of what we'll be tasting. There are several first dishes, a few main courses, and a list of desserts. Without reading through it, I place the menu back down and look across the table where Mara is sitting. It's hard for me to see her through the large centerpiece, which seems unnecessary and mostly annoying. Through the flower petals I can see that Mara is studying the menu, careful not to look up at anyone else. She's wearing a dark cardigan, which looks like something Bonnie would have picked out and I wonder if Bonnie and her are starting to bond. Bonnie hasn't ever mentioned to me seeing Mara since the engagement party and I wonder now if I need to warn her too. Does she know who Mara is? There's no way, I think. She would have mentioned something to me.

I look over to Garrett, who is sitting with an arm around Mara and reading the menu that she is holding. He looks so protective of her, like he is guarding her from something and I think that something is me. Garrett looks up and catches my eye a moment. With a quick smile, he looks back down and kisses Mara's forehead.

"Everything sounds delicious," Bonnie exclaims, putting the menu back down on her plate. "Food at weddings is so important. You remember the Holmer wedding last year? Everything was inedible! And there was just so little of everything! I'm telling you, they ran out of hors d'oeuvres just minutes after the cocktail hour began."

"Remember the first dish?" Caroline chimed in with a chuckle. "Two slices of tomato and they called that a salad! Everyone was hungry!" Everyone at the table let out a little giggle, lightening the mood.

"We cannot let that happen with us!" Bonnie exclaimed, just as the man in the tuxedo returned followed by two waiters carrying trays, from which they placed a plate in front of everyone.

There were three different first dishes to try, the man in the tuxedo explained. "Taste the dish in front of you and then pass it along so everyone can taste everything." In front of me is a Waldorf salad, the blue cheese, grapes and nuts carefully arranged on top of a bed of lettuce. I put my fork inside and take a bite. It tastes like a regular salad, but I feel like my mouth is full of sand.

"These scallops are heavenly," Caroline says, closing her eyes. "I think I'll just keep this plate to myself, no need to taste anything else!"

"Pass it over!" Caleb chortles as he stabs his fork into a scallop on her plate.

"Here, have my scallops, they are divine," Bonnie says, passing her plate to Garrett. "How's the artichoke tartlet? That one sounds interesting!"

"Tartlet is good," Garrett responds. "Mara, Dad, how is the salad?"

"Good," Mara and I say in unison. We're both caught off guard as though our words clashed in the air. I motion to her to go ahead. My opinion here doesn't matter.

"It's good," Mara repeats. "Kind of boring. Just a salad."

"I agree, Honey," Bonnie says. "No one remembers the salad! The scallops will be remembered!" The dishes are passed around and I taste the scallops and the artichoke tartlet. It's like my body is revolting against this wedding, not letting me taste any of the food. All I feel is the texture of sand in my mouth and a metal aftertaste. The feeling reminds me of the accident; going to the hospital and having my forehead stitched up. I remember having that same taste in my mouth.

We taste the main dishes, a filet mignon, rosemary chicken and a pumpkin ravioli. I try to wash the flavor out of my mouth with water, but to no avail. I'll have to take everyone's word that every dish was *magnificent! Scrumptious! Packed with flavor!*

After the meal, Garrett excuses himself to the bathroom and Caleb gets a phone call that he says he has to take. A moment later, Bonnie and Caroline decide they need to get inside the kitchen to speak with the chef about a few of their observations. Mara and I are left alone at the table. She's still sitting across from me and I can see through the centerpiece that she is biting her nails.

"Please don't hurt my son," I say with calm authority. It's ambiguous whether it comes off as a threat, but I want Mara to know I'm serious. There haven't been any new letters since the one I received before the engagement party. I'm not sure if that's a good sign or not. Or if it's just because I confronted her. "Do you really love him?" I ask not expecting to get a real answer, but with hopes that I'll be able to read her expression. Her face freezes like a deer caught in headlights and she sits motionless, a fingernail still trapped in her teeth. I'm trying to find my answer, but then I notice Garrett jogging back to the table.

"Where is everyone?" he asks, quickly placing his arm around Mara, who continues biting at her nails.

"Bonnie and Caroline are in the kitchen," I respond. "Caleb got a call. Anyway, I better be going." I stand up and throw my napkin on the dirty table. "Tell Bonnie I had to run to the office." I walk around the table and give Garrett's shoulder a squeeze before I head toward the doors of the ballroom. Mara's expression is still stuck in front of my eyes. What did it mean?

Chapter 34
Mara

I wasn't sure why I went back there. But I somehow found myself sitting on that blue couch, the cushions so hard that my body almost ached. I held my purse tight on my lap, afraid the contents would fall out. I peeked inside again and saw the light reflecting on the shiny metal of the gun. My heart pounded, I had never taken the gun out of the house by myself before. My father always did it, carrying the gun in his belt or in the portable case. He would have told me it wasn't safe putting the gun in my purse. That it could roll around, hit something that could jam the trigger or injure the cavity. I wasn't wearing a belt, and lugging that square case was unappealing. Instead, I held my purse tight, making sure the contents didn't move around too much.

I quietly let myself into the apartment and sat down on the couch to wait. While I waited, the sunlight coming through the windows started to fade, the shadows around the room grew larger. I couldn't stop myself from staring at the metal wall hangings, whose shadows grew like demons climbing up the walls. I thought about turning on the lights, but it was hard to move from the stiff couch.

Later, I heard the footsteps approaching the door and then the key being slipped into the lock.

The door handle twisted and in he walked. He threw his keys on the counter and went straight for the kitchen without noticing me. A glass clanked on the counter and a bottle cap fell to the floor. Liquid gurgled as it filled the glass. Then, with a flick, the lights came on.

"What the fuck?" Paul yelled, almost dropping his glass when he noticed me sitting on the couch. "What are you doing here? I told you I never want to see you again!" I sat still, watching him puff out his chest and narrow his eyebrows. "Are you deaf? Get off my couch! I swear, I'm going to fucking kill you if you're still here in 30 seconds."

I didn't move.

"I'm serious! I'll kill you," he said, taking a drink from his cup. "You deserve it anyway."

"So kill me," I responded, with one hand in my purse wrapped around the gun. "What's stopping you?"

"If that's what you want," he said. "I always knew you were a sick mother fucker. Everything you put your sister through. The world would have been better if it had been you instead of her!" He slammed his glass on the counter and started walking toward me, his arms swinging like they had a purpose.

Immediately, I stood up and held the gun in front of me, pointing right to the middle of Paul's face. "Bang!" I said. When he jumped, I began to laugh. "Aren't you going to kill me?"

Paul stood still with his arms raised in surrender.

"Maybe you should have died instead of her!" I screamed.

"Me? I fucking loved her!" Paul yelled. "She died because she always did whatever you wanted! You know why they were late that night? Why they were speeding to meet you? Because last minute Shannon decided she wanted to go to your stupid birthday party! We had plans that night, we were going to a concert. Halfway there, Shannon tells me to turn around and she calls her parents to come get her. I said 'why don't we both just go to the restaurant?' but she was adamant that I go home and that she go with her parents. If you weren't so selfish, I would have taken Shannon to the restaurant and we all would have had one big happy dinner! You happy? You got what you wanted? So you see, you sit around blaming everyone and hating everyone, but it's all your fault. Everything that happened that night, was your fault. If you were less selfish, Shannon would still be here. Your parents would still be here. You understand?"

I held the gun strong in front of me, even though I felt my arms quivering.

"So shoot me," Paul said, shrugging his shoulders. "You already killed your family. What's one more person? Besides, it's not like I have something to live for now anyway."

I held the gun out, but my arms were starting to ache. Slowly, I dropped it down and stood silently in front of Paul.

"That's what I thought," he said. "You're too chicken shit to actually do anything."

"I'm not," I responded. "You're just not worth it."

Paul turned around, his back toward me, and went into the kitchen. I heard a second glass hit the counter, another pour of liquid and he returned carrying another glass with the clear brown liquid inside. He handed the glass to me. "You hate me for no reason other than your sister loved me," he said.

"That's not true," I responded, thinking about my sister's twisted ankle, the bruises on her arm and the scratch on her cheek from a few weeks ago.

"It's true," Paul responded. "I know a lot more about you than you think. Shannon told me everything. All about your problems. You wanted her to stay and take care of you forever."

I shook my head, while taking a drink of the alcohol he gave me. It burned my throat. It was like a real fire had sparked in my mouth and it would now raze my entire body from the inside.

"Anyway, you're directing all your anger at the wrong person," he said.

"I didn't kill them!" I screamed for the first time. "It's not my fault!"

"Then whose fault is it?" Paul answered.

"Maybe it's yours," I responded. I looked down at the gun still in my hand. My hand was heavy from all the power and responsibility wrapped up in that tiny machine.

Chapter 35
Garrett

Stressful barely describes the last few months. Not only has my mother gone crazy with wedding planning, forcing Mara and me to attend multiple pointless meetings and events, but work has also become more difficult. The business is strapped for cash, many of the recent investments are not going as expected, and we lost a few bids on new investments we wanted because we couldn't organize the financing. On top of all that, I'm losing my father. I feel him slipping away from me, our conversations becoming less candid, the reek of disappointment following us around everywhere.

Just yesterday he stopped by my office, tapping the door frame like he always does. "Any news?" he asked. I knew he was asking about 706 Highland, a new deal I was crunching the numbers for, but that wasn't what I wanted to tell him.

"Actually, yes," I responded, beckoning my father to step inside.

"The seller called me again, they want to know if we're in or out, otherwise they might find a new buyer," he said. "Are we ready to make a position?"

I shook my head. There was something off about the numbers, they were too good to be true, which always made me suspicious—usually for good reason. I think back to 762 Hamilton, the last property that had inflated numbers on a spreadsheet. After weeks of digging around, I found the issue: an extra zero was typed in the valuation of the lot. Just one small number, but it cost us months of investigating and almost made us pay exponentially more than what the property was worth. In the end, we dropped the deal. Months of wasted time researching, negotiating, and setting up renovation plans.

"By the end of the week," I said. My father nodded and pivoted toward the door.

"Well, keep me posted," he said, just as he was about to slip away to avoid any real conversation.

"Wait, Dad," I said. I could see his shoulders straighten like an electric shock got him right in the shoulder blades. He turned his head, keeping his body facing out the door. "Do you have a minute? Mom and I went tuxedo shopping this weekend. We picked out a few options for you. You need to go try them on."

My father let out a sigh so big it could have caused a hurricane. "Sure, Son, just tell me where," he said as he stepped into the hall and disappeared from my view. I also wanted to see if our weekly golf session was still happening. We'd missed it the last few weeks. A few work emergencies and then some urgent wedding meetings kept getting in the way. The distance between us was growing.

I need a break. I'm sure Mara does too, so I planned a surprise getaway for the two of us. It will be a full weekend without any discussions of wedding logistics, family time, or burdening obligations. Just the two of us, a small cabin, a beach, and a few bottles of wine that I bought for the occasion.

I'm waiting for her when she finishes work that afternoon. I've packed a small suitcase for us, with bathing suits, and the minimal amount of clothing needed for a beach getaway. When I was packing, I remembered how much I love that about Mara—that she didn't need extravagant clothing nor did she put in much effort with what she wore. She kept it simple, often lounging around in pajamas almost to the point where it could have been too much. She could get ready in minutes, going from sweats to date night attire in less than the time it takes most girls to dry their hair. All I packed for her were two bathing suits, three sundresses, jeans, and two t-shirts and I was sure that was more than enough.

My car is parked outside the new office building for CADD. They recently moved to a bigger space to accommodate the growing number of employees. I hadn't been inside this new office, but Mara says it's barely bigger than the previous and they are all still squished inside. She shares an office with the new community outreach director and the new grant writer, who she says never stop gossiping. Apparently, they went to college together and still act like they think they're in a sorority. Mara's impressions of them always make me laugh.

I'm smiling to myself, remembering the way Mara imitated the grant writer talking about how one of her dates had food in his teeth ("Like, what was I supposed to do? Tell him? That would be so embarrassing! Of course, I still let him kiss me! If I didn't, he would have been totally offended! It was, like, a really nice restaurant!") when I hear the knock on my window. I'm startled a moment and then I see Mara leaning forward looking in.

"This is a no parking zone, Sir," she says as I roll down the window. "We're going to have to tow this baby." She pats her hand on the roof of the car.

"Maybe I can convince you to change your mind, Officer," I respond, playing along.

"Are you attempting to bribe me, Sir?" Her face is so straight, it's almost hard to tell if she is joking.

"Of course not, but I am attempting to kidnap you for the weekend," I say. I'm never as good as she is at acting. "Want to hop in? I wouldn't want to make a scene."

"Kidnap me?" she responds without breaking. Her tone shows feigned disbelief. "Sir, we were just dealing with a small parking ticket, but kidnapping is a felony. I'll have to punish you." She's still, holding my gaze with her serious expression. I suddenly feel uncomfortable, wondering if I crossed a line or said the wrong thing. The feeling makes my heart pound and my

245

brow start to sweat. After what feels like minutes, she opens the car door and slips inside. "Where are we going?" she says with a smile as she leans over to kiss me on the cheek. She's dropped the banter and I feel myself starting to relax.

"It's a surprise," I respond, feeling like I'm regaining control. I'm not sure what it is about Mara, but she makes me uncomfortable to the point that it's exhilarating. I've never felt that way with anyone before. I'm always in control, always leading. I always feel like I know what to say or do. But not with Mara. With her, I sometimes feel like I'm watching my steps, tripping on my words. Like the wrong move could be dangerous.

Our destination is a few hours away. We're going to a new complex that Derby Ventures just purchased. We usually stick to office buildings or skyrise apartments, but we're trying something new: a vacation-style beach complex. The property has six small cabins on a private beach. The cabins are unfinished, but one had been furnished to show potential buyers. I'd visited with Caleb a few weeks ago. When we were there, all I thought about was how nice it would be to be there with Mara. I imagined us sitting on the couch facing the floor to ceiling windows watching the waves roll by or drinking coffee on the wooden balcony, tasting the salt from the air. My father doesn't know I'm taking Mara there this weekend. I took the key from our lockbox before leaving work. He'll never notice, anyway. He never checks the lockbox. I did, however, check with my mother that there were no wedding appointments for the weekend. We were free, she said, surprisingly. It must have been the first weekend in months without vendors to meet or something to do.

During the drive Mara tells me more about her officemates. I try to empathize and wrack my brain for any office drama that may be comparable, but I don't have any. There are several employees other than Caleb and me, but they are all men and most office conversations revolve around sports or work. I couldn't even tell you if my colleagues were single or married, it never comes up. When the conversation lags, I try to think of a new topic. I bring up a TV show we watched, but that conversation soon dies, and then I talk about a new restaurant that everyone seemed to be talking about. I feel the elephant in the car, the one topic I want to avoid this weekend: the wedding. I'm, of course, excited to get married and have Mara as my wife. But does it have to be so stressful?

It's just after sunset when we arrive at the complex. I pull the car inside and park in front of the furnished unit. I walk around the car to open the door for Mara and help her out. She smiles at me and I know I did the right thing, planning a vacation for us. I can see the real Mara coming out of her shell. The carefree, fun, and confident Mara, the one I'm sure was dominant before her family died. Trauma does that to someone. It takes their best self and slams it away, laughing hysterically whenever it tries to surface. Years of this internal struggle make it hard for trauma victims to return to who they were, that's what a

247

therapist I recently spoke with said. I had tried to get Mara to speak with the therapist, but she wasn't interested.

We walk up the stone steps holding hands and I notice the lights are on inside. I wonder if the lights have been on for weeks since Caleb and I had visited and I worry about the electric bill that's coming. I slip the key into the front door and it creaks open. There are voices inside; did we leave a TV on? I don't even remember seeing a TV. I let go of Mara's hand and motion for her to wait by the door while I go inside. I walk through the foyer and still hear the murmuring of a conversation. I can't yet understand what is being said, but a few more steps take me to the living room where I see the electric fireplace is on and two glasses of wine being held up by whoever is sitting on the couch. Their voices are low and they don't seem to notice me coming in. Could it be the previous owners? We hadn't changed the lock yet, are they still here enjoying the property that we paid for? I clear my throat, ready to reprimand them for trespassing. The two people look up at me behind the couch.

"Garrett? What are you doing here?" my mother asks. She turns to my father. "Did you know he was coming?"

Suddenly I feel Mara breathing behind me.

"How lovely," my mother continues. "What a nice little vacation for the four of us!"

Chapter 36
Mara

"We find the defendant guilty of a wet reckless," the jury foreman said, his eyes glued to a small scrap of paper he was holding in his hand. "And not guilty of vehicular manslaughter." The foreman looked up at the judge and then sat back down, his eyes still focused on the small piece of paper, as though he wasn't sure he had read it right.

The judge banged his gavel. "You're a lucky man, Mr. Derby," the judge said. "A wet reckless is much less severe than a DUI and it seems the prosecution did not meet the burden of proof to convict you. This is a lucky break for you, and you should take it as such. If something like this happens again, you will not be so lucky. A DUI after a wet reckless is a severe offense, Mr. Derby, do you understand that?"

"Yes, Sir," Robert said from the defense table. He looked straight at the judge, his eyes never swaying. During the entire trial, he kept his head facing forward, never letting his gaze stray. He never looked back, never at me.

"Good," the judge continued. "I'm ordering a limited suspension of your driver's license. You can drive to and from work and that's all. If you are ever pulled over somewhere not between your residence and your workplace, your license will be revoked for five years. If you are ever pulled over and any alcohol is found in your blood, that means a blood alcohol content of 0.01% or more, your license will be revoked for five years and you could face jail time. Is this understood?"

"Yes, Sir."

"I'm also fining you $1,000. I'm sure that for you, Mr. Derby, this is just pocket change. I'd fine you more, but that's standard for what the jury found. When you write the check, I hope you realize how easy you got off," the judge said. "And I don't want to see you in my courtroom again. If I do, I will be sure to order severe penalties." The judge banged his gavel again. "And I guess that's all then." He stood up and left the courtroom.

I sat still in my seat in the back of the courtroom. I'd been attending the trial daily for the last month, even though I promised my grandma I wouldn't. She said it wouldn't be good for me. It would make it harder for me to cope. But she was wrong. I needed to be there. I needed to see the murderer sitting at the defense table, his wife behind him every day. I needed to know what would happen.

A low murmur rose over the crowd in the back of the courtroom. People stood up, putting notepads back in their bags. Surely there would be articles about this online later in the day. Tabloids had been covering the case writing all sorts of ridiculous headlines. *Real Estate Tycoon Derby Faces Jail Time. Derby Family Shows Support During Trial. Experts Predict Harsh End for*

Derby Family. I was sure all the tabloids would go crazy over his acquittal. No one was expecting this. I didn't get up. Instead, I watched Robert Derby shake his lawyer's hand and turn around to talk to the team of lawyers standing behind them. The team members were all smiling, patting each other for their unexpected win. What scum, I thought. Lawyers don't realize that their wins come on the backs of poor people who can't afford to fight them.

"What a turn of events," someone said to me. I looked up to see a woman in a white blouse standing next to my bench. "Are you covering this case?" I shook my head and the woman moved in the pew to sit down next to me. "You've been here every day," she said. "Are you related to the victims?"

I looked at her and immediately tears filled my eyes. I looked down at my lap, where my hands were shaking. My nail beds were bloody from all the picking I had been doing.

"I'm Cindy Fowler. I'm a civil justice lawyer," she said, sticking out her hand to me. I looked at her hand, afraid of offering my bloody one up to meet hers. "Have you thought of filing a civil case for manslaughter?" She put her hand down realizing I wouldn't shake it. I shook my head and she continued speaking. "You deserve some compensation. I can help you with that. Pro bono. I'll only take a cut of whatever we win." I sat silently. "Think about it." She handed me her card and placed her hand on my shoulder. "Look, I know I can't imagine what you are going through. And I know that nothing can bring back your family. You feel like there is no such thing as justice, especially after what happened today. And you're right. There is no justice. But sometimes we have to settle for compensation instead of justice. It won't make everything OK, but it will help you in the future."

I looked up to Cindy's face. "OK," I said. "What do I have to do?"

"Come to my office tomorrow," she said. "We'll get everything started." Then she left.

I was alone in the courtroom, except for the ghosts. My parents stood in front of me, their faces mangled from the crash, blood dripping down their necks. They stared at me, like they needed to tell me something, but I just couldn't understand. "What?" I yelled. "I'm sorry!" I scrunched my eyelids as tight as I could, trying not to see them, but even with my eyes closed, the image was stuck in my memory. When I opened my eyes, I saw my fingertips covered in wet blood. It was no longer just the drips oozing from my nail beds, which were raw and scraped up. I didn't even remember picking at them so hard. The blood was also from my parents, covering my hands until they were completely coated.

Chapter 37
Mara

"You can fix this," Paul said when he showed up at my doorstep. "I have an idea."

I walked back inside my house and sat on the couch, waiting for Paul to enter. These surprise meetings were becoming more frequent. At first it was just me, showing up at his apartment. I always had a reason, I wanted Shannon's purple shirt, or I was looking for that shot glass she bought when she went on spring break with her friends. Paul hadn't moved any of her stuff—it stayed in the closet, in the cupboard, on the bookshelf waiting for her as though she could come back any minute. I didn't mind that, it was better than him throwing everything out like he was trying to erase her memory. Every time I showed up, Paul handed me whatever it was I needed, often with a scowl or a comment under his breath. I didn't care how he acted, I was there for Shannon's things after all. He never touched me again, except an accidently brush of our fingers when he handed me something.

Then, one day, he showed up at my house. "I need that shot glass back," he said.

"Why?" I stood, blocking the doorway with my arms crossed.

"None of your business!" he shouted at me. "Now give it to me, or I'll come in and take it." I closed the door on him while I went inside to get the shot glass. I thought about throwing it at his feet, showing him that I'd rather shatter it in a million pieces than give it back to him. But in the end, I just handed it over.

The back-and-forth continued for months, each of us showing up at each other's place needing something of Shannon's. Neither of us ever argued, we just handed each other what we needed and went on our way. Until that one time. Paul showed up at my house with eyes that were red and puffy. "What color were Shannon's eyes?" he asked, barely waiting for me to open the door.

I thought about it a few moments before responding. "They were like hazel, sort of. Sort of dark greenish, with some brown specks."

"I think they were light green, but sometimes they looked brown in the light," he responded, pushing himself inside for the first time. He sat down on the couch and we spent the next hour trying to define the exact color of Shannon's eyes. In the end, we settled on seaweed green, maybe not the most flattering color, but it seemed to capture the right essence. Then Paul left. My next visit, I asked Paul if Shannon had still slept with her retainer. He said he didn't know she had one, and then I had to go home to find it so I could prove it to him.

Our meetings were calming, it was like there was something still alive about Shannon when we talked about her. And as the two people who knew her best, we were the only ones who we could really ask our silly questions to. I still hated Paul. I hated him for taking my sister from me, for making her fall so deeply in love that she never wanted to be without him. I hated him because I still wasn't sure if he was good to her, and I was sure I'd never find that out.

I started visiting Paul every time I had an attack. When the anxiety got too great, when the demons inside me started taking over. I'd rush over to Paul's and we would debate about the way Shannon used to scrunch her nose when she was suspicious about something or how she'd always tap her foot when music was playing. Focusing on Shannon brought the calm back.

"Get on with it," I said to Paul after he followed me inside my house. "What do you mean, 'you can fix this'?"

Paul sat down on the plush chair on the side of the couch. I was suddenly hit with a memory of Shannon sitting cross legged in the chair reading a book. I'd never understand why she liked to read there, the lighting was terrible and it was right in front of the TV.

Paul handed me a thick paper on cardstock that looked like a poorly designed wedding invitation and sat back. I picked it up and started reading.

You can make a difference at the second annual CADD gala!

Cocktails! Paparazzi! A silent auction with amazing getaways and more!

"What is this?" I asked, throwing the flyer back down on the coffee table. I had heard about CADD. It was that charity that horrible man started. He thought he could use our family's tragedy for his own benefit.

"We need revenge," Paul said. "Look at this guy! The two of us are sitting around arguing over Shannon's dirty underwear and this guy is becoming a celebrity for what he did! That's fucked up! He can't be allowed to do this!"

"What are we supposed to do about it?" I responded, angry with Paul for bringing that flyer into my house. I didn't want to know anything about that murderer. I definitely didn't want anything with his name on it in my house.

I was supposed to believe that justice had been served. That everything was all over. That's what the contract said at least. A couple months ago, my lawyer Cindy Fowler had called offering a settlement from Robert Derby. $100,000 and an agreement that I wouldn't pursue any further actions. Cindy said it was a good deal, especially since he was acquitted in the criminal case. I could hear that Cindy wanted me to accept it. She had been working on my case pro bono for a year and every month she seemed less and less dedicated. She told me it was time to move on. I agreed to the settlement and deposited the check in my bank. It didn't feel like anything to me. It made no difference. An extra $100,000 and I still had the same empty feeling inside me. Except after signing the agreement, I no longer had hope that maybe it could get better.

"He needs to know how it feels," Paul said. "He gets to go on living like he's a king! That's what rich people do! They can do whatever they want, even murder, and they get away with it. There is no justice for people with money!"

"That's life," I responded, still not understanding Paul's point. "It sucks."

"Well, we can fix that," Paul said. "You have to show him how it feels."

"Me?"

"Yes, you, Mara," Paul said, his eyes burrowing inside of me and creating a fire. His eyes were starting to frighten me. They were turning black and it was like the devil was coming out of them. "You have to fix this, because it was your fault."

"Stop it," I retorted. Paul shrugged.

"Can I use your printer?" he asked me. I nodded and he went into my parent's office. After a few moments I heard him typing and then the printer came alive. When he returned he was holding a sealed white envelope.

"What's that?" I asked.

"Don't worry about it," he responded before letting himself out.

Chapter 38
Robert

"What are you doing here?" Garrett says, grabbing Mara's hand. She's standing behind him, like she's hiding from us.

"I'll ask you the same question," I respond. "I own this property. I'm allowed to come whenever I like. Your turn."

"I thought we'd take a small weekend trip," Garrett says. "But how did you get... I have the key..."

"There are multiple keys, Garrett," I say. I'm angry at him for showing up like this with Mara. It wouldn't bother me so much that he would want to use one of the properties for a vacation. It bothers me that he took the key from the office without saying anything. And it bothers me that it's with Mara. I think about the two of them secluded here and it worries me.

"But I didn't see your car..." It's like Garrett is trying to rationalize how it's possible that Bonnie and I are here.

"We had a bottle of wine at dinner and decided to take a taxi home," I respond, careful not to look at Mara when I say it.

"I guess, we'll go find a hotel," Garrett says suddenly, looking back at Mara behind him.

"Nonsense!" Bonnie shrieks. Her voice increases several octaves with each glass of wine. "There are two bedrooms here. We can all stay, it will be fun. A good opportunity for us all to get to know each other better." She's smiling at Mara like she's trying to convince her. No one but Bonnie seems convinced.

"Fine," Garrett responds and pulls Mara away to the cabin's second bedroom. It's meant to be a kid's room, with white bunk beds and pastel blue décor.

I look at Bonnie who is sitting, calmly drinking her wine, and a wave of emotion runs over me. It's half disappointment, half relief with a little frustration mixed in. Bonnie and I need a weekend away. We need to work on our marriage in a setting without distractions like the club or any of the other social places we frequent. We need some time alone to remember who we are together when we're not pretending in front of a crowd. We need to remember why we got together in the first place. But now, any hopes for that have been squashed. We'll end up spending this weekend pretending like usual, and most likely talking exclusively about wedding plans. I'm of course disappointed at this. The relief comes because I'm no longer afraid that Bonnie and I will realize we have nothing in common anymore. We'll be too busy pretending to be the perfect couple—a great example for the future bride and groom.

"How funny that we all ended up here," Bonnie says to me. Her voice has become less candid, the voice she uses when other people are around, instead of when it's just us. "What do you think we should do? Mara may feel awfully uncomfortable, she is so shy sometimes, I wonder if she talks to Garrett when it's just the two of them."

"Let's all just try to enjoy the weekend together," I respond, although I don't think it will be any bit enjoyable. Garrett hasn't been speaking with me lately. He avoids me at home and has canceled our weekly golf trips. Whenever he speaks to me, he sounds like he is bearing terrible news, his tone darkens and he becomes deeply serious. We used to speak candidly all the time, now I'm afraid to say what I think around him. Afraid it will offend him, make him angry, or cause him to do something rash.

"Garrett is so thoughtful, wanting to bring Mara here," Bonnie says. "I just wish she'd let us get to know her better, you know? So we can see what he sees. She's just so quiet! She seems so uncomfortable all the time! Maybe us here all together will be a good thing." Bonnie seems like she is still trying to convince herself that this weekend won't be disastrous, that maybe it will still be the fun getaway we—or at least I—had hoped for. "Why don't you go get them? See if they want some wine? We have another bottle if we finish this one." Bonnie coaxes me to get up and I reluctantly comply. I put my wine glass down and walk through the hall to the bedroom where

Garrett and Mara will stay. The door is closed. I try to listen in through the door, but I hear nothing. No sounds, no muffled voices, no creaking from the wooden floor. The silence worries me. I knock.

"Garrett? Mara? Would you like to join us for a glass of wine?" I ask through the closed door. I feel like a dad of a teenager, trying to break through a shell of angst against parents. I suddenly hear Garrett's deep voice and then the door opens.

"Sure, Dad, give us a few minutes," he responds and then closes the door back in my face. I return to the living room and fall back down on the couch next to Bonnie, who already retrieved two more wine glasses from the kitchen. The two of us sit silently, as though unable to start a conversation until our guests join. The only sound is the crackle of the fire from the electric fireplace. I'm staring at the flames, watching them dance above the fake log. It's a nice touch in this room, I think, it gives a cozy ambiance and I wonder why more people don't use electric fireplaces. I'm still staring at the flames ten minutes later, when Garrett and Mara finally emerge. They sit down carefully on the loveseat at the right side of the couch. The seat is barely large enough for two people, causing them to sit with their legs touching. Garrett has a hand on her knee and his other arm wrapped around the back of the loveseat. Bonnie hands them both wine and they sip silently.

"Such a lovely cabin this is," Bonnie says, her voice like a knife cutting through the silence. "I can see why you wanted to come for the weekend. A great getaway for young lovers!"

"Yeah, it's nice," Garrett responds and the conversation feels like it's over. "I think we'll go for a little walk on the beach. It's not so cold out." Garrett looks at Mara who nods and places her glass down on the little yellow coaster on the coffee table. The two of them stand up and I realize they are already carrying sweaters as though they were never planning on sitting with us for long. "Have a good night," Garrett says as he leads Mara to the porch facing the ocean. There are a few stairs from there down to the sand and I watch as the two of them descend and start walking along the beach. They're holding hands, both looking out to the water, the wind blowing Mara's long hair in every different direction. It's a romantic picture, their outlines in the darkness, even I can see that. But the sight worries me. It's like I am seeing a new side of them, how they are when it's just the two of them, and I feel more afraid that this wedding will move forward.

Chapter 39
Mara

"Get out of my house!" I screamed, but Paul pushed himself through the threshold and plopped down on the couch. "I don't want you coming over here anymore." I had stopped showing up at his apartment. Retrieving Shannon's things wasn't worth the eerie feelings that came from being around him. I hadn't seen him for a week, the longest time since we started our back-and-forth. He had shown up at my door a few times, but I pretended not to be there. This time, he was waiting for me when I opened the door to leave for work.

"Do you think hiding from me changes things? That if you don't see me, you can pretend that everything is all right?"

"Get out, Paul," I yelled, but I could feel myself weakening. My voice shook and I watched as Paul's pupils became black and started to hypnotize me.

"Come on, Mara, you can't run away from this," Paul said. His word lassoed me in, pulling me back inside the house. I would be late for work, I thought. But it didn't matter. Nothing mattered. My life was a monotonous cycle of work, home, sleep. I was spiraling through the cycle faster and faster each day, hoping to get to the bottom.

Maybe hit the ground and stop the endless rounds of meaningless pain.

My legs turned to stone and I couldn't move. The lasso pulled me toward Paul, tightening on my torso. I could feel the ropes burrowing into my ribs, my stomach, squeezing me like a wet towel, wringing out all the anger that was soaked inside me. "How can you live with yourself like this? Knowing you have the ability to avenge your sister's death, but you choose not to?"

I was hypnotized, unable to respond. Paul leaned forward and pulled a folded envelope out of his back pocket. He tossed the envelope on the table. "I got you something," he said. "Aren't you going to see what it is?"

The lasso pulled me forward until I was sitting on the couch next to Paul. My arm reached forward and picked up the envelope, even though my head raged against the decision. *Don't touch it!* I wanted to yell to my hand, but it was no use. I had lost control over my own body. I opened the envelope and inside was a small rectangular piece of paper. *Admit One to the second annual CADD gala*, it said.

"I'm not going," I said. The strength in my voice even surprised me.

"Yes you are," Paul responded. "You have no idea what that ticket costs. I'm pretty sure they can fund the whole charity with what I paid."

I dropped the ticket back down on the coffee table, but I couldn't stop myself from looking at it. My eyes examined the shiny white ticket, the cursive font telling me that I would be admitted to this exclusive event.

"Who's Amy Barnes?" I asked, reading the name on the ticket.

"Well, you can't exactly show up as Mara Sanders, can you?" Paul responded. I didn't respond.

"You're just moving on, aren't you?" Paul continued. "That's it? They give you a little money and then everything is OK? You don't care anymore? You disgust me, Mara. I'm actually surprised at you. I thought you loved your sister as much as she loved you. But it seems you don't. You don't care anymore and you're going to let that scumbag murderer continue living the good life. I don't know how you live with yourself."

"Anyway, if you change your mind, take this." Paul pulls a small phone out of his pocket and drops it on the coffee table in front of me. "We don't need the police on our tracks after you do this, understand? From now on, we communicate only through these phones. I programmed the number to my burner in the phone, OK? Call and text me there. Don't be an idiot." Paul stood up and walked out the front door, slamming it behind him.

Alone with the ticket and the phone, I felt my knees start to shake. Paul was right, I could barely live with myself as it was. How could I have fought with my sister like that? Over something so stupid. Everything could have been avoided if I had just let Paul come to my birthday dinner. Paul

265

was right, I was disgusting. I was horrible. I didn't deserve the family I lost.

I picked up the ticket and put it back in the envelope. I slipped the envelope into my purse and stood up. I needed to go to work, but instead, I marched back into my bedroom and curled up on my bed. I held my knees in tight, trying to stop my body from shaking. I could feel my insides rattling around, shaking so hard that everything could explode. *How could I live with myself?* The question kept popping into my brain, each time louder than the last. *How could I live with myself?* The question took on a life of its own and began whirling around the room, forming a tornado. *HOW COULD I LIVE WITH MYSELF?* The tornado roared around me, pulling me in every direction around the room until the answer came to me. I couldn't. I couldn't live with myself anymore. I didn't want to live with myself anymore. I wanted it to be over: the loss, the loneliness, the abuse from Paul, which was the only thing that could calm my anxieties.

I had the power to end it. I could go to the gala, get my revenge and then end everything for myself. It would be simple. I had the gun. I knew how to use it. Just four shots was all it would take. Three for Robert Derby's family and one for me. I could avenge my family's deaths and then join them above. The tornado around the room had stopped, leaving everything in its place.

I walked back to the living room where the small phone he left me was sitting on the table. I flipped it open, thinking about the last time I ever used a phone so archaic. I opened the SMS icon and texted Paul: *I'll go.*

Chapter 40
Mara

"Maybe Italy," Garrett says with his arm around my shoulder. He kisses my temple and I can feel strands of my hair getting caught on his lips. "We can start in Milan and work our way down, end somewhere on a beach in the Mediterranean." I look out at the blackness of the ocean beside us as we walk on the sand. The black water stretches back as far as I can see, sprinkled with the reflection of the moon dancing on the ripples. The breeze rips through my hair, chilling my face, but in a good way, like it's massaging me. Garrett continues talking when I don't respond. "Or a Caribbean cruise," he says. "Those can be nice. One of the guys at work just came back from one. He said he and his wife really enjoyed it. Whatever kind of honeymoon you'd like, we can plan it."

I look up at Garrett and smile at him. "What?" he says as he smiles back. "Caribbean cruise?" My smile widens and he kisses my forehead again. "You got it."

We continue walking silently on the beach. Our feet sink into the cool sand with every step and we teeter a little as we gain our balance. The walk is calming, therapeutic, a perfect moment after the surprise we just received. Garrett brought me here to get away. To avoid his family and all the pressure we've been feeling. Every free moment we're being dragged to taste something or choose something, or explore different options for a wedding that no longer feels like it's about us. But no, his father couldn't let him have one weekend of freedom. Instead, he ruined it by joining in on our vacation.

Avoiding Garrett's father has been getting harder. Through all the wedding planning and family obligations that Garrett has begged me to join, I've been seeing him more and more. But now it's worse. Now when I see him, he has this look on his face like he's smelling something bad. Like he's trying to get rid of the stench, but isn't sure how. We avoid eye contact. I try to avoid being near him and I'm pretty sure he does the same. But nevertheless, here we are caught together in a tiny beach cabin.

If it were up to me, Garrett and I would disappear. We would elope and settle down somewhere far away from everything we know. We'd live together, just the two of us, on an island or a small village where we could start over. We'd each only have each other and we'd work together to build a life. Maybe we'd open a small restaurant, or a shop selling local souvenirs. We could change our names so it would be a real new beginning and no one from our old lives would be able to find us.

As though someone could hear my thoughts, my purse buzzes. I turn to check my cellphone, but it's still. Then I feel the burner phone next to it vibrating. Paul. My heart gets caught in my throat. I quickly silence the phone without taking it out of my bag.

"You can take it if you want," Garrett says. "It's OK."

I shake my head, but then I feel the phone buzzing again. I've been avoiding Paul for the last few months, trying to get him out of my head. But he was making it nearly impossible. After the CADD fundraiser last year, he showed up at my door.

"I was wondering what happened," he said. "There was nothing in the news about it, so I knew you chickened out."

"I didn't chicken out," I responded, trying not to look him in the eyes, afraid he would hypnotize me again.

"So what happened?" he asked, grabbing my wrist. His fingers burrowed into my skin and I felt the bones starting to crunch.

"I changed my mind. That wasn't the right place. We'll find another opportunity." I tried to free my wrist, but Paul just tightened his grip. I could feel my hand starting to go numb.

"If you say so," Paul responded. "Just remember, the sooner you do this, the sooner you will feel better." Then, he let go of my wrist and left. I gently rubbed my skin with my other hand, trying to ease the burning sensation. That was right before my third date with Garrett. The date when he picked me up and took me to dinner. The date when I first found out that Garrett's last name was Derby.

The next time I saw Paul was a few days before the first time I went to brunch with Garrett's family.

"This is perfect! Mara you are an evil genius!" Paul said to me when I told him I had started dating Robert Derby's son. "I underestimated you."

I smiled coyly back at him. It was a nice compliment, the first one I had ever received from Paul. I pretended that it was all part of my plan, even though it wasn't. I hadn't started dating Garrett as part of my plot for revenge. I started dating him because he was nice to me, something I hadn't experienced in a while.

"Now you can really get them good," Paul said. "Go to brunch and then WHAM! You've got them all in one place and there will be no witnesses. Smart Mara, smart!" Paul squeezed my hand before he left, transmitting encouragement and fear all at one time. I suddenly felt good about myself, like I did something right for a change. Something my sister would be proud of.

After that brunch, I felt ashamed. Not only had I let down Paul and my sister, but I had also embraced Robert Derby. I was helpless at their house, unable to move, afraid to seem suspicious or make a wrong move. That's when I started pulling away from Paul.

"What's wrong with you?" he said the next time he came over. "Do you actually like that

271

pathetic rich boy? Do you think he's dating you because you're special? You're a charity case, Mara. That's it! Poor you with no family. Garrett's dating you to try to make up for what his dad did."

"Garrett doesn't know," I contradicted.

"Maybe not consciously, but subconsciously, he thinks being with you absolves his family's sins," Paul said. "You'll see. Once he's had enough, he'll dump you like the trash you are, and then it will be too late for you. You'll have failed at everything."

"Stop!" I yelled, making Paul laugh.

"You're only angry because you know I'm right," Paul said. "This isn't over. You owe me."

Once my grandma died and I moved into Garrett's apartment, my meetings with Paul stopped. But he didn't stop trying to contact me. The burner phone was constantly buzzing, ringing, displaying all caps text messages that I was sure he could tell I had read. Part of me told me to throw away the phone. But the other half of me told me to keep it. Maybe I'd need it one day. I didn't want to see Paul anymore, for now. I didn't want him in my head anymore. But he wasn't only in my head. I started seeing him in the shadows across the street when I walked places. I saw him standing on street corners outside my office building. I could never tell if it was really him, or if the static in my mind had conjured the picture. I started carrying my gun everywhere, just in case. In case I needed to protect myself. Even now, I have the gun tucked inside my purse.

"Everything all right?" Garrett asks, startling me from my train of thought. My hand is still in my purse, holding the phone. The buzzing stopped. I look up at Garrett and nod, then look back down into my purse. The phone lights up one more time before I turn it over and let go. *WTF Mara? We had a deal. This isn't over.* I read the message quickly before closing my purse. "Sylvia nagging you about CADD stuff?" Garrett asks. "She's a workaholic. We'll have to talk to her about you cutting back there so you can relax more and take more time off."

I fake a smile to show Garrett that everything is fine. He wraps his arms around me, shielding the wind that was massaging my back. I try to breathe deeply and I look back toward the cabin we walked from. In the distance I see the figure of a man. I squeeze my eyes shut, sure they are deceiving me, but when I open them again, the figure is still there. It's not moving, just standing there under the moonlight. The sound of the water turns to static in my ears and the static fuzzes the outline of the figure. My eyes are stuck and I can't look away.

"Guess my dad wants us to come back," Garrett says, nodding at the figure behind us. "It's getting cold anyway."

Chapter 41
Garrett

I'm panting as I run down the sand. I can feel my cheeks heat and I know I can't keep going much longer. *Don't stop*, I reprimand myself, *you have to keep going, you can't slow down now*! My chest feels like it's going to explode and my lungs will burst open, but I keep running. My legs start to sputter out of control, flipping forward and catching me, although with each step I'm sure I'll fall. My legs suddenly feel like they are no longer under my control, they keep going, sloppily hitting the sand over and over until one of them just stops and I flip forward catching myself with my hands. I look back, behind me toward the cabin. It's far, but not as far away as I thought it would be.

It's a crisp morning. The sun is shining bright, but the air still holds the cold from the night. It smells like salt and my lungs burn as I breathe in. I hate exercising, but the wedding is coming up and that's just what people do before they get married. Not Mara, of course. Her body is perfect and she doesn't need to torture herself to look good. Me, on the other hand, well, I still have work to do.

When I stepped out in the morning, Mara was still sleeping. I left her a note telling her I was going for a run and that I had my phone with me if she needed something. Still laying on the sand,

I pull my phone out of my pocket and brush the sand off it. No calls, no messages. I push myself up and dust the sand off my body. It's still early, but I can feel the air temperature starting to rise. In just a few hours, it will be a perfect beach day.

I start walking back to the cabin, my legs feeling like lead. It seems like the cabin isn't getting any closer, no matter how many steps I take. Ahead of me, I notice another jogger. He's wearing black sweats and his body is bouncing over the sand in a rhythm so steady, it's like his legs aren't even touching the beach, he's just gliding above it. I start thinking about how clumsy I am, wondering what this guy would think of me if he saw me running. The runner smiles at me when he is a few feet in front of me. I give him a smile and a nod and continue walking my heavy pace forward. Then, suddenly, I feel myself almost fall back from the impact. I'm so startled by it, that the wind blows out of me and I am not sure what happened.

"Oh, uh, sorry," I call out to the jogger who is now behind me. I rub my shoulder, which is aching from the hit. It's disorienting. The jogger, who was going so smoothly just ran right into me and kept going. It somehow must have been my fault. When the jogger doesn't look back at me, I turn around again toward the cabin and continue walking. Then, suddenly, I'm on all fours and my back feels the blow of another impact. "Excuse me?" I try to remain polite, but my patience is waning. I look up and see the jogger in his black sweat suit standing in front of me with his arms crossed in front of his chest. "I'm sorry, dude, do I know you?" I realize it's the second time I've said sorry, when I haven't done anything wrong. Have I?

"You should," he says, reaching his arm down and offering me his hand. I hesitate before taking it, but then I grab it and pull myself up. His hand is strong, with veins popping out around his wrist. "Because I know who you are."

I shrug. A lot of people know who I am. That's what happens when your father is an extremely rich real estate investor who ended up with his picture in the tabloids for a year after a horrible car accident that wasn't really his fault. I'm pretty sure I know where this is going. It's not the first time someone has approached me, or Caleb, and tried blackmailing for money. But these things never work. We have nothing to be blackmailed about. We've been prepared for this scenario our whole lives and know there is no such thing as secrets when you are in the spotlight. Last time this happened, I was approached by a guy who said he would tell the IRS about my father's foreign bank accounts if I didn't write him a $100,000 check right there. I didn't write him a check and we never heard anything from the IRS. My father asserts he has no foreign bank accounts and I'm apt to believe him.

"What do you want?" I say to the jogger. "I don't have any money on me."

"I don't want your money," he says. "I just want to tell you something about your girlfriend."

The way he says *girlfriend* makes my stomach curl. "No thanks," I say. "I'm pretty sure I know everything I need to know about her." I start walking toward the cabin. I wish my legs would go faster, but they feel so wobbly in the sand.

"You know that she almost killed you?" the jogger says. "She was planning on it, at least." I continue walking without looking back. People will say anything for money. "When you met her, she had a gun strapped to her leg. Bet you didn't notice it under her long black dress." I picture Mara in that beautiful dress she wore to the CADD fundraiser all that time ago. I'm sure it's just a coincidence that this guy knows she was wearing black. A lot of girls wear black. I don't look back.

"Remember the first time she came to brunch? Did she seem a little fidgety to you? She almost killed you then and your whole family," the jogger yells. "And she would have been right by doing it." This makes me stop. How did he know about brunch with my family? How did he know she was fidgety? I turn around and the jogger is right behind me.

"Do you know who Mara is?" the jogger says. "She's the one survivor of that family your father killed." He has this smug look on his face, like he's telling me something new.

"She told me," I respond. "That doesn't matter."

"But she didn't tell you about the gun, did she?" the jogger says. "How she wanted to kill you for revenge?"

"A lot of people say those kinds of things," I respond, remembering how Mara said she wanted to kill me, but that it was just a figure of speech.

"But not everyone who says it actually carries a gun with them and knows how to shoot it," he says.

"Mara doesn't have a gun," I respond, although as soon as I say it, I am not sure. It's never come up. I mean, how is something like that supposed to come up?

The guy laughs. "I think you'd better get to know your girlfriend better before she kills you and your family."

"She's my fiancé," I correct him. I've moved past feeling annoyed and now I'm angry.

"Oh, that's right," he says. "I saw her with your mom at the wedding dress place." He winks, making my stomach flip again. "Just know, this isn't over, Garrett. There's no happy ending for people like her. Or people like you, you don't deserve it." He turns around and starts jogging again, away from the cabin.

"Who are you?" I yell at his back.

His words come to my ears through the wind and it's hard to know if I hear them right. "Just ask Mara," he shouts. "She'll know." By then, he's far along the beach, getting smaller and smaller in the distance, gliding over the sand just as he was doing before our confrontation.

I stand still, staring at the figure disappearing in front of me. He becomes so small that it feels like everything that just happened was part of my imagination. But then I look back and see the imprints of my hands in the sand. No, it wasn't my imagination. It happened. My heart is pounding now, even harder than it was when I was running. I'm not sure what to make of what just happened. I have to get back and talk to Mara.

Chapter 42
Mara

I'm alone. The fact is glaringly clear from the stillness in the room. I roll over in the bed and suddenly feel a thud as I hit the floor. Something's not right, how did I fall off the bed? The night before starts coming back to me. I slept on the bottom bunk of a bunk bed, with Garrett on top. Every time he moved all night, I felt the bed shake like an earthquake was about to crack open the floor. Now, I feel like I just stepped off a boat, the stillness seems oddly unfamiliar.

We're staying in the model unit at a beach resort Derby Ventures just bought. We're in the bunk beds because Robert and Bonnie are in the master bedroom. I rub my shoulder and stand up, looking at the top bunk. As I expected, it's empty with just the faint indention in the pillow that suggests Garrett slept there.

The walls of the room are light blue with white clouds stuck on. There are white curtains covering a square window and letting light shine through. I walk to the window and look outside, expecting to see the beach, but instead I see a small path and another cabin in front of me. I look down on the white dresser and there's a note on top. It's from Garrett. *Went running. Be back soon! Call if you need anything, I have my cell.* I put the note back down and lie on the bottom bunk. I pull the covers to my shoulders and my knees into my chest, but my eyes are wide open. My throat is dry and my mouth has that taste it gets when I sleep after a few cups of wine, like rust is decaying into little pieces of sand.

I'd like to get up, get some water, brush my teeth. But I won't. I won't leave this room until Garrett comes back. I don't want to run into Robert or Bonnie and be forced to sit pleasantly with them, or my other option would be to rudely run back into the room.

Last night couldn't have been more uncomfortable. Garrett asked if we could sit with them for a drink. I would have said no, but I was trapped. Trapped in this little cabin with all of them. Trapped by Garrett's request. When we went to walk on the beach, I thought we'd be free, but we weren't. I kept feeling that shadow behind us, like we were being followed. When we turned back toward the cabin, I was sure we'd meet that shadow, but then he was gone. Maybe I had imagined it after all.

I stare at the bunk above me, the crisscross on the bottom of the mattress, and wait. What am I doing here? I feel ashamed that I can't leave the bedroom. How could I ever marry into this family when being around them—even with Garrett by my side—makes me feel like I'm being eaten alive by ants? Why can't Garrett and I just get away from them? My thoughts start going down a dark path when I hear a faint tap on the door. I recognize the sound of Garrett's knuckle, the way he holds his index finger like a hook whenever he knocks on anything. It's a movement he got from his dad, I've seen Robert do the same thing.

Then the door handle clicks as it twists open and Garrett steps inside, closing the door behind him. His face is white, but his cheeks are red, giving his face the contrast of a made-up Russian doll. Salt lines the edge of his hair and runs down in front of his ears. He looks as though he just ran a marathon—dehydrated and ready to collapse—although there's no way he could have been gone that long.

"How was your run?" I ask as I sit up on the bed. His eyes pierce into me and I realize it wasn't the run that made him look completely spent. I suddenly notice sand coating his legs and hanging on to the fibers of his shirt. "Are you OK?" I don't think I've ever asked Garrett that before, he's always the one asking me.

"No, actually," he says, but his voice is calm, as calm as though he just said *it's a beautiful day outside*. Sometimes it irks me how calm he always is, I can't understand it, although I want to try to feed on it. I want to suck it up, catch the calm like it's contagious, but apparently it's not. "Mara, the strangest thing happened…" Garrett sits down on the bed next to me.

In my mind, I see the figure on the beach. The dark shadow, it's outlines blurred by the static in my mind, and I now know the figure was real. That shadow has been haunting me for months, it was only a matter of time before he infiltrated into my new life. "Paul," I whisper under my breath.

"What?" Garrett says, but before I say it again, he continues. With every breath, his calmness is evaporating. "Some guy accosted me on the beach! Can you believe it? He was trying to blackmail me or something. I'm not sure, it was different than the other times I've been blackmailed. Usually they are really straightforward with what they want, but this guy, hell, this guy, I still have no idea what he wants."

"What'd he say?" Suddenly I have hope that maybe it wasn't Paul. Maybe I am just being paranoid.

"Something about you and a gun," Garrett continues. "It made no sense. Do you have a stalker or something? Maybe I should call the police."

"No," I say and my heart sinks. "Don't call the police."

"Do you know who it was?"

"Paul." I feel defeated, saying his name out loud to Garrett. It's like by saying his name, I've let him into this part of my life, the part I was trying to protect from him.

"Who's Paul? Your ex or something? He kept saying you wanted to kill me. That you brought a gun... that you wanted to kill my whole family at brunch! Can you believe someone would say that? How did he even know about brunch?" As Garrett rambles I can see something is clicking in his mind. His expression changes. His eyes narrow like he's focusing on my face. I look away, shame starting to pound down on my shoulders. "Mara? Do you know anything about this guy?"

The shame is getting heavier, making my shoulders slump farther and farther down. Another inch, and I might fall to the floor again. There's buzzing in my ear and I suddenly wonder if a bumble bee somehow got into this room and is humming in my ear. I try to swat the bee, waving my hand by my ear, but the buzzing gets louder, causing me to swat harder. I'm frantically swatting, still sliding down under the heavy blanket of shame pressing down on me. I'm falling down down down, but it seems the floor has dropped as well. I keep waiting for a thud, any notification that I've hit the bottom, but it doesn't come.

"Mara? Are you OK?" Garrett asks, his voice suddenly gains the calmness back, the calmness he always has when he asks me this question. And then there's the thud. My bottom hits the floor, sending a shock wave up to my head. I look up and catch Garrett's eyes, which have now lost their focus and are expressing worry. "Mara, I'm sorry. I didn't mean to upset you...I shouldn't have brought it up..."

"It's OK, I'm OK," I say, pulling myself back up on the bed. I'm not sure what I should tell Garrett. He's been so understanding and I am not sure where I'd be crossing the line if I confessed more. "It's nothing, Paul's my sister's boyfriend, well, her ex-boyfriend, or…" My voice trails, is he her ex because she died when they were together?

"I'm so sorry," Garrett says, wrapping his arms around me to tell me I don't have to say anymore. This is what happens every time I bring up my dead family. It's like Garrett thinks his embrace can erase the hurt. "Let's just forget about it and try to enjoy the weekend. It's going to be a really nice day today. Maybe we can get some breakfast somewhere or…" I know he wants to say *go to the beach*, I mean, that's why we came to this cabin in the first place. But the shadow is still hanging over us and we both know we won't be going to the beach this weekend.

I nod and Garrett kisses my forehead. "I'm going to get in the shower, then we can go, OK?" he says. Again I nod, and he stands up and leaves me in the room. Although, this time I don't feel alone. The shadow is there, hanging over me, blocking the sun from the window. The figure that won't leave me alone. I have to end this. Take care of things. I have to fix this so I don't lose Garrett. I check my purse, my gun is still tucked inside, next to my two phones. I pull out the burner phone, which for the first time in months has no notifications.

My fingers start typing before my brain knows what I am doing. *Where are you?* And then I press send.

Chapter 43
Robert

"Where's Mara?" I ask when Garrett steps into the kitchen. He pulls a single mug from the cupboard and pours himself a cup of coffee from the coffee maker on the counter.

"She stepped out for a bit," Garrett responds. He brings his coffee to the kitchen island where I am sitting, drinking my coffee and eating a bagel. There's a brown paper bag on the counter with bagels in it, and I push it toward Garrett. I had run out to a bakery that morning, hoping that the smell of fresh bagels would bring everyone together. Garrett peeks inside the bag and grabs a cinnamon raisin. It makes me smile, knowing that I still know him well enough to know his favorite type of bagel. He opens the cream cheese and starts lathering on a thick layer.

I'm wracking my head to think of what I should say. This is a perfect conversation opportunity, Mara is out, Bonnie is in the bathroom completing her hour-long morning routine. I clear my throat and crunch into my bagel, the noise making the lack of conversation that much more apparent.

"What are your plans for the day?" Garrett asks. It sounds like an innocent question, but it feels like there are layers of meaning behind it.

Like my answer could be used against me in court. I remember the last time I felt that way.

"I'm not sure," I respond. "We weren't planning on doing too much. Probably go into town. Bonnie likes the antique shops. We'll probably have lunch there. Maybe a walk on the beach later. We'll see." I pause to gauge Garrett's reaction, but his face is expressionless, except for the rhythm of his cheeks as he chews on his bagel. "What about you?"

He shrugs and then swallows. "I don't know. We're probably just going to relax around here."

"When's Mara getting back?" I'm not sure why I find her absence so suspicious. I guess because it would seem to me that if you escape to a remote beach cabin with your fiancé, you'd want to spend the entire time together. But as it seems, I don't understand Mara. I don't understand anything about her.

"Probably soon. Why?" Garrett asks, taking another bite.

Now I shrug. "Just curious." I pause, knowing this is my last chance to try to have a real conversation with my son this weekend. "Garrett, are you happy?" It's a question I've often asked my sons, although not lately.

"I am," he responds, almost robotically. He didn't even take a moment to think about his answer. Maybe that should be a good sign, but to me, it's a sign that he's just saying what he thinks he's supposed to.

"Are you sure? Because I'm worried about you—"

"Dad, have I given you any reason to think that I'm not happy?"

"Well no, but something is off—" I stop as Garrett rolls his eyes.

"You need to stop it about Mara," he says. "Your thing with her, has nothing to do with who she is. It has everything to do with your own issues."

"What?" I'm taken aback by Garrett's sudden psychoanalysis of me.

"You don't like her because she reminds you of what happened." Garrett's words sting me right in the heart. "You don't like her because you feel like she hasn't forgiven you. No matter how much money you pour into stopping drunk driving or no matter how nice you are to her, you still feel guilty whenever she's around. Am I right? Is that why you want me to break up with her?"

For someone who doesn't know the whole story, Garrett's observations could sound very right. But there are deeper layers. Beyond the guilt I feel—when she is around and when she isn't— there are the letters. The threats she's been sending for a year now.

"No Garrett, that's not it at all," I respond.

"Really?" He leans back. "Then what is it?"

My mouth drops open. "I... I don't trust her."

Garrett lets out a smirk. "Maybe you should try talking to her. Maybe you should try to have a simple conversation with her. Then maybe you will see she's more than just your victim. You say you don't trust her, well that's just bull. It's a dumb excuse you have for not even trying." Garrett takes the last bite of his bagel and brushes his hands in the sink. I can see he is about to storm out of the kitchen and I have to stop him.

"She's been sending threatening letters," I say.

"What?"

"For a year, she was putting threats in our mailbox. According to those letters, she's planning something."

"I don't believe you," he says. He turns like he is about to leave the kitchen, but then Bonnie glides in, wearing a silk bathrobe. Her hair is perfectly blown dry, each strand in place and her face is made up just to hide her wrinkles. It's a look that takes her an hour every morning, but is designed to make it appear that she just woke up that way.

"Good morning, Dear," she says as she walks with her arms outstretched to Garrett. They embrace and he kisses her cheek. "Where's Mara?"

"She stepped out," Garrett responds coldly.

"I was thinking maybe the four of us could go antiquing this morning," Bonnie says as she pours herself a cup of coffee. "They have some lovely shops in town. You remember those brass candlesticks on the mantle? I got those at one of the shops here years ago. They were made in the

1830s in Italy. The shopkeeper told me he could tell from the designs on the base. They don't make things like that in America."

"We'll see, Mom," Garrett responds with a smile. "You two should go without us and I'll let you know if we'll join."

"Oh, I'm sure Mara would want to join," Bonnie says. "Sometimes you can find great centerpiece ideas in antique shops. We could get lots of inspiration and buy whatever she likes that could be part of the décor at the wedding. We still need a theme for the opening cocktail hour."

"Feel free to choose a theme and get whatever you think will fit," Garrett says. "I'm sure Mara will be happy with whatever you choose."

"Well that's no fun!" Bonnie exclaims as she looks into the brown bag of bagels. She pulls out a half of the whole wheat one I bought for her. "She's the bride, she needs to be involved!"

"Don't worry about it, Mom, just do what you want." Garrett starts walking out of the kitchen back toward their little bedroom.

"Garrett," I say, not wanting him to rush off. I'd be happy to give up my romantic vacation with Bonnie just to spend a few tensionless moments with him. And to save his life.

"What?" He stops, his hands on his hips.

"Just text me, OK? We'll be in town."

He raises his eyebrows and nods before turning around and going back into his room.

"Poor Garrett," Bonnie says, scraping the thinnest possible layer of cream cheese on her bagel.

"Poor Garrett?" I laugh in response.

"Yes! He came here for a romantic vacation and now look, he's alone in a bunk bed! Mara went to do her own thing, and he doesn't want to spend his weekend with us! That Mara is always doing her own thing. Even when we went shopping together, I could see she was somewhere else. She's not always with us. I hope Garrett understands that."

I nod, surprised at Bonnie's intuition. I hadn't voiced my concerns to her. I didn't want to upset her, nor did I think she would share my opinion. But maybe she's been having her own struggles with this, which she'd been hiding behind endless wedding planning.

"Bonnie, there's something you should know about Mara," I start, watching her nibble on her bagel.

"What is it, Dear?"

Once I start, the words just tumble out.

Chapter 44
Garrett

"GARRETT!"

I hear my mother's scream through the walls of the cabin. I'm lying on the top bunk, scrolling through my phone and trying to pass the time until Mara comes back. I should text her, but I don't want to sound needy. She slipped out when I was showering and just scribbled on the same note that I had left her earlier. *Something came up. Need to step out for a little bit. Don't worry.* I wasn't sure what "a little bit" meant, but it had been at least an hour already.

I start thinking about the last thing my father said. That she had been sending threatening letters. It doesn't make sense. But maybe it does. Yesterday, I thought I knew her. But today, I'm told she carries a gun. Sends threatening letters. There's no way this is the Mara I am engaged to, unless I have been horribly wrong about her. I'm suddenly angry with myself. Have I let myself fall for another broken girl? Is Mara really no different than my previous girlfriends? Just with different baggage packed up in the same heavy suitcases?

"GARRETT!" My mother screams again, making the door rattle. "Can you come in here?"

I sigh as I put my feet on the rungs of the ladder taking me down from the bunk. I can only imagine what my father may have said to her. I walk into the kitchen. My father is sitting in the same place. My mother is leaning over the island, a barely nibbled bagel in front of her.

"Did you know about Mara?" she asks. Her tone is both accusatory and afraid.

"Know what?" I respond, crossing my arms. Any other answer would make it seem that I was holding some deep secret about her, which I wasn't.

"That she's, you know," my mother says.

"She's what, Mom?" I want her to say it, reprimand me more for the mistakes I've made.

My mother lowers her voice to a whisper. "She's the girl from the accident?"

"Of course, I know," I say. "But there are a lot of other things about her." My voice rattles, making my statement seem false and untrustworthy. Am I trying to convince her or myself?

"Did you know from the beginning? Why didn't you say anything? Is that why you started dating her? Are you trying to fix things? Garrett, it's not always your responsibility to fix people!"

"Mom!" I yell, looking at my father, who's staring at the counter. His expression evokes anger in me, like he's suddenly turned my mother against me.

"Garrett! This is serious!"

"Why is it such a big deal?" I'm screaming now. I hate screaming. Especially at my parents.

It makes me feel like a pathetic child. "It's a coincidence! We were dating before I knew the connection! Why does it even matter?" The more I argue, the less I believe myself. But I feel trapped. I can't leave my ground just yet.

"It matters Garrett!" my mother yells. "What will people say? This will get out, you know. You'll be back in the tabloids, everyone will be talking about this! How you started dating the girl whose family was killed in your father's accident! Why does she even want to date you?"

"Why does she want to date me?" I'm still screaming. "I don't know. Maybe because I'm a nice guy. Maybe because we enjoy each other's company. Maybe she likes me. Wow, I would think that my parents would think more highly of me!" *Maybe because she wants to kill me?* I try to shove that thought away.

"It doesn't make sense!" My mother yells. "I don't like this. This is a serious problem. I don't understand how you don't see that."

"What's the problem?" I say, lowering my volume. "Why is it such a big deal?" *How could I have missed all the signs?*

"Because you'll never know if she's dating you for you!" My mother is still yelling. "You do this all the time, Garrett. You date people who you want to fix, but you need to stop doing that! You need to date someone that lifts you up!"

"Don't bring up the past, mom, it's not relevant!" I'm getting angry again. Angry at myself for making the same mistake again and again and again. "Why would she want to date me because I'm Robert's son? That would make no sense." I pretend my logic is solid as a rock and I don't understand why my parents can't see that. *She's been using me. We're not safe here.*

"This can't be happening!" My mother starts putting her hair behind her ears over and over, a habit she has when she is nervous. "I'll need to call Eric. We need to change wedding plans. Garrett, you can't go through with this. Oh, but if we cancel, it will also be a scandal! What are we supposed to do?"

"You know what, Mom? Call the wedding planner. You can cancel the whole thing. It's not what Mara and I want anyway. We're just going through with this for you!" *Maybe I can get out of this without admitting I made a mistake. Can I take care of this on my own?*

My mother's eyes pop open. They are so large they look like they will fall out of their sockets. "Garrett! How could you say that?" My mother sounds like she is about to cry. "Robert? Don't you have anything to say?"

I look to my father who is still sitting quietly, staring at the counter. He looks up, his eyes darting between the two of us. "I don't know, Bonnie. Something doesn't feel right to me."

"I can't believe you two," I say, exasperated. "If it wasn't this, there would be some other reason you wouldn't like Mara. There's always something. You don't want me to be happy." *But you want me to stay alive.*

"We do, Darling! What about Ainsley? You would be so happy with her!" My mother sounds like she is begging. *Maybe she's right. Life could be so easy.*

I roll my eyes. "No, Mom." I turn around and go back to the bedroom. I can't be around them anymore, listening to them berate Mara, when they're really berating me. My bad choices. My naiveté.

My phone is still in the room, lying on the dresser next to the note Mara left. I check it, hoping to see a message or a call from Mara, but there's none. I start composing a text to her.

Where are you? I delete it.

When do you think you'll be back? Delete.

What's going on? Delete.

I miss you. I press send, hoping that portrays the right message. That I want to spend time with her, but I understand that sometimes she needs her space. I don't want to sound desperate or angry. Now I'm afraid she might not come back.

Suddenly I hear a phone vibrating under the covers of the bottom bunk. I lift the quilt that was carelessly strewn like a teenager had been forced to make his bed. There's Mara's phone and I see my text message lit up on the screen. Where would she go without her phone? I think for a moment whether I can unlock the phone, check if she has any weird messages, but I don't know her password. It's the least of what I don't know about Mara.

My mind drifts back to the jogger on the beach this morning. Part of me wants to forget the whole encounter, while the other part of me thinks that maybe there was more to it that I need to better understand. Mara has a gun, he said. What if I believe it? We'd been living together for a while now, I think it's something I would have noticed, but maybe I am just that oblivious. I feel an anchoring to search through our bag, but I remember that I'm the one who packed it. I check my phone again, even though I know it's impossible for her to respond to me. Maybe I don't know Mara at all.

Chapter 45
Mara

I quickly throw on one of the dresses Garrett packed for me and scribble on the note he left when he went running. I grab my purse, tossing my phone on the bed. Better that my whereabouts aren't traceable. Then I tiptoe as quietly as I can out of our room. As I pass the bathroom door, I hear Garrett humming under the drum of the shower. The door to the master bedroom is closed, but I can hear mustering around on the other side. I hold my breath, hoping not to disturb the house while I sneak out.

Paul responded to my text message immediately. He was staying in a motel on the edge of town and he'd wait for me there. He said it was just a short walk from our cabin. This last sentence pierced my stomach, as it only proved that Paul knew exactly where we were staying.

Stay away from me, I say in my head, practicing what I may say to Paul. I'm walking down the road that leads to our cabin. From there, I'll hit the main part of town and on the other side of that is Paul's motel. *If you talk to Garrett again, I'll...* what would I do? Even in my own daydream I'm stuck in what I want to do to him. I pull my purse closer to my side and stick my hand inside. The touch of the cold metal instantly comforts me. I'm safe. I'm protected. I can handle this.

I turn off the side road onto the main road in town and I'm immediately in the downtown area. It looks like the kind of town that only exists in movies. The sidewalks are clean and lined with grass that separates them from the street. On the other side of the sidewalk, there are tall windows showing the shops and restaurants that I assume are the biggest industries in the town. I pass by a creamery, where a young man is filling the freezer with tubs of ice cream. Next there is a candy shop, with a machine already turning taffy in the window. A souvenir shop has beach paraphernalia and t-shirts on headless mannequins. I peek through the window, I'd like to get a sunhat if we are going to spend any time lounging on the beach, but I keep walking.

It's not long before I'm on the other side of town. The shops become more spread out and side streets peel off in different directions. I look for the street I need to veer off on. It's still up ahead and I quicken my pace feeling impatient at how slow I am on my feet. Eventually I reach the street, which is more like a highway and I turn left. I immediately see the sign for the motel.

In the parking lot I recognize Paul's car. A black convertible Miata that sits so low to the ground, I wonder how Paul gets in it. I walk past it, suppressing my urge to drag my keys along its side. Paul's in room 209, so I walk to the end of the motel and find the stairs that zigzag up the building. My hand is still in my purse, my fingers curled around the gun giving me strength to move forward. On the second floor, I walk down the open hallway until I get to his room. When I am about to knock, the door opens.

"There you are." Paul is smiling at me. He just got out of the shower and has a white towel wrapped around his waist and another one hanging over his shoulders. He motions with his arm to invite me in. I step past him, tightening my fingers on the gun. The rumbling sounds of the highway make my skin vibrate.

"Great town," he says over the sound of a passing truck. "I went for an amazing run on the beach this morning. Have you been there yet? It's beautiful." He's smiling at me, knowing his words tell me so much more than what he said. "Guess you really lucked out with that boyfriend of yours." He takes the towel from his neck to rub his hair. "I mean, fiancé."

"Couldn't you get dressed?" I snap at him. I don't want to see his bare chest that could have been carved from stone if not from the little hairs on it.

"I'm on vacation, Mara. What's the big issue? Can't a man just enjoy himself on vacation, or is that offensive to you?"

"It's offensive to me." My palm is sweating around the gun.

"Wow, someone has a lot of confidence today." Paul grabs a pile of clothes from a chair and ducks into the bathroom. When he comes out, he's wearing khaki shorts and a navy-blue t-shirt that he easily could have bought in town. "So, what's up?"

"What's up?" The words are like vomit in my mouth. "Why don't you tell me? Why are you following me?"

"Mara, you came to me, remember? You texted me this morning asking where I was."

I roll my eyes. "So it's a huge coincidence that you're here in the same town as me, Garrett, and his parents?"

"His parents?" Paul looks surprised. "I didn't know they were here with you. I guess you've totally forgiven Robert Derby then, I mean, going on vacation with him and all. You're just enjoying the high life living on his money. I can't believe you're so easily bought. Shannon would be so disappointed in you."

"Shut up, Paul!" I yell. "You don't know anything what you're talking about."

"Actually I do, Mara," Paul yells louder, just as a car horn blows. He stands tall with his hands on his waist. "I think I know exactly what I am talking about. A year ago, you cared about your family. You wanted to avenge their deaths and now you're eating from the hand of their murderer. And you like it! You're disgusting, you know that?"

"Stop it."

"You know, though, since you're all there in that cabin together, this would be a great opportunity for you." Paul takes another step closer to me. "Why not prove it that you haven't forgotten your family and stop chickening out with your revenge? You could do it easily now in that cabin."

"Shut up."

"What? Mara? Then why did you come to me? You came to me, because you need me to give you the confidence for what you want to do. You came to me because you know I'm right and I can convince you to do what you need to do. Isn't that right?"

"No Paul. I came here to tell you—" Paul steps closer to me so that his toes are up against mine. His hands are still on his waist, but it feels like he is strangling me. My instincts tell me to fight back, to squirm, to get out of his hold, but I stand still.

"What, Mara?" It feels like his grip is tightening on my throat, but I can see his arms on his waist. The heat from his body and the smell of hotel soap are swirling around my head. I can't breathe. I need to fight back. I step backwards and pull the gun out of my purse. I hold it up in front of me, pointing it straight to Paul's chest. He laughs, but doesn't move. "You remember that this isn't the first time you've pulled a gun out on me?"

"Leave me alone," I yell. My voice is strong behind the gun.

"You came to me, Mara. You came to me first after the funeral and you came to me today. If anything, I should be telling you to leave me alone. Especially with what a shit you've been. You lie and you fail and you pretend like you want to fix things but you're too scared to."

"Leave me alone," I repeat. "And Garrett. I don't want to see you or hear anything about you again. Understand?"

"But we aren't finished, Mara," Paul responds. "You know that. That's why you're here. You want closure as much as I do. That's why you keep coming to me." Suddenly his face changes and a grin sprouts from his lips. "You know what, I just figured it out. The issue is, you're too chicken shit to get revenge, but you want it. That's why you're here. That's why you keep coming to me. You women are all the same. You wait for men to read your minds. No matter how long it takes, you'll never just say what you want to say, you just wait and wait and wait until we figure it out on our own. I have to commend you on your patience, but seriously it would just be easier for all you women to just come out and say what you want to say."

"Thanks for the tip, Paul," I respond. "But you're wrong. I'm not here for any reason other than to tell you to leave me alone." I'm still holding the gun straight in front of me.

"Fuck you, Mara. You're such a liar. I know you Sanders girls, you're just like Shannon, I know exactly what you want even if you won't say it. But just like I always gave her what she wanted, even when she refused to admit it, I'm going to give you what you want." Paul rocks forward like he is about to lunge at me. Outside a truck is chugging along, sounding like a nuclear generator about to explode. My instincts take over. I need to save myself before I asphyxiate, my body is squirming, fighting for my life and my brain takes a back seat. My body is fighting, fighting to stay alive and then, BANG! Silence. I breathe in deep, my throat sore, desperate for the air it needs.

When I've caught my breath, my eyes focus on the hotel room. Paul is no longer standing in front of me. He's on the ground, his navy-blue shirt almost black and clinging to his body. His face looks like it's mid-laugh, like he is still processing a hilarious joke he just heard. He's so quiet, I almost don't believe it's Paul lying there. He'd never be so silent.

I relax my arms and put the gun back in my purse. There is a feeling of calm over me, a feeling of peace. Like the inner demons that have been plaguing me since my family's death have dissipated. I step over the body, careful to avoid the blood that has started to soak into the carpet. I check the floor and grab the bullet casing from the gun and Paul's burner phone, which is sitting on the dresser. I quietly let myself out of the hotel room, placing the "Do-not disturb" sign on the outside door handle.

Once I'm out of the room, my heart starts racing. I look around to check whether there are any cameras or people around, but I don't see any. Maybe Paul was right, I was too chicken shit to do what I wanted—until now. I finally did right by my sister, freeing her and me from the monster who had kidnapped us for the last few years. I rush down the stairs and through the parking lot, back to the road that will lead me through the downtown and back to the cabin.

I feel like I should be more anxious, but I'm feeling calm, like I finally did the right thing. The only question is whether others will see it that way. I'm sure it won't be long until Paul's body is discovered. But I also know from my dad's long experience as a police officer that it isn't easy to find a murder suspect unless there are witnesses or other clues left at the scene. I'm sure I left none. I'd learned a lot from my dad's years on the force. Maybe not the lessons he'd have wanted me to take, but these lessons will save my life.

I'm almost running back to the cabin. I need to talk to Garrett. He's the only person I can trust. And I'm going to need him.

Chapter 46
Mara

My pace slows as I get to the downtown area. I stop in the candy shop where I saw the taffy turning earlier. A bell rings when I open the door and the man behind the counter instantly smiles in a Pavlovian response. "Good morning," he says to me. "Want to try a piece of taffy? Here's a buttercream one." He holds out a small brown square in his gloved hand. I walk over and take it from him and pop it in my mouth. It's chewy and sticking to all my teeth like it might force my mouth closed for good. But my jaw fights back, pulling apart the sticky candy.

"Do you have a wet wipe or something?" I ask. He raises his eyebrows like he'd expected a different response. But then he nods and turns around, grabbing a wipe from the back. "I'll also take some of that taffy. Give me a few of each flavor."

He fills a brown bag and hands it to me. I pay and take the bag and wipe with me outside. I stuff the taffy in my purse and pull out Paul's and my burner phones, which I scrub down with the wipe. Once I'm sure they're clean, I remove the batteries and toss the phones in a trash can. I keep walking and toss the batteries in the next trash I see.

Once I turn off to the road that leads back to the cabin I'm forcing myself to move forward. My legs are lead, so heavy and stiff that it takes all my effort to move. I'm afraid of reaching the cabin. Until I do, I can pretend that everything is normal. That Garrett and I are living our happily ever after and I just stepped out to buy some taffy. I can pretend that I didn't just kill someone. But I did just kill someone. And I'm not sure what I'm supposed to do next. Do I pretend nothing happened and just offer him taffy? Do I confess to Garrett? Or do I turn myself in? Get the punishment a murderer deserves—the punishment that I was angry that Robert avoided.

Even with my snail-paced walk, I eventually see the cabin in front of me. It looks like the cover of a magazine or a romance novel where there's supposed to be a happy ending. I hold my breath as I approach the front door. I turn the handle but it's locked. For some reason, I hadn't expected that and it catches me off guard. Like I've been kicked out or something, or I need to beg to be let in. I knock quietly, and seconds later the door swings open. Garrett's standing there, his bottom lip tucked in his teeth. I've seen that look before. It usually comes out when Caleb is teasing him about something or we're doing some wedding prep activity that his mother forced upon us. It's the look that says he's stuck in a situation he wants to get out of, but he'll politely hold his tongue until it's over. I've never seen it directed at me.

I smile at him and hesitate before leaning in to kiss his cheek. He let's me, and puts his hand on my back to guide me inside. The house looks empty.

"Where's Robert and Bonnie?" I ask.

"They left a little while ago to go antiquing. They wanted to know if we want to join them for lunch." The statement is an accusation, meaning that I'm the one who could be keeping Garrett from a family lunch.

"Um, sure, I guess," I feel like I don't have another choice in response. I quickly feel relief that I didn't bump into them when I was gone. I walk into the kitchen where there are coffee mugs drying in the rack next to the sink. "Is there any coffee left?" I ask. Garrett is still standing by the front door, his arms down by his sides.

"I can make some," he responds and starts walking toward the kitchen. He opens the coffee maker and pours in the grinds. "Where did you go this morning?"

"I bought some taffy," I say, pulling the brown bag out of my purse. I place it on the table. "I tasted the buttercream, it was really good."

"You left your phone here," he says.

"Oops," I respond, but that wasn't a mistake.

"Mara, what's going on?" He's staring at the coffee maker, where the brew is starting to drip into the pot. "I thought we'd have a nice weekend together, but Saturday is already half over and I haven't even seen you."

"You went running in the morning," I remind him and he rolls his eyes. He's usually so patient with me, he's never reacted to me this way. I'm bursting to tell him everything. My heart is pounding so hard and I know that is the only way to get relief, but I also know I could lose him for it.

"Mara, I'm not sure I can do this," he says, grabbing one of the clean coffee mugs. He pours my coffee and adds enough milk to turn the liquid light brown—exactly how I like it. He hands it to me and I sit down on the barstool in the kitchen island. "I suddenly feel like I know nothing about you. Like you have a secret life behind my back and I can't live like that. I'm not sure what's happening, but..." his voice trails off. "You have a gun?" his voice cracks as he adds the last question. "I just..."

"You're right," I say, looking around the cabin to make sure we really are alone. "Maybe you should sit down." He leans back on the counter, telling me he's comfortable where he is. "Ok, but please let me finish before you say anything." I pull the gun out of my purse and place it on the island between us.

"What the—" Garrett's eyes pop and he stands up straighter. "Mara!"

"It belonged to my dad," I start. "He was a police officer." I realize I'd never told Paul much about my family. "I inherited it when he died."

"OK, but why is it here?" Garrett's voice sounds rash and frantic.

"I've been carrying it with me for a while now. Just in case."

"In case what? You need to kill someone?" Garrett raises his voice. "I just don't see a reason anyone—"

"Please let me talk," I say quietly.

"What were you planning on doing with that thing? Why didn't you tell me about it? Were you planning on killing someone? Did you kill someone?" His words tumble out so fast they are almost scrambled before they reach my ears.

"Yes." I say and relief immediately flows over my body.

"Yes, what? Yes, you killed someone? You're planning on killing someone?"

"Please Garrett, let me talk and then ask questions. You're right that I need to be honest with you. If we're going to get married—"

"*If* is right," he says.

"Please," I say and he motions to me to continue. "Let me finish before you speak, OK?" he nods in agreement. "I'm going to tell you everything from the beginning. When I finish, you can decide if you want to be with me. I'll start by saying that I want to be with you. That you saved me and that I can't imagine living without you, OK? And you're right you deserve to know the truth, so that if you want to stay with me, you know exactly what you're getting." I wait for him to nod again before I continue.

"When I first met you at the CADD fundraiser, I was there for revenge," I say, watching Garrett's eyes focus on me. "At first, I thought I wanted to kill Robert's family so he could understand how I felt."

"Yeah, you told me this already," Garrett says.

"But I don't think you realize I was serious," I say, taking a sip of my coffee. "I had this gun with me and I thought I was ready to pull the trigger. But I wasn't. In my mind, it all sounded so easy, like I could just get my revenge and that would be it, but I couldn't. For a while after that, I still thought about revenge."

"So why didn't you do it? You had so many great opportunities. Is that why you were dating me?" Garrett cuts in again.

I shake my head. "I didn't really want the revenge. It wasn't my idea. It wasn't me. I was being manipulated. Paul, the jogger you ran into on the beach this morning. It was him."

"Who's Paul?"

"Paul was Shannon's—my sister's—boyfriend. He was, I think he was abusive to her, he was a violent person. But my sister loved him. And after she died, we started talking. Paul was my only connection to her. He had all her stuff. I used to go to their place and we would talk about her. But then, he started manipulating me, probably like what he would do to Shannon. And he somehow put it in my head that I had to kill you. I was so broken. I felt like I had nothing to live for with my family gone. He was the only person I could talk to and so I started thinking maybe he was right. I could get revenge and kill myself, then I'd be at peace. I know it sounds totally ridiculous, crazy even. But I've always had these weird mental issues. Like maybe I'm schizophrenic. I don't know, I see things, hear things. Sometimes it's hard to live in my head. I need someone to quiet the static.

"Then I met you, and I felt like I wasn't alone anymore. Maybe I did have a chance at happiness. Maybe someone would notice if I were gone. The static started to fade. And yeah, I was struggling with your family, I feel so fake when I am around them, and it's hard for me, I feel like I am betraying my family and that's what Paul kept reminding me. I tried to push Paul away, but Paul wasn't so happy about that. He started following me and threatening me. He wouldn't leave me alone. So I started carrying the gun with me. Having it made me feel safer, I never planned on using it. But then, you told me about this morning, with Paul accosting you at the beach and I needed it to stop. I shot him."

"What?"

"I shot him."

"There are other ways to get someone to leave you alone. Like restraining orders, or getting the police involved."

I shake my head. "Maybe, but this is what happened. That's the whole story. Now, I understand if you don't want to be with me anymore or if you want to turn me in to the police, I get it. I'd want the same thing. It's up to you."

"Did you have the gun with you when I first brought you to brunch with my family?"

"No." I shake my head again.

"And the letters?" he asks. "What about those?"

"The letters?" I respond. But then I remember Paul using my printer. The clean white envelopes. "From Paul. I didn't send them." Garrett's face softens.

"So what now? Do you need me to be your alibi? Are you going to need a lawyer?"

Again, I shake my head. "No. I don't think they'll connect Paul's body to me. No one know we were in contact. For the last year, we've only talked through burner phones and the phones are gone now. They won't be traced to us."

"Are you ever going to be able to forgive my dad?"

"I don't know," I respond, and suddenly I hear the floor creaking behind me. I turn around and Robert is standing in the doorway of the master bedroom.

"Dad? What are you doing here?" Garrett says. "How long have you been standing there?"

"Bonnie forgot her lipstick," he says, holding up a tiny gold tube in his hand. "I'm sorry, I've..."

Again my heart starts racing. It's pounding so hard that my chest is about to rip open.

"Dad, how long have you been in there?"

"I've, uh, I, I stepped in just before Mara got back," he says bashfully. "I'm sorry, I didn't mean to eavesdrop, I didn't want to intrude..."

"But you heard everything?" Garrett says. Robert slowly nods his head and lowers his eyes. Sweat starts to form along my hairline and down my back. Now Robert has all the tools to get me to stay away from his son.

"I'm sorry," he says, his eyes still on the floor.

"I have to go," I say quietly. I grab the gun that's still on the island and shove it into my purse and I bolt from the kitchen. I jump out the front door and start running. I'm not sure where I'm going, but I won't stop until I get there.

Chapter 47
Garrett

I stare at the open door and then at my dad, who is still waiting near the door of the master bedroom. "I wanted to sneak out," he says, motioning to the door. "When I got Bonnie's lipstick. I didn't know how to leave without disturbing you..."

"So you heard everything," I say. He nods. It's almost a relief really. If I were the only witness, I'm not sure what I would do with everything I just heard. My heart is telling me to forget all of it and go find Mara and tell her I'll protect her. My head is wondering if I should still be listening to my heart. But my father knows. My father who I used to be able to speak with about things. He was always a good confidante, until we started to drift. I can trust him to guide me.

"I better go," my father says. "Bonnie's been in the car... I'm surprised she hasn't stormed in here yet." My father takes a step toward the open door.

"Wait, please," I beg. "Can you tell mom to wait? Tell her we need a few minutes."

My father nods, motions for me to wait a minute. He steps outside, leaving me alone with my thoughts. I'm not even sure how to sort them. *Revenge. Manipulation. Schizophrenic. I shot him.* I feel like I'm supposed to have so many questions, but I'm not even sure what to ask. Would she really have killed me? Was she really carrying around that gun all that time? How come I never heard of Paul before? Was it really him sending the letters?

I start thinking back to if there were clues. Sometimes she was protective of her purse. I tried to bring it to her once when we were on our way out to dinner, but she protested and grabbed the purse herself. Was the gun in it then? Did she bring it when we went out to dinner? Other images start to run through my head. Like the bruises on her arms that sometimes mysteriously appeared. Were they from Paul? Sometimes her purse vibrated, even when her phone was on the counter. Was that Paul calling her burner phone? Once I swore I saw a flip phone on the coffee table, but Mara had laughed when I asked her about it. "No one's used those since 1999," she had said. I laughed in response, thinking I must have imagined it.

My father steps through the open door and closes it behind him. "Bonnie is going to go antiquing by herself. I told her I'd meet her for lunch in a few hours."

I nod, looking to my father for what to say next. He comes into the kitchen and leans against the island. We're both standing, just leaning on the granite looking at each other in silence.

"Well," my father says, as though he has something to say, but he doesn't continue. The silence lingers, getting heavier as the seconds pass.

"What am I supposed to do?" I finally blurt out. "Just tell me what I should do now."

My father purses his lips, munching them together between his teeth. "Well," he says again. "I can't really answer that."

"I should go to the police," I say. I'm not really sure if that's what I want to do, but I say it, fishing for a response from my father. "I mean, she *killed* someone. There are laws against that."

"I killed someone," my father says. "I killed three someones."

"But that's different, Dad," I say, almost annoyed at the comparison.

"Is it?"

"But you didn't mean to do it," I reason. "It's not the same."

"Maybe what I did was worse. I killed three innocent people because I was stupid."

"What are you saying?" I'm annoyed. I want my father to just tell me the answer. Tell me what to do, like he did when I was a child. When he knew the answers to everything.

He shrugs. "I can't really tell you what to do," he says. "You have to figure that out on your own."

"Really? I would think you would definitely know what to do. You probably want me to go to the police so they can lock Mara up and then you don't have to worry about her anymore. You and mom would be so happy getting rid of her. Then you can invite Ainsley to dinner again and we can all be a happy family. Isn't that what you want?"

"No, Son," he says. "I want you to be happy. You have to decide if you can live with what Mara told you. And if you really love her. And now that you know everything, if you think you can build a life together."

"Won't you always be worried that she's going to come over with that gun and shoot us?" It's something that I think I might be worried about.

"If that was her plan, she would have done it already. And she wouldn't have confessed everything to you."

"I don't know, Dad," I say, rubbing my hand on the back of my head. "It's too much. She's schizophrenic."

"No one is perfect. She can get help for that."

"Why are you fighting for her? Why are you suddenly so sympathetic to her?"

He shrugs again. "I don't know. I killed her family. If the tables were turned, I'd hate me too. I'd want to kill my family. She's young, she has issues. But I see that she makes you happy. And she did what she did to protect you. That says something. She didn't choose the easy option."

I let out a deep sigh. My father is not being helpful at all. I still feel stuck. I have no idea what I am supposed to do.

"Look, I'm going to go meet Bonnie. You should stay here and think. I love you, Son." My father steps toward me and wraps me in an embrace. My body goes limp in his strong arms.

When he pulls back, I feel my feet falter, but I catch myself. He nods at me and steps out the front door.

I look around the empty cabin. The whole interior is brightly lit from the sun shining through the huge windows. I can see the sand and the beach through the back balcony. It's almost a violent scene, with the waves crashing onto the sand, shooting white dots of foam into the air.

There's still coffee in the coffee pot and I pour myself a mug. Instead of adding sugar like I normally do, I add milk, as though I'm making the mug for Mara. The house is silent, so much so that I feel like I can hear the silence. I start tapping my foot on the floor, just to add some noise. I take a sip of the coffee. It tastes like her.

I try to make sense of the thoughts in my head. Maybe I can organize them in lists so I can review them all one by one. *Mara killed someone. Mara has been carrying around a gun. Mara thought she was capable of killing me. I love Mara. I love the way she looks at me and the way she makes me feel. She could be dangerous. She could be schizophrenic. She killed someone.*

The thoughts in my head jumble on top of each other, making it impossible for me to organize them in a list. I slam the coffee mug down on the island, spilling the liquid on my hand. Then I walk to our bedroom with the little bunk beds and white dresser. I notice her makeup bag is open on the dresser and something yellow inside it catches my eye. I take a deep breath, wondering if

319

it's some other weapon she's been hiding all this time. I walk up to the dresser and gently stick my hand in the bag. I grasp the yellow thing between my fingers and pull it out. It's a carnation, laminated in clear plastic. On the plastic it's written *Lead me to the water.*

I hold the laminated flower in my hand and I'm hit with a flashback. Knocking on her door, her opening it in a tan dress. I'm handing her a bouquet of yellow carnations which she puts in a vase on the counter. Then I see the dead upside down flowers that were pinned to her bedroom wall. I realize I bought her this flower and she saved it. She's been carrying it around with her since our fourth date. *Lead me to the water.*

I put the flower in my pocket and head out the door. We both need a new start. Away from these worlds that have been forcing us into roles we don't fit. I jump into my car and start driving. Downtown I stop in a flower shop and buy a bouquet of yellow carnations. Then, I get back into my car and turn the key into the ignition. I'm about to back out of my parking space, when I realize I don't know where to go. I start driving slowly through town looking at everyone walking down the streets. There's lots of families out; couples holding hands. The sidewalks are packed with people eating ice cream and carrying big shopping bags. But I don't see Mara.

After an hour of driving slowly down the main road, I go back to the cabin. I park and take the yellow carnations with me around the cabin to the beach. The tide has gone out, making the water seem far away in front of me. I start walking down the sand and then I see her. It's just a black dot bobbing above the water in the distance, but I know it's her. I start running toward her, the water soaking my shoes and the bottom of my pants as I go deeper. I keep going and the water gets to my knees and then my waist.

"Mara!" I yell. It looks like she's floating, bobbing back and forth with the tide that has calmed significantly since I last watched it through the window. My heart is pounding as the thoughts swirl through my head. What is she doing? Why is she just floating? Is she...? "Mara!" I scream again.

Suddenly she raises her head. "Garrett?"

I smile with relief when she calls me. I'm holding the yellow carnations up high so they don't get wet. "What are you doing?" I yell as I get closer.

"Swimming. How did you know I was here?"

I can't help but laugh. "Lead me to the water," I said. "I knew I'd find you here."

Epilogue
Mara

I'm looking at myself in the mirror, but it's a person I hardly recognize. The pink flush on my cheeks, the absence of dark circles under my eyes. I want to touch my face, but I know I'm not supposed to.

"You're gorgeous, Darling," Bonnie says, squeezing my shoulders from behind. "Your parents would be so happy for you." I place my hands on top of hers on my shoulders and smile at her in the mirror. "Now, I think it's my turn," she says with an indulgent smile. I get off the chair and she replaces me in front of the mirror. Bonnie immediately starts explaining what she wants to the makeup artist and I walk into the bedroom where my dress is hanging up on the outside of the closet. It's not a typical wedding dress, nor was it purchased at one of the many expensive boutiques Bonnie took me to. It's just a plain floor length white dress I found at the mall. It's simple, clean, and doesn't call for any unwanted attention.

On the dresser sits my bouquet of yellow carnations, like the ones Garrett brought on our fourth date and then when he found me floating in the beach. That was one year ago. At the time, I wasn't sure what I was doing floating in the water. I thought maybe I could drift away from everything, be carried by the peaceful water to a better place. But then I heard Garrett splashing behind me and I knew the better place was with him.

"Let's fix things," he said, standing with the water up to his chest, holding the flowers in the air. "Whatever it takes. I'm here for you." He led me out of the water and back to the cabin, where we showered off and drove back home, listening to music the whole way. The next day, I went to see a psychiatrist. After an hour of talking, the doctor prescribed me the pills that my mother didn't want me to take all those years ago. At first I didn't want to take them, but Garrett insisted. It took a few weeks before I started feeling the effects, but when I did, the change was obvious. I no longer heard static in my ears and my heart seemed to find a steadier rhythm inside my chest. I continued seeing the psychiatrist and sometimes Garrett joined me there for a couple's session.

We never mentioned our wedding, which Bonnie had disgracefully agreed to cancel, or at least put on hold for the time being. At first, she resisted, saying she didn't know what to tell her friends. But eventually she came up with something that was satisfactory enough.

In the meantime, I quit working for CADD. The psychiatrist helped me see that working there wasn't helpful for me. It meant I spent a lot of my day thinking about my family's accident, which wasn't productive. Instead, I stayed home and started rewriting my memoirs. At first, I tried to copy what I had written years ago and shredded after the editor rejected me. But then I realized the editor was right. What I had written wasn't publishable. It was a mash of incoherent thoughts and feelings that only made sense in my head. This time, I focused on the story. On my sister. When I finished writing, Robert brought it to a friend of his in the publishing business. They're still editing, but they expect to publish it next year.

A few months ago, Garrett brought up the question that I knew he had been wondering about. "Did I still want to get married?" I did, I told him, but not the way we had previously planned it. He agreed and we started planning a small ceremony just for close family.

In the meantime, my psychiatrist wanted me to work on forgiveness. This was the one thing blocking me from moving on and focusing on my own happiness. I needed to forgive Robert. Forgiving didn't mean forgetting, the psychiatrist emphasized. It just meant that I needed to accept and stop blaming Robert today for what happened those years ago. It didn't mean forgetting my family, or abandoning them, or betraying them, it just meant accepting the present.

The psychiatrist also helped me work through my manipulation issues with Paul. I was used to leaning on my older sister for guidance. When she wasn't there, there was a void in me looking for someone to tell me what to do. Paul filled that void and I listened without thinking for myself. It was easier to accept his guidance than grieve for myself. Of course, I never mentioned to the psychiatrist what had become of him. When she asked if I still heard from him, I would shake my head and say he disappeared. A few days after I killed him there was an article in the newspaper about his body being found at the motel. The police had no leads, but an investigation revealed that he had severe gambling debts and had borrowed from several loan sharks with shady backgrounds. It turned out that the motel was also a short drive from one of the casinos Paul would frequent. A few months later, I called my dad's old boss, the local police chief, to ask him about the case. I explained to him that Paul was my sister's boyfriend and that was why I was curious. He agreed to look into it for me, while keeping my interest secret—no need to dig up more about my family's accident, as the press would be sure to pick up on any connection to the body and real estate tycoon Derby. The police chief came back to me saying the case had been closed after investigators followed all leads to dead-ends. "I'm sorry," the chief said to me. "I wish there was real justice in the world, especially for you after everything you've been through, but that's just how life is. It's not like the movies where all murder cases are solved before the commercials. In real life, murders go unpunished everyday, but you already know that." If only he had known that real justice had been served.

"Mara," Bonnie suddenly awakens me from my daydream. "What do you think?" She bats her fake eyelashes at me and smiles.

"You look beautiful," I respond. She helps me into my dress, I grab my bouquet, and we leave the apartment together. Downstairs, a Lincoln with its chauffeur is waiting for us. He greets us and helps us into the back of the car and we start driving. I'm staring out the window as we drive, thinking about how calm I feel. I feel like I'm floating in water, weightlessly bobbing in the waves.

When we arrive, the chauffeur stops the car right in front of the gates and opens the car doors for us. "You'll have to lead me to where we're going," Bonnie says. "I always find these places so confusing."

I nod. I know this place like the back of my hand. I could navigate it with my eyes closed, crisscrossing down the dirt paths right to my family. We enter the gates and I lead Bonnie through the identical rows of gravestones. We walk down a small hill and at the bottom, I see that Garrett, Robert, Caleb and Caroline are already there, drinking champagne around a small table that the cemetery allowed us to set up. A pastor is also there, dressed in black robes as though he wasn't sure if this was a wedding or a funeral.

When Bonnie and I approach the graves, Garrett comes up to hug me. "You're so beautiful," he whispers in my ears. I look over at the graves belonging to my parents and sister. Dried flowers taken from the wall in my old bedroom are draped over the headstones and candles line the bases.

"Shall we get started?" the pastor asks. He seems eager to get this over with. I can understand him. I'm sure this is the first wedding he's performed in this place. I nod and Garrett and I take our places in front of the graves. The pastor begins to read from his book, but I barely hear what he is saying. I'm looking straight at Garrett who keeps making silly faces at me, trying to get me to laugh. I try hard not to, but every once in a while, I break, causing the pastor to look up from his reading like he fears the interruption. After the "I dos" Garrett pulls me close and kisses me. Then Caroline brings us two champagne flutes and we all cheers.

As Caleb and Caroline continue to make toasts to Garrett, I turn to look at the graves. When I used to come here, I would have this urging feeling, like if I felt strong enough, I could change the past and bring my family back. I used to hate myself for not being able to feel strong enough to fix things. Now, I look at the graves and I just wish my family would know I've found some peace.

"I'm proud of you." I feel a strong hand on my back and turn to see Robert standing next to me. "And I know they are too."

I look at him and smile. Tears start to form in my eyes.

"Maybe this isn't the best time to say this to you," he starts saying. I notice we're both looking at the graves instead of making eye contact. "But I want to apologize. For everything. For the accident, and for not supporting you and Garrett in the beginning. I've always felt guilty for taking away your family and it's a feeling I'll never get over. I wish there was something I could do to fix things."

I look over to him and smile. The tears are welling up in my eyes, about to start trickling down. "Thank you," I respond. "But you did do something. You've given me a new family." It's the truth. It may have taken a year, but I've become more comfortable with the Derby's. Yes, they are sometimes superficial and flawed, but they also care about each other. And for some reason, they now care about me.

"We'll always be your family, even though we can't replace who you've lost," Robert says and it's exactly right. It's one of the things I've come to appreciate in Robert, he seems to have a higher level of understanding than others in his circle.

"I'm happy they got to see this," Garrett says, suddenly appearing on my other side and nodding to the graves in front of us. "This was the best idea you've had."

"It was Robert's idea," I say, smiling at my father-in-law. It was his idea. When Garrett and I started talking about getting married again, Bonnie wanted to start planning a huge party. When Garrett and I said we only wanted close family, Robert had asked who would come from my side of the family. When I had no answer, he suggested we get married here.

Robert winks at me and Garrett and then steps away back to the small table where there are now only empty bottles of champagne. Garrett wraps his arm around me and we stand there silently for a few moments.

"Who's hungry?" Caleb suddenly shouts. "Let's get over to the restaurant for dinner." We look back and nod at the group, which has now started walking back toward the parking lot. Garrett holds out his hand for me to take and follow them out.

"One minute," I say. He nods and begins walking away, leaving me alone in front of the graves. I continue to stand silently for a few moments. I wish I had something profound to tell them. Something to say about what they just witnessed. I bend down and place my bouquet of yellow carnations on Shannon's grave. "Thanks for leading me to the water," I whisper before turning around and following Garrett up the small hill.

Want to know what happens with Mara and Garrett one year later?

Go to my website www.avivagatauthor.com to get the FREE bonus chapter.

Acknowledgments

This book may have one author, but there are many people who contributed to it. First of all, I want to thank my husband Ori who helped me come up with the idea for this story. The idea for this novel was almost a year in the making. It started with a discussion of why terror attacks were usually conducted by men. Then the conversation morphed into why mass shootings were usually conducted by men. Together we questioned what would drive a woman to initiate a mass shooting. From that discussion, we developed Mara's motivation and the story unraveled from there.

I would never have been able to come up with the idea for this book on my own. It's different than the ideas I usually come up with. My husband was the main driving force for helping me break barriers and write a story unlike anything I would have on my own. A big thank you goes to him for his encouragement and hours of brainstorming. He is always supporting me and pushing me to dream bigger. I also want to thank him for being a wonderful husband and father.

I also want to thank my friend Naomi Caplan for reading the very first draft of this book. When I sent it to her, it felt unfinished. I had a nagging feeling that something was missing, but I couldn't figure it out on my own. Naomi's insights and comments turned this story into the complex novel that it became.

I also want to thank my dad Nahum for reading the rough draft and the second draft. My dad has always been one of my biggest supporters and provides endless encouragement for my writing.

Thanks also goes to my Grandma Dorothy and my Aunt Gail and Uncle Mark for reading the manuscript while quarantined during the COVID19 pandemic. I hope my book provided them with a much needed distraction!

Thanks also goes to all the other hands that touched my book: Caitlin Graham, an Instagram friend who did a wonderful job editing. Isabelle G, who did the final round of proofreading. Angela Stevens for designing the cover.

The biggest thank you goes to all my readers, especially those who leave me reviews on Amazon and Goodreads. Reviews (and recommendations!) are the best way to give back to an author you like. They help other readers decide whether to read a book and encourage writers to keep going.

Learn more about me by following me
on Instagram @aviva_writes
Facebook.com/avivagatauthor
or check out my website,
www.avivagatauthor.com

Made in the USA
Monee, IL
05 February 2021